In the Slammer
with Carol Smith

Novels
False Entry
Textures of Life
Journal from Ellipsia
The New Yorkers
Queenie
Standard Dreaming
Eagle Eye
On Keeping Women
Mysteries of Motion
The Bobby-Soxer
Age
The Small Bang (as Jack Fenno)
In the Palace of the Movie King

Novellas and Short Stories
In the Absence of Angels
Tale for the Mirror
Extreme Magic
The Railway Police and the Last Trolley Ride
The Collected Stories of Hortense Calisher
Saratoga, Hot

Autobiography
Herself
Kissing Cousins

HORTENSE CALISHER

In the Slammer
with Carol Smith

A Novel

Marion Boyars
New York • London

First published in the United States and Great Britain
in 1997 by Marion Boyars Publishers
237 East 39th Street, New York NY 10016
24 Lacy Road, London SW15 1NL

Distributed in Australia and New Zealand by
Peribo Pty Ltd, 58 Beaumont Road, Kuring-gai, NSW

Library of Congress Cataloging-in-Publication Data
Calisher, Hortense
    In the slammer with Carol Smith/Hortense Calisher.
    I. Title.
    PS3553.A4155   1997
    813'.54—dc20   96-23858

British Library Cataloguing in Publication Data
Calisher, Hortense
    In the slammer with Carol Smith
    1. American fiction—20th century
    I. Title
    813.5'4[F]

        ISBN 0–7145–3020–4 hardcover

Typeset in 11½/13½ Caslon by
Ann Buchan Typesetters, Shepperton, Middlesex.
Printed and bound by Redwood Books, Trowbridge, Wiltshire

In the Slammer
with Carol Smith

Alphonse was my wino friend; when he was off the sauce he still thought he was an actor. That's the wrong way round for a wino; it's when you're high you're supposed to give yourself airs, but the wrong way round is what we people are. He and I met leaning out to look at the river, in that jog the West Side Highway takes before the cars go back on Riverside Drive, Seventy-second Street. He thought I was normal because I still had the bike.

'This wall — they got it just right for leaning,' I said. With some guys the woman has to speak first. He had a thin, Picasso boy's profile; that's why I could. And it was true about the wall. Stone. The right height for most elbows. The city fathers must have put it up a long time ago.

'You a college girl?'

I was pleased. When I am, I can speak the truth; when I'm angry, it goes off. And I still do wear my hair that way, long. Pinned with the barette. 'I was, once. I'm twenty-eight.'

'I'm an actor.'

Right then I thought: he knows. That what I am is what

I do. That all the profession I have is to go on being that. Else why would he fling out this way, with what he is?

'Character?' I say. What other kind of actor could he be, with that Adam's apple, and the skinniness? Unless he was a transvestite — which I didn't think.

'Some. I'm on unemployment.'

'Gee. That's the cream.' Did I believe him? I think I didn't, even then. Takes one to know one. But I gave him the advantage. Like he is giving me.

'Not that easy,' he says. 'Not as easy as you think.' He's repeating, see, for confidence. Sometimes it makes me feel sad, seeing others using my same tricks. Sometimes it makes me feel safe. Like if I cared to, I could have a relative. I wouldn't of course. It isn't that safe.

But I can't help giving him the look — like he's a high class dog I might be thinking to buy. Or like at someone who might buy me. 'I don't know any you unemployment footdraggers anymore. I'm on welfare. A branch of it.'

He nods. Maybe he is too. If he is, he knows that family welfare is not the only kind. And that I'm not any widowed mother or healthy dependent. It's not just an informal once-over he's giving me.

'What you looking at?' It burst out of me. I can never help it. It's what we all say, when people look too long.

'I'm not,' he says too quick — as if he knows that. 'I'm looking at the bike.'

'It's an Italian racer. Until it got too rusty it used to fold.' I don't like to own things, except for the barette. So when I socked half the disability allowance for the bike, my SW was too encouraged. 'Guy in a garage I know gave it to me,' I told her. 'It was left.' But she wasn't fooled; maybe she passes by that thrift shop window on the way to me. 'Oh Carol, that's real health,' she said. And gave me an allowance replacement because she knew I wouldn't ask. For a social worker, she's not bad.

'How many speeds it have?'

'I don't know. I've never let it out.' I don't ride it, only walk it. But it looks so good. So me, as I ought to be. Like the barette. 'Anyway, I don't own it. Belongs my neighbor's kid.'

He does give me the focus then. When he pulls the pint bottle out of his chino pocket, and sideswipes a slurp without even a gander at it, is when I cotton to what he is — and when he stashes it again. They never trust a bottle to any bag they may be carrying. 'You shouldn't say that to a stranger.'

'Say what?' But I already know what I shouldn't have said; I almost always do. And that he's right. But unless he's one of us, how did he know?'

'Name's Alphonse. What's yours?'

'Carol.' It always helps me to say. Sometimes I go around saying it to people: I'm Carol. Try not to: the SW says.

'You know what, Carol?' he says. But not dirty intimate; it's only the drink's made him debonair. 'Making like you have a neighbor? With the way you look like. Some guy who's dangerous might think you have a pad. And want to crash.'

Why does honest advice make me see red? Maybe because I've had so much of it.

'Maybe I do have one.' But I've never said that before. It's a hard path I walk. You don't have to walk it, the SW says. 'I know' — I yelled at her last time — 'and that's *my* disability.' That shut her up.

He shakes his head, solemn. 'The shoes are good. Even that skirt and blouse can pass these days, though you've buttoned wrong. Lipstick, even. Hair? Who knows a real mess nowadays from a fake one? And the bike, a touch of genius. I was fooled, first off.' He shakes his head. Drunks do sermonize. 'But not with those fingernails of yours. Like some cavewoman digging herself an exit.'

I like a sharp tongue. I have one myself, now and then. And his same eye for detail. 'I have this nail downer. Sometimes I scrub till I bleed. Sometimes I let go, like this. On purpose.' And not only with the nails. 'But today, where I stash the bike, they stole my support gloves.' That did happen, once.

This time his headshake admires me. 'To crash with a bike. In a garage?'

Used to. When I was on the street. But couldn't stand having to do a trick with that guard. 'No one's followed me yet, Alphonse.' And no one will. Where I hang out, I'm normal. I'd kill — I tell the SW. She only smiles.

He's slipping out the pint again.

'I only spoke to you because winos aren't dangerous.'

I mean to hit home but he only shrugs, wipes his mouth and stashes the bottle again. 'Good old Tokay. I'd offer you. But now we're telling I can see what you're on. That prescription drug, isn't it, Carol. The one makes a person shift from foot to foot. That's rough.'

It is. Worst of all, that people can see. 'Why's it any rougher than you?'

'They want me to stop what I'm on. People who say they care. Or the doc. But they won't ever want you to, will they.'

That's the burden of it. He's put it sharp. Like the nurse

when she twiddles the scale for you. Saying: why do I bother, I can see your bones. 'I don't go to the hospital anymore.' I whisper it.

'They can't get me to go in,' he says, proud.

'Oh. Alphonse.'

'Don't read me the book, Carol.'

No. But he looks so good still, the head up, the mouth not loose yet, the shock of hair as thick as mine. Too good to waste yourself, boy — or girl — is what they tell you. They even wanted me back in school; they know better now. 'How old are you?'

'Didn't want to say. After you did. Twenty-eight.'

He sees round my disability. I see round his. The wall stays the same.

'See you,' I say. 'Gotta keep walking.'

'Parting is sweet sorrow,' he says. 'But gotta keep to my task.' He pats his hip where the pint is. 'Bye.'

When I get back to the pad I do have, the SW is sitting on the stoop. She comes once every eight days, never drops in. Once last year, she did. Upstairs, I was just sitting there. But the time I've wasted, being checked up on; it all came up in my throat. 'What are you, a lezzie, this extra snooping?' I said. 'You're not eating, I knew it.' she said. 'You're thin as a ghost.' And she brings out a salami from her bag. But that was last year. I eat now. It's part of my job.

So is this room-and-a-half, with a real cot in it. Up four flights, toilet, running water; renting in the barrio can still be a bargain if you don't mind the Spanish screeching, day and night. The woman next door, Mrs. Lopez, scrubs her two front rooms like she does her kids' necks; the grandmother in the back bedroom, her mother-in-law, won't let her in to clean. The week I moved in, Carmen Lopez knocked on my door, bringing me a hospitality bowl: a lemon, an orange, half a papaya with the stone still in it, a can of coconut milk and a packet of Goya seasoning. We swap cockroach recipes; she started me on the sprinkling; now we do it together. Better than pushing them back and forth, she says. Bicarb-and-borax works best. When she caught her husband knocking at my door one night she came at him with one of her four-inch heels; his forehead has a dent. The women are the queens here; they build up the men to think they are the kings. Now when he carries my bike up the stairs for me she calls out — 'Whatta guy!' — first in Spanish, then in English so I will hear. Angel, her oldest, I have promised to let ride the bike when he is ten; he is oiling it. They keep winning me over, it's hard not to be.

The SW, Mrs. Gold, wanted me to call her Daisy. 'I'll call you Gold,' I said '— that's professional.' She has to call me Carol; that's what her job tells her to do. I have to admit this helps. We both know that getting me to admit things is prime. Only I get so sick of what we both know.

'I liked your hair blonder,' I say fast, the minute I see her on the stoop this time. I have to get my oar in quick. Between us, I rate as the one on the fashion beat, but we won't have any of that upstairs. As we climb, we both check. In my book, she's tending to fade. My guess is the hubby was the one to leave. Once she brought her two kids along here, but it wasn't a success. Divorce brats, with that special kind of ego. The Lopez kids have the charm. 'You bring your kids on account of that crack I made,' I said to Gold —

meaning when I asked her was she lezzie, but she only laughs, which is better than when she sighs at me. I was a swinger once, but always with guys. Now I don't do any of it. Maybe I did it to show I was vulnerable, she says; that's her school of thought.

Upstairs I go quick to the sink and soap the nails, but she saw them when I fumbled the key; she isn't fooled. 'Okay, Gold, so let's get to the Try-not-to's,' I say. 'Open the fridge.'

It's secondhand from the donation center, but works.

Tacked on the door there is a list of meals — each item with a check. When she first got me onto that, I used to draw up menus to shock: pigs' knuckles with whipped egg-white, ice-cream with snow peas, but that was juvenile, and god-awful if I was honorable enough to eat them. Now the meals are so balanced they could spin on a dietitian's nose. Inside, when she opens up, the milk carton smells sweet — and has a red ribbon on it to show the level. The eggs are pillowed in their grey paper-carton casket: I couldn't resist sticking a tiny flag on it, American of course. There isn't a single festering dish in the box.

Gold reaches in to flip the ribbon.

I say, 'I couldn't find a rubber band.' We both giggle.

'Oh, Carol. If you could only be casual.'

'If I could, Gold, you wouldn't be here.'

A sigh. 'Still, wish my kids could see that squeaky-clean box.'

She's always posing me and her kids against each other. That is something she doesn't know and I'm not telling. 'No you wouldn't. Gold. Because I cheat. Last night was when I ate every old leftover in the box.'

'At least you eat.' She is moving the milk carton aside. And there are the medicines. One has a seductive nipple-shape. The other squats in its box like a poltergeist. They are a new trust.

She checks. Both are empty. 'You took them all? And I mean — take.'

'No throwaways. I remember what you said.'

'What did I say?' She is truly puzzled. Her own slogans, don't they register with her anymore? I wrote what she said in ink inside the box where I stash the barette; have even been considering a decal of it over the toilet — and she can't remember it?

'To remember the pills, "you have to take the pills."'

'You have a mind like a steel trap, Carol. When you want to.'

'Trap?'

She squinches her eyes. 'So, what was the week like?'

'Mrs. Lopez and I did the roaches. Twice.'

'Good.'

'But they all went downstairs, to the tenants below. Is that right?'

'Carol. I am not answering anymore of your questions about the state of the world.'

'Yeah. Maybe there's some pill you could take. So you could answer.'

I'm serious. Since the state of the world has got me where I am, maybe everyone should be taking pills for it. You take pills like I do, you better believe there's one for every situation.

'What's Mrs. Lopez's opinion? On the roaches?'

'She says we're doing a community service. If the downstairs wants, it can always join in.'

She hoots. 'You wanted moral advice. There you are.'

But I'm not sure she isn't hooting at the Lopez's. And now, she sniffs. All the cartons and cans of the week, and the food papers; they're piled under the sink. Along with maybe a sanitary pad. When Angel comes to tinker with the bike, he usually cleans under there, not saying anything. But it's not the weekend yet.

'I forgot,' I say. 'I was so busy eating.'

'I'm no martinet, Carol. I'm not even a very good house-keeper myself. I just hope you can learn —'

'To live indoors. To love it even.' I look at the TV, the radio clock, the toaster, all the stuff for starting over, given me by kind persons along the way, whose names I should remember: a little hurt comes each time I do. 'So's I can be happy as a clam, being me in a house.' And forget the outside. 'Maybe by summer I will.'

'Not like last summer. Please.'

When I never went out. 'Once I decided I had to hate the heat — I hated it.'

'This year — try not.'

'Okay.' She's very tiring. But that is supposed to be good for me.

'Anything else you want to tell me, Carol.'

'Don't want to, Gold. I have to.'

She ignores this. This is the waiting game. And some-times, I win.

'Mrs. Lopez sounds like a practical person, Carol.'

'She is. She is the only nice practical person I know.' I give her a stare. 'And want to know something? She spends a lot of time on the street. They all do, here.'

'Puerto Ricans are a tropical people. They like to think

they're still there. And you haven't seen them in winter yet.'

'Maybe I should have been a tropical person.' I go off a little, dreaming. 'Gee. Then there wouldn't be any difference, except maybe a straw curtain. Between the outdoors and the in.'

'Maybe you could be — yes I can see you in one of those countries.'

She fires up easy; that's when we get on together best. 'But we're not exporting you yet. Meanwhile, looks like you're learning some useful Spanish.'

When they start on that we're not far from what the want-ads would call my 'secretarial skills.' For the job that wouldn't be just me being me.

'I only speak with Angel. He's in trouble too.' Imagine coming here only eighteen months ago, along with that grandmother. And then being an Angel, in a U.S. school. 'And he understands about the street.'

She is digging in her purse. Now out will come the week's supply of pacifiers. Suddenly, I begin to weave. Over to the right foot. Over to the left.

'Carol. You know you're doing that. You're doing that on your own. On purpose. You've been off the compazine for weeks. And the tofranil.'

'Have I? I never look at the boxes. They're all so much alike.'

'What you're on now doesn't have that side-effect. Come on. Stop.'

'Why? It's good to have a purpose, didn't you say?'

'And stop being sly. It's bad for you.' And then I see the tears in her eyes. 'Oh Carol. You've come so far.'

She puts her arms around me. We weave back and forth

together. Like we don't know who the enemy is, but we have the same one. 'Yes, I'm learning Spanish,' I whisper. 'Downstairs, those men who hang around the bar next door? One of them whistles at me. I'm standing on the stoop, doing left foot, right foot, maybe it's not the medicine only; it's when I'm thinking: will it be outside, or inside? And a guy who lives in this building, he says to the guy who whistled 'No, Pedro, no. She is touched by God.'

'So? That's not so bad to be. With a little help.' She's holding something out to me. It's a doctor's prescription.

'On my own, I'm to go get it?'

'On your own. You're responsible.'

A word I no longer go for. Once you have to be told to be that, you aren't. The prescription is ordinary black-and-white, like for cough syrup, for anything. 'I won't fill it at the drugstore around here,' I say, though I don't know why not. When I bought the barette they said, 'Come again.' The barrio can be very polite.

When she is leaving I say: 'You going back to the office, Daisy?'

She turns to look at me. 'Yes, Carol. Why?'

I'm not good at thanking people.

'You got a lunch-spot on your plaid.'

She went to the big Rite-Aid blocks away to fill the prescription. It was so early in the morning that no one else was in the store. Behind the counter the pharmacists were cold as ice in their white smocks; if you were setting up a new record, this was the place to go. There was a guard at the door to watch you didn't lift anything from the too friendly open shelves. 'That's not my problem, buddy,' she said to him as she left. Walking back to the pad she said to herself: I'll always do the dose inside.

In front of the sink she had the impulse to empty out the whole bottle, but resisted. You're just a sink. I can swallow too. The one-a-day she tipped into her palm was brightly striped. Too fancy for a placebo? The world runs on trust.

Now comes the bad moment of the morning, the tug. Will she take to the outside, or the in? When you've had a little warmth you want more. That's the rub.

Three mornings she went to lean on the stone wall. Turned out, so had he, never on the same days. When they finally met and exchanged this she said, 'Pure coincidence.'

She had combed her hair through. 'That's a great ornament you wear,' he said. She stood there feeling the breeze the phrase made. He had on an orange sweater instead of the brown. 'Orange looks good on you,' she told him.

He said: 'It's my other one.'

So all was understood.

When he said 'Want to join the Cat Club? It's where some of us crash?' she said, 'Why not?'

On the subway she said, 'It's not a halfway house?'

'No way.'

'Can I just visit?'

'That's what we all.'

The Cat Club was a storefront in the Village. The tenement above had been condemned as unlivable. 'Until the landlord comes back from Florida and fixes it up. She won't; she's notorious. Her former husband or her brother — we don't know which but he hates her guts — comes in from Long Island City now and then to check the building.' Along with his girlfriend. 'Older even than him, and all in fur. Hil-ari-ous. He's a broken down gigolo; in his day the Village must have been steamy with them.' Alphonse had stopped to buy a bottle beforehand. He took a swig, swinging his long haircut, which was tidy but not greased. 'Long Island City. On a Sunday. They live in the carpet-cleaning warehouse the girlfriend owns. No wonder we're their bright errand.'

She watched the stations foam by; this was an express. 'That from Shakespeare?'

'Dunno. Never did him.'

'Could be a film title. Maybe should be.'

'So you went to college,' he said. 'So did I. Adirondack

Community College. My cousins still own land up there. Buy their kids snowmobiles. Hunt wild turkey in the fall. Can't see why they never catch any. Turkeys have the last word.'

She is quiet, searching for what she can say next. Not what kind of actor is he. Nor if he ever really has — acted. Nor what had brought him to the city. No questions asked is only fair; he hasn't asked her that much. What you can't ask really tells you what you want to know. One foot up on the wall, elbow on his knee, he hasn't forgotten her, merely recognized her, in the same trust. If you haven't been on the inside somewhere, why would you make such a business of being out?

'You're not a gigolo,' she said. Neat. Took care of everything. And she made him laugh.

'If you're so smart, why're you such a — a pixie?'

She didn't need to answer that. They were safe in the routine. He was blunter at it though than she was.

The club was on a street so meager and crooked that the city still disdained it. Once the storefront had sold wallpaper that still patterned the inside in faint pinks and greens, so the window looked frugal and occupied. The cat, a yellow tom, sunning in the window by day, he said, and now shining its eyes at them in the dark, completed it.

He could tell she didn't want to go in.

'Not afraid of cats, are you.'

'Not — categorically.'

'Oh wow, Carol.'

But she still stood there. Then she too began to laugh. That cat looked so much like a nurse, the ones at the Receiving Desk, who do just that, and no more. With a stony purr.

'We go in the back, Carol. Just we.' He touched her hand but didn't take it. 'In or Out is always optional. Nobody has a key. Nobody.'

The back alley was murky, offering anybody that dead-end feel of being at the bottom of trouble until morning. No garbage cans though, no smell. Attached to the rear of the house was an old added-on wooden shed, dank with weather but still firm. Its iron bolts were gored deep in, two sets of them. He tripped them, one-two and a three. 'Couldn't have done it, on brick.' Inside the shed the back door to the house proper was ajar. It was all so flimsy, so outdoor connected that she still felt safe.

'We're in the basement.' They crept down the battered steps.

All along she'd wondered whether the 'we' meant only a friend, man or girl, though she'd plumped for girl. It wouldn't be one of those imitation pads, though, that she'd encountered in her singles-bar days. It would be a real one.

It was. But communal.

'Floor's concrete, or we couldn't have done it. The city socked a sewage violation on the old girl once, when there still were tenants.' He smacked his lips. 'Pure poured concrete.'

An odd rejoicing. But she could see what he meant.

Only one of the bed-downs set at intervals along that poured gray was really a bed — an old painted-iron one with a naked metal spring, underneath it what might be sleeping bags. The other bed-downs were more like piles of preferences. Some of the stashes were familiar ones. Army blankets went with knapsacks, and a predictable owner. Tartan coveralls, stolen from the city shelter, or the churches.

Old moth-holed polo-coats, once royalty in the thrift-shops. A couple of beach umbrellas neatly stacked, by some nomad capable of carrying two, or unable to pass either of them by, wherever found. She's seeing all the angles, once again. Boots and more boots of course, everywhere. One cane, leaning up against a pile covered with the granddaddy of capes — or the grandma. Each heap is one person's answer to winter. Not always a barricade. Sometimes an embrace.

Nothing thin enough for summer? Yes, there — a washline hung with shirts of all sorts drying stiffly in the chill.

'We been hanging the shirts over the underwear. Neater.' Alphonse said. 'What you looking for, hey?'

The walls have no pin-ups. 'Rules.'

'No rules, though. People change.'

'Oh. The membership. Or you mean — in themselves?'

'Hey. Don't look so terrified. We don't do anything. Strictly come and go. Maybe we're the only club in the world with no membership.'

He saw that she was soothed. She could belong.

That summer is a game of pick-up sticks: those long slivers of wood, tinted magenta, frog-green, pumpkin and dragonfly-blue, which one shook into a teepee, from which each player by turn tried to extract one sliver without making the whole feathery shape slide. If one succeeded, the heart flew. If not, the sticks lay, a malevolent nest. The airy heap, each time tossed, was never the same as before. The failed nest always was.

The yellowy stick, safely pulled, is for when she got her prescription refilled in the neighborhood pharmacy after all, where no one looked at her cross-eyed. The blue and the green were for her first shopping tours, the one for the vegetables, at a stall, easy, the other at the supermarket, on a kind of catch-all sortie for boxed goods. So many she'd never seen, they helped pull her along the aisles. Sometimes she even purchases for Mrs. Lopez — 'You going A&P, carita, buy me Armour Baking Soda. Not just for the bugs. Make-a the cold-a box no stink.'

In her own hoard under the sink she now had a line of cleansers, with names either out of woolly-bear country:

Soft-Scrub, Easy Fluff, or from flash television: Electrosol, which was for the dishwasher she didn't have. Imitating Carmen Lopez, she was loathe to reveal she had never cleaned a house or stocked one, until she realized that Carmen knew. 'No, I can't buy you bleach, Carmen,' she dared to say to her one day. 'I'm an environmentalist.' Behind her, memory unfurled a line of Boston faces at her back, dim but strong.

The red match-sticks were for the painfully long bus ride to the Club, during which she'd clench her fingers onto the seat in order not to jump off and away. At the end of that first run, when the only riders by then, a tourist couple, said to the driver: 'Is this SoHo?' he answered, 'No-ho, this is No-ho,' including her in his jolly black-and-white smile. Puzzled though, when she said with a relieved gust of breath, 'Puns are everything.' Meanwhile, with each ride another color bloomed at her, returning: the happy, fuzzy peach of a girl's sweater, the seal's-fur shine purpling a raincoat, a man's camouflage jacket, toad-spotted or brown. Dogs too were said to see only in shades of gray, as she had been doing up to then; if a person had acquired dog-seeing, or been immured in it, could that be called a 'skill?' She knows better than to ask Gold.

The night Alphonse had first brought her to the non-club — her own term for it that she kept secret — the man who belonged to the iron bed was already there. 'We don't come 'til dark,' he said to her, nodding at Alphonse. 'But it is already dark.' Though it wasn't quite. He lent her a blanket so that she could sit on the cold floor, like the other people shortly to drift in would soon do. 'Name's Mungo.'

The name went so well with his bluff red face, walrus

mustache and worn safari khaki, that it took her some while to catch on that he might have tagged himself with it. He had twitched the blanket off the bed, then immediately pulled out another from beneath the bed to make it up again. His orderliness was several times interrupted by his itch to lend. He never ate at the club, never stayed longer than it took to finish the two bottles of fizzy water he brought with him, but came earliest in order to clean out the night's collection of milk cartons, paper cups, take-out boxes, soda cans and wine bottles, that others had left.

Nobody brought food that looked like it came from a home. It would have saved money for her to raid her own shelves, but she too purchased on the way. Mungo never slept on his bed; it was his hallmark, his bike. As his self-assurance wore off, usually with the last of his water ration, his sporty get-up and otter mustache wilted also, making for an uncertainty whether he was the hunter or the animal hunted. She suspected that like her, he too had a pad. Nothing in his talk ever indicated so. Nor was it ever noted aloud by any there that Mungo, like Carol herself, and above all like Alphonse, was in fact a regular. Or at least a 'faithful', a word once dropped by Alphonse himself, to mark someone long gone, who had again turned up. In the eyes of all the Cat Club was committed to serve the drifter, occasional or serial, which each of them still was. Or had once been. If she could understand the balances here, she would maybe better understand her own, but that was not why she came.

Whenever anyone new came, one of the others stayed with him or her for the night, ministering to whatever needs. Sometimes a regular slept over but never steadily.

Now and again one disappeared, forever, far as the Club knew. There were crises, violences, but, in the phrase of one of the occasionals, a woman who called herself Mavorneen, 'Those always valve out. Like a bath-tub don't run over.' Many of the names here were elaborately self-pointing; you call yourself Mavorneen surely because you want to hear people calling you that. Ordinaries like Carol were happy 'just to be —' as she once said, when pressured, '— echoed enough.'

Preferences could be loud here, and mostly abided by, if remembered, but it was easier to forget, rather than rebuff. Forgetting was natural here. The past wasn't forbidden altogether, but habitually ignored. Little blurts gave you inklings of a person. Now and then somebody let loose with a wild riff.

'On medical know-how, you people could run a health column,' a transvestite said, after a lively general discussion as to whether he should soak his swollen high-heeled foot or bind it, and at which clinic he would be best served. Hard drugs were not barred; nothing was. But most exaggerated conduct, not finding much of that at the Cat Club, eased itself out. Medications, on the other hand, were rife; comparisons could be made as at a bazaar, and even swaps. While it was okay to exhort against medical aids, including the psychological, to proselyte for those was frowned on. No one here would ever remind her to take her pill, although once she and Mavorneen, shrugging at each other, had gulped theirs at the same time. Though never repeating that. Sex happened. People went upstairs for it, to the least shaky parts of the condemned house.

Little was repeated here, individually. Instead there was a flow.

'It's a halfway house,' she said to Alphonse.' 'Only — only not to get to the other side.'

Rumor persisted that he had started the place after his girlfriend O.D.'d. Nobody could corroborate. 'Not everybody's a sex nut,' Mungo said. 'Though I fathered two children myself.' After that blurt he had not been seen again.

'It's my ace-in-the-hole,' Alphonse himself said. 'Case I get thrown out of the Y.'

Everybody there laughed. When she was a kid, the Young Men's Christian Association was the norm. Or the Young Women's, in college, for those who were too square. Now, whether or not it was the norm again, it wasn't for those here.

'He could almost qualify, Arturo could,' a girl said. A dancer who did ruffly steps while she was talking to you, she Hispanicized all names. 'Lucky he drinks.'

Everybody fed the cat. It was the only one who had rules, in the form of a calendar you checked once you'd done it, over which was scrawled DON'T FORGET THE WATER BOWL. All this was done behind a screen that separated the front window from what had been the store proper, in which there was also a narrow stall with a rear toilet better than the basement one, and a sink. Alphonse bought the cat food, anyone who could contributing, and whoever volunteered did the cat's box. The cat didn't seem to care who took care of it. Sometimes it prowled the vandalized upper house, where a window was left open for it. There was no light in the store window, but by night the cat was there, paws folded, eyes slitted, under the street lamp. Daytimes, children tapped to it, through the pane.

Now and then Carol too disappeared from the Club, if only so that she could drift back. Once, after such an interval, Alphonse said on her return, 'You have good manners,' so there was no need to explain. On very hot nights she might go to one of the docks on the lower river, a family one, not the gay one where she might be unwelcome. By day she might stay in the pad, cleaning herself, keeping up her Lopez connection. To Angel, who wanted to know where she went, she said — after a gap meant to show she was making things up: 'Turkey country. I have a brother there.' He asked if he could come along. After which she answered: 'Not on the bike.' Kids understand the future; it propped up the now. They didn't really believe in it.

The summer went, like a picture she was in.

Gold took vacation all of August, like she always did. Time out for me, else I might have told her about the Cat Club, which I must not do; that would be joining up with her, over the long-term case that is me. Last time she comes, end of July, I am there of course, though I had spent the night before on the street. I do that the day before she comes; it keeps me limber against her influence. Summers though, the pad itself has a pull. Carmen gave me a window-blind that grades the sun down to lemony. 'I only have one window,' I grudged at her, but she has such courtesy you find yourself saying thanks. Lopez could fix the jammed window in the back, that opened on the air-shaft — she said. 'Only put a security grill, so nobody can come down from the roof.' So, since her husband don't work Wednesday, that has been done and afterwards she is introducing me to the tea called maté; she is not Puerto Rican like him but South American.

She has brought the black gourds you drink it from, and the metal straws. The gourds have metal bases. I look closer — 'Silver.' — and she nods; the Club has made me talk more. The gourds were a wedding present from her six aunts when she married Lopez after Angel came. She is wearing her hair very high these days, in a basket of curls which her face is too strong for, and has bought a couple of housedresses in too small a size; Lopez has a woman in the bar downstairs.

'I had aunts,' I tell her. 'They had a house full of games.' Telling her is only dropping it down a slot, like you do the lapel clip-on the museums give you on entry; when you leave it vanishes, but you've paid. I could almost say where the house was; the location would mean nothing to her. It was like an old nag of a horse, that house, its bones poking up like haunches from the lawn, and had a real horse to match, so old that we never got to ride, but there was a game of parcheesi always set up and ready for us in the window-bay.

The maté is bitter, which I like. Sipping, I see the iron cage Lopez has put over the air-shaft window in the back half-room, which is now a tiny cell. 'Looks like I keep a gorilla here.' Angel, who is oiling the bike he now comes to see every day after school, and nagging his mother for money to buy an ice-cream stick with, says, 'Would the gorilla be touched by God?' Carmen, mouthing him to hush, says 'Get out of here, Angel. Go ask your father for the ice-cream money. You know where.'

We both stare at her. She doesn't like him to go in the bar.

He runs up again to say, 'Carol's lady is sitting on the stoop.'

'Hah, she don't know we have bells now,' Carmen says. Lopez fixed the old wires. She is still building him up, for me to hear. 'We go now. Come, Angel.'

'No, stay. You never met the SW.'

So she is still there, in her high-collared, no-sleeve starchy pink when Gold walks in. Out of breath, and the way the summer city can do to people — creased and lowdown from what they usually are. But also more faded on her own. I want to build her up. 'Carmen, this is my social worker; she knows about the roach campaign. Gold — you met Angel; he's her boy. This is Carmen; she —.' Knows about the medicine in the fridge, though I have never said. I see I don't have to say any of it. They both know their place in my life.

'You give her some maté,' Carmen says. 'I bring another cup.'

Gold knows what maté is but has never had it. 'Not too addictive. Like coffee. And other kind substances.' She makes a face. But when Carmen comes back she accepts the tea, extra-polite lady-style — like she's accepting it.

'Carmen's six aunts gave her these cups,' I say. 'For her wedding. They are gourds really. What you call them, Carmen?'

'Calabash.'

We sip. The straws are silver all the way. 'Those aunts —' I say '—were they all on one side?'

'Two my father sister, four my mother.'

I hold my breath. 'Mine were both adopted. The diddly two of them.' What's 'diddly?' A word you use when you don't say more. But I have mentioned the house, almost.

Gold's eyes are wide, her mouth too. She knows that history, which we never discuss.

'Say where —' I say to her. 'I want to. But I can't.'

'In Dedham, Mass.' Then she covers up, by sucking the straw.

Angel bursts in, his father behind him. Lopez has brought up ice-cream bars for Carmen and me. And for 'the lady.' 'We are having maté,' Carmen says, haughty. 'Angel, go put those in the freezer.' She smiles at me. 'I save for us.'

It's different when you introduce a man. 'He fixed the wires,' I say. 'From now on, Gold, you can use the bell.' I see he is disappointed in Gold.

She wants to notice only me. 'I know Carol for three years now,' she says to him, almost with an accent. Though she scores me, for talking slum.

'Carol teach me to talk,' Carmen says. She brings Lopez a maté. In the wedding picture his chest sticks out like an apache's; now he is just a greaser with a beer waistline. But he still likes his women slick.

'Yes — you have conversation now,' Gold says to me. 'And I must go.' She digs in her bag.

'Come on, Angel,' Lopez says. They leave. Carmen is listening for whether the two of them go all the way down-stairs to the bar again. We hear their home door open and close, one flight down. 'No, stay —' I tell Carmen, who is making like to follow them. She needs to be away from Lopez. So she half stays, washing the cups. I am watching Gold, who is still digging.

'I hate that bag,' I say. Because of what it has in it.

'So do I —,' she says. 'But I must carry it.'

I used to think it had all our case-records in it, and that mine must be what made it so heavy, but no, she said, 'those stay at the office; we don't take them into the field.' Which is what they call visiting the 'clients' — 'going into the field.' 'Sounds like you're picking flowers,' I said. I wouldn't say that now, the bag is so worn. Three years of me, and all her other cases. Rent vouchers, for those who aren't able to deal on their own moneywise, blanket coupons, and the food stamps I wouldn't accept. And the prescriptions.

Usually those are clipped neat; today they are loose in the bag. She hands me mine. 'The substitute, Ms. Mickens, will bring you the next. Watch your step with her. She's new.'

I will, I know what that means. Rules. Meanwhile Gold is wanting to say goodbye to Carmen who is bent over the sink, but her ears are sticking through those curls. I am not sure how to balance the two of them.

'I had a medal like that once,' Gold says to her.

On a chain always around Carmen's neck, I don't know for which saint. But I know what the tiny leather doll hanging next to it is for. The Lopez's are more tropical than they are Catholic.

'You did, Gold? I didn't know you were Catholic.'

'I was. Gold wasn't. And the little charm? What's that for?'

What's come over her? A good SW doesn't ask. And a client's friend — in the record I am the 'client' — comes under that.

'You say, Carol. My English no good.' But Carmen's teeth shine. Against her, Carol looks musty, older, though their children are the same ages. Carmen will get plumper, but she'll stay hard-colored.

'It's to keep the bull in the barn.'

'Hmm. I should have had one of those dolls.'

'I give you, missus. I get more.'

'Thanks. Too late to shut the barn door. . . . Well, Carol, *hasta la vista*. Keep well.'

'Have a good vacation.' Her gray is showing. 'Get blonder.' I feel generous. 'And remember me to the kids.'

'Their father has them.' She is looking at me like at a person. Like I am one. 'I'm going in retreat. Up Hudson. I'll send you a card, hair freak.'

She never told me anything personal before. I don't even know her maiden name. 'In retreat? Don't do that. I had a college friend did that. She came out a nun.'

'Oh, Carol. Know something? You're great.' She shoulders the bag. 'And I have to — get the year in repair. I have to.' She is gone.

'So what means "re-pair"?'

How can I say? It's what I'm in. 'Have to get you a dictionary, Carmen. So you can pick these things up on your own.'

'Also you.' She squeezes the dishrag, draping it carefully over the sink's edge; there's no hook for it. 'That lady, I think she is no more good for you.' She drops a Spanish phrase I don't catch.

'What's that mean?'

A shrug, a headshake, a smile; she's not going to say. '¡*Cuidado*!' she shrieks suddenly, stamping her tiny foot.

'What, what?' I know already.

'A roach.'

'**D**oes being well scare you, Ms. Westmount?'

August twenty-fifth. Mickens and me. For the third time.

She's the same as she was the first time, fresh-crowned with her SW degree 'from Brandeis,' cool as her vinyl rain-cape, stiff as her brand-new jogging shoes — and hell-bent on not being anybody's substitute.

That first time, she found Lopez's gimpy bell-system pronto — which was more than the firemen could when the second-floor-rear's oven exploded. And she was up the four flights to me before you could say crackerjack; she has never sat on a stoop.

I was scattering the bicarb-borax when she banged on the door, and in answer to my 'Who is it?' yells back like they're calling out the troops: 'The visitor!'

That'll be the substitute, I think; they're always louder than the original. So when I open up and she walks right in past me, I let her. Those thick shoe-soles of hers send up the powder like we're on maneuvers. With a SW you always are, but the dust is not usually that visible.

Her pitch is total honesty, she tells me. Even though I wouldn't know her name is BRYNA, except for her fourteen-carat gold bracelet saying it. 'Total' means she interviewed my own neighbors before visiting me, but didn't say. I only catch on when she asks me do I really feel touched by God? I say 'I could only wish. It would save everybody energy.'

The new style in social psychiatry is not to pussyfoot anymore 'but to confront.' She is up to her earrings in the new style. And even that first time, making sure I expect it. She's read my record *in full*, and knows I have 'the requisite IQ.' What she's really saying is that she's got my number — which if she has, she will be the first, not excluding me — and that I am to play pattycake with her confront.

And now this double-whammy question. Does being well scare me? When after what happened over Gold's last prescription, I am scared, yes. To unbutton my lip to this dame about anything.

... When I brought in that prescription to the drugstore down the corner, the pharmacist, who is also the owner, gives me a smile; by now he knows me, I don't mind. He takes the folded white slip into the back, like always. But after a minute he comes out again. He is a nice, shriveled little man in a dirty white coat. 'I can't fill this, Miss. Some mistake maybe. Is this yours?' On examination it wasn't. Not for me, and not for tofranil or compazine either. Or for what I'd been getting. 'For a controlled substance,' he says. '— one on special register. In the name of Daisy Gold.' 'They mailed me a mistake,' I said. 'I'll have to go to the office.' He could give me one of my usual, to tide me over, he said; 'I know how that office goes, Miss; you could spend the day.' And he did give me the one pill. Calling me 'Miss'— but he kept that prescription. . . .

I did go to the office. I'm responsible. They took a long time looking up my case, which is listed as I want it, under Carol Carol. Though the other names must be in it for the record, Gold always did her best for me, in those conferences, where they decide. This time I did my best for her. When I said to the worker at the desk, a youngish black man: 'I'll need a new prescription, my bag was stole,' I could even hear her voice. 'Say "stolen," Carol. Stop putting on.'

She wasn't too honest to have faith.

'Would you repeat the question, Mrs. Mickens?' I say now. I know quite well the substitute's not a Mrs. Just like she must know what I'm not.

'*Miss* Mickens.' But she repeats the question.

'I'm not Westmount.'

'We know.'

Gold always said 'I.' Her and me. 'We' was the office.

'Westmount is in Montreal,' I say. 'A suburb.'

'A fancy one. Like all your names. For fancy places.'

Miss Evanston, Miss Bridgehampton, Miss Paget — that's Bermuda. The list is long. All in memory of the nice home-places a nice orphan college girl at a democratic college got invited to for the school holidays. Places as good as anywhere for stopping up your ears against the call of the wild. Around the country-club pool, in the borrowed bathing-suit.

For a time, all that girl thinks to do is to swing. So did a

lot of others then. So do a lot of us always, until after
graduation we are pulled back — all but a few of us. If the
suburbs don't do it for sure, the city job will. Or the family
job.

But there are always some, a few, who are determined not
to have just a single history. Funny how you think you can
manage that — when you're young.

. . . Bomb camaraderie. In the basement of a brownstone
front — so appropriate. Amateurs, playing the matchstick
game. The others around that work-talk table all have
parents who are too rich to love. They envy me my aunts,
and my orphan freedom. I marvel at the electrical
know-how and other survival lore that the top private prep
schools seem to provide. Later on in the afternoon the
lace-curtained windows in the house across the street will
shatter in the blast. I'm told I wasn't there; those who
should know keep telling me that I'd gone for sandwiches.
I can't recall. But the weather-in-the-streets later — I too
would have wanted that. So, like the others, I went on the
run. . . .

'Eastlake. Northwood.' Mickens is being chummy. 'Why?'

Nine out of ten she's hoping to do a paper on me. Funny,
how it squints the eyes.

'I was seeking direction,' I said.

When she's about to leave she recalls that I haven't
answered the first part of her question.

Does she mean that I am well? Or may shortly be
considered so? The balance is hard. And winter is coming.
To stay on the outside, you have to be just well enough.

'I wouldn't know,' I say. 'But by the time Daisy comes
back, I may.'

'Daisy? Oh — Mrs. Gold. I'm afraid — she's not coming back.'

Mickens is not 'afraid.' One thing the pills do, they make you see other people's body movements. The involuntary ones you no longer have. She has planted her feet. She doesn't know what 'afraid' is. 'You may as well know. Mrs. Gold is no longer on the job.'

I expected that. Those druggists have to report.

I look her over. Showing nothing of what I may be thinking. This makes her nervous. She knows she's not real enough. For these lower depths.

I stare until she falters. This takes experience.

Shrink back only a step like she has, and you're in the pad's little half-room, if you can call it that. I don't have anything more to put there. You could crowd an extra cot in, if you needed. The guy beneath me has a Moog. 'Good heavens,' she says, pointing. 'What's that?'

Lopez's handyman jobs will never earn him a license, or a union membership. The bell downstairs, when pressed, often gives one a shock. Up here he's criss-crossed scrap metal every which way over the window on the shaft, and daubed it black. It takes up all the wall.

'Why — this is almost a room,' she says, turning slow on her heel. 'You could have a desk. And a chair. I could get you the vouchers.'

Some SW's keep wanting to give you. It's the way they see for you to live. Or that's how they view giving. Last thing they want to do for clients is to identify with them. Giving keeps them from doing that.

To me, they always want to give a desk.

'No thanks.'

'Why not?'

Because, in the end all furniture blows away, in the bomb blast. Silent though some of those may be. Nest down in any alley, and you're safer. Only have enough blankets. Then you're in control.

'Just take down that awful black thing, Carol. And you could have a workroom. We know you worked for environmental causes. Or you could do just typing. You're very literate.'

They're ganging up on me like always. I can hear them saying that: she's very literate. A SW is a gang all-in-one. With concealed weapons ever to hand.

The best thing you can do with empty house-space is to keep it that way — clear. Fill it, and the day will come when you know better. And watch out, meanwhile, that you don't fill your head to match.

'No, no.' I remember my manners. 'Thanks very much. But no.'

'Why not, Carol dear? It could be a darling space.'

So now we have the intimacy needle. And the 'we-girls' one.

'It's where I keep the gorilla,' I said.

At the Cat Club, the cry to-night is — 'Everything's at sixes and sevens.' Nobody knows who started it.

'Why isn't it at twelves and thirteens?' the dancing-girl asks. 'Wouldn't that make more sense?' How, she doesn't say. Nobody has to make sense here, but she won't relax. She is our house-fly, Alphonse says; there's no getting rid of her. 'Because ever so often, a go-go girl has no place to.'

'It refers to dice,' a big-breasted woman named Margaret says. One of those sweet fatties who dress like they haven't heard of jeans — a gingham housedress and a bow in her hair — she never seems to feel the cold. Alphonse has started to call her Mavorneen, saying to me, 'We have to have one from time to time.' More and more he's on top of things, or on the bottle less and less, though alcohol is cagy. When I came in tonight he whispered: 'I'm on the wagon. Wagon's full of nails.'

Seems the couple from Long Island City, the owner's manager and his 'common-law wife,' are expected to come by. Alphonse saw them parking their truck, a new gray-and-red Ram with a long wheelbase but empty, in front of the greasy spoon hash-house on the Avenue. The woman stayed in the cab while he went in; maybe they expect the owner also. 'Her hair is as red as her fur.'

'In summer?' the go-go says. 'Only cats wear fur.'

Ours is where we can't see him, in the ground-floor window, in front of that screen — but we know he's there, paws tucked in. Cats don't fade.

It is now mid-September. When the desk Mickens insisted on sending me finally came, Angel and I upended it against the wall opposite Lopez's construction. Then we hung the bike on it. But insurrection worries me. I mustn't let it go too far.

'They'll be having lunch, that couple. I know their routine.' Alphonse is in real pain, real white, but he hasn't jacked out the pint bottle; maybe it's in the corner he jokes is his office, in with the cat stuff, the cleaning rags and the packets of toilet paper, the flat kind he cadges from a public restroom somewhere. His own private stash of belongings wanders the place, a couple of bags giving way whenever we're crowded, but always very neat. If ever I forget the necessaries, he's said he'll lend me. But when I roll up or stretch out on the newspapers he keeps stacked here, my one thick sweater does me, along with the trenchcoat some worn-out debutante left at the thrift, alongside me my shoulder bag, that almost matches it, in the bag a pewter flask that keeps water fresh, matchbooks, and an airline pillow I've had forever. Winter tricks, that I keep as reminders. On top I scatter summer: Handi-wipes, Kool-aid. I never bring anything to leave.

'The old girl, our landlady, she has other Village property,' Alphonse is saying. 'The kind she keeps up all right, all right, you bet. That pair will be making the rounds there first. The old woman must pay them a price. They'll leave this place until last.'

'Whatever could go wrong?' I say, checking the floor, which has been swept, each stash on it practically geometrical, the drying underwear all disposed under the shirts and tee-shirts. It's not perfect here. There's that acrid smell of jeans-crotch and cheesy underarm; you can't wash a human being at a launderette. And transiency casts its cloud; you would never mistake this joint for more than a shake-down. I find that reassuring. But on the up-and-up we have all done our best. At least on this floor. Above, all is ruin, but not ours.

'Everything's neat beyond the call of duty, Alphonse. If you ask me, the brass here is kind of a nag.'

He loves it, when we call him the brass. But now he looks shamed. 'I never told you the real deal. The old lady down there in Florida, she once got her mug in the papers as the worst slum landlord in Manhattan. Now she's moved up in the world, to a suburb of Palm Beach. But he and the redhead, they hate her guts; this here was to be their revenge. Nobody's supposed to live here; she's holding to sell for the land. The deal they cut with me; I was to sneak people in; they would keep hands off. Over the summer. We were to trash this place, but still occupy it. A health menace, so they can turn the old lady in. But I couldn't hack it. Not that deal.'

'Hey —,' I say low. 'Hey.' We look at each other across the others.

'Oh wow —,' the dancer says. 'Let's. Like it could be an art piece — performance art.' She does a twirl. 'Let's trash.' She does a great scoop of a twirl, calling out 'La Trasherero' and swirls a curtsy to the floor. Her black ballet slippers are split and chalky, but I see there was more to her than go-go once.

'But we only just tapped into the electric again,' a kid who did that bypass for us wails. He's thin from AIDS but did a very good job; his uncle, an electrician, threw him out, right while he was learning the business.

Big Margaret beats her breasts; she's always at them; her pills are for fits. 'Hopin' to bake bread, I was.' In her stash she carries old kitchen appliances, a toaster and a countertop oven, but the kid hasn't let her plug in, for fear the newly spliced bypass might blow.

Both of them have been here for longer than what Mungo, who as a former sailor claimed to be learned on all the varieties of time round the atlas, used to call a 'fortnight,' saying life went better by those than by the week. At the moment the Cat Club is down to us five. The kid won't give his name; we call him Ace. The names come easy. Getting in here is like what coming out of zero tundra into the warm igloo must be. We plug into a house.

But how is it they don't stay on and on? — Alphonse said to me soon after I arrived. 'Beats me.' At the onset he'd been prepared to have trouble moving folks on in a kindly way. 'So that more could benefit.' Each time he worries himself somebody might be getting to be a fixture, then can't believe it when one day they don't turn up. He says he can forget them after five days. But down in his heart he wants all of them to stay. That's why he hangs onto me. But one day I'm going to disappoint him too. This place is not the outside.

'Trash this place. This place? I couldn't do it, understand?' he says, appealing to the three of us.

We do. He had to do what he saw could be done here. He couldn't resist.

The kid is fiddling with Margaret's toaster. A kind of nineteen fifties job with an arrow design on its chrome. 'Know what you'd be, Alphonse? If you wasn't a wino? A parole officer.'

Out of the mouths of babes. Alphonse — he's an improver. You could almost marry him to Mickens, if he wasn't one of those timid almost neuters. Not just merely off the sex sauce, like me. Or maybe he wasn't so neuter once?

'That pair won't be coming this late,' I tell him. 'It's ten pm.' Just when any like us start to come in. But not those daytimers. The Club is on another time, really. On the outside, you still have to deal with those others, the workadays. Even while you're walking their pavement, or hanging around stuck straight up in their sun.

'Never fear, that pair will be coming. I got a letter last week. Asking why no housing complaints?'

He goes off to the toilet. He used to do that to retch, but not any more. Nobody ever remarks, either way. When you luck into the use of an in-house toilet and no questions asked — you know your luck.

'Hey — this toaster tests okay,' Ace yells. His face falls then — or what's left of it. 'So old though. I dunno we should.'

I feel so cozy here. There's nothing like meeting your kind. And like —having something to risk. This Ace would understand what I did with the desk.

'When they come,' Margaret asks '— can't we hide?'

On this big square of poured concrete with no closets, no curtains, only our three stashes for furnishings and the one tiny stall, where could we hide that big butt of hers, those breasts that just looking at makes mine feel sore?

Alphonse comes back. He shows us a patch he's put on his arm. You wear one, and it's supposed to keep you from smoking. 'Somebody told me it works for wine.'

The go-go girl gives up on him. 'I gotta lead on a job.' She twirls out, taking her gold-leather backpack with her; we don't ask where.

I stay the night. We make toast.

Once the sun is up, Margaret and I climb to the third floor. Her weight makes it risky; half the risers are bunged in. The violations stare at us as we pass. Ripped off banisters, plaster hanging from the lath at every landing, water-stained ceiling far above. A smell of rot. In places here and there you can see the brick. The ladder to the roof is on its chain, but the landing up there is caved in. On each floor doors on either side of the staircase are open; if you want you can peer in and see how people have lived. At the third floor front Margaret says 'Italians lived here. Fifty years in one place maybe, like my folks. The kitchen — see that old-style white tile? A tub over there, once. Mondays the work-shirts. Saturday before, the kids. Same soap.'

An easy chair is still in the front room by the window, its bottom stuffing half on the floor. When it holds her, she crows. I sit on a plank over the radiator. Gone to rust, it hadn't been worth stealing. 'Ours was a cold-water flat,' she says. 'Two front windows, like here.' I say, 'Don't lean. The sills are crumbling.' The air blows in free. Only the street level is boarded up.

'We always leaned,' Margaret said. 'The mothers, that is. We kids got socked for it. For our mothers, talking window to window, it was like a club.'

Sun climbs high. We have no watch. She has one in her slip hem. 'But it's squashed. I stepped on it.' The slip, which has pockets in the hem for valuables, was a gift from the staff when she left Valatie.

She spells that for me, like for a spelling contest. 'Vee ay — *vah*, ell-ay — *lah*; tee. But it's pronounced Valaysha.' She wouldn't have had to explain; on the street you get to know them all. Rockland's not bad, they say. Manhattan State is the worst.

She is only on a one-month try-out pass to her family. The pass is in the hem pocket, along with her medication. 'I don't report in, I go back to first base.' But she is on her way back there. Her folks hassled her.

'Ace skipped, before it got light,' she says. 'You were sacked out. He took my little oven. I'd have guv it; I can't keep it upstate. But maybe to take it set him up.'

Not my hang-up, lifting stuff, but I know what she means. I've watched people hoard a piece of crap to their hearts one night, toss it away the morning after. And not always crap. Or if it's money, gone before you can say Jack Robinson — leaving them nothing to live on for the week.

Still — I like knowing. I am not a Christian, never been baptized. My one aunt was, the night one; though she never was at church, she taught in a rough school. Which she claimed was enough religious instruction. How can we really be Christian, she said — unless we know thieves? I feel akin to that. Unless I wise to what others on the outside, sleeping in my alleys, walking my paths, are capable of, how can I be one of them?

Down below, the street is September for sure. That foggy pall is no longer summer, no matter how hot. Look at the city from up above this time of year and it's like draped. Season's last call. First call from winter, my element.

'Mid-morning, my gut says.' Margaret brings out a cardboard cake box from one of her homemade folds; she was a seamstress by trade before she went in. One-and-a-half deli sandwiches and a jelly doughnut are stuffed in. We eat, me taking the half. Camaraderie is where you find it. And sandwiches.

When the car draws up in the street down below, its top shines like a beetle crawling toward its burrow. The persons who get out — you can tell they have breakfasted. The man carries his belly like it is satisfied. The woman saunters in her fox fur. Rushing the season. Maybe it was in storage in the warehouse. The wig doesn't match. Red fox is more orange. But who's this third person, short and stumpy, also in fur?

'Must be the old girl herself,' Margaret says. 'Florida to the city, sure. You wear your mink no matter what.'

We wait. There's no reason for us to hold our breath, but we do.

'Get yourself up like a customer, don't you,' Margaret says to me then. 'That brown skirt. That tan blouse. Thrift shop, I know the score. But it's the picking that counts. Got all your marbles too. But you don't talk much. They give you shock?'

I shake my head. But it knows it should speak. 'My think-track. It sticks.' Or it piles up. 'Long time ago, things blew. I mean really blew. A bomb.' How it helps to say. And who better to, where it can slip into those loose hem folds. 'After that, I was a long time on the run. I didn't do it, they said later; I only thought I did. But you turn yourself in; they tend to believe.'

'You been in the slammer?'

'Not for long. They said I wasn't responsible. But in the end they want you to be. That's when I got started on the hospital.'

'Which one?'

A private one, she wouldn't know of it. She didn't.

'Boston. My two aunts had left me a trust.'

'A truss is for hernia. Old-country stuff.' She looks at me sideways, like maybe I am screwy.

'Here, it's money.' Game stakes, left over from obedient Sunday afternoons in the bay window.

'Ah-hah. So you couldn't get the disability, huh. Not till you use up the truss, huh?'

I look at her. The all over fat, so queerly placed. The sneakers, on slab feet. A sweet two hundred pound subnormal, in teenage clothes. But on certain things, all the Club's clientele will know the score.

'Not back then, no.' Not until the halfway house. Such a dedicated one, the SW up there advised. But how naive a one though, for the swingers some of us had become. — You've such a good environmentalist record; you even marched — they said. — But over-night stands are not allowed here.

'This is my third pass,' Margaret said. 'I'm not mental; I got a wrong gene. But my folks, they won't take me for good. There's a guy at Valatie, he would. A guard. I made a communion dress for his son's kid. When he retires, he'll sign me out, he might even marry me. If they say okay.'

'I know an ashram would take you.' Women kitchen-slaves. Long days of fostered male calm, lean brown rice. Not to eat at all makes the head sing. Top slaves get to wash the Swami's feet, and maybe sing with him. 'But I wouldn't recommend.'

Talking at cross-purposes is the safest. Even on the ward, we all know how to dream the past. And to forget the future. To be on the run is the best of all.

'Finished, hon'? You don't want your crusts, I'll take.' Margaret's voice is dulcet, like the kids in my grade school classes, who were always willing to nibble the leavings of the thick sandwiches our hired-girl had forgot to trim — since bits of crab or ham or turkey adhered to them. Mothers urge a child to eat the crusts. Maiden aunts teach it not to. When I catch myself at that I am still shamed.

'What you suppose they're doing down there?' Margaret whispers. 'I got to pee. I'll go use the one here.'

'None of them work, up here. The plumbing is cut off.' And the basins gone.

'Okay. I'll hold off.' Her compliance is so humble. Her smile so sweet.

I feel like an attendant. They're not nurses. There's not enough distance between the patient and them. The world is full of them. 'Go if you have to, Margaret.'

She too likes the sound of her name.

'Nah. But Jeez, it's hot up here.'

Framed in the window, she sits rubbing those breasts. I kneel at the other window, chin on the sill. Doze off and I could be in the hospital common-room, among such silent figures as hers. Or weaving ones: right foot, left foot, blotted here and there in the medicinal dusk. Time for my pill now, but I am dozing. What's going on down on the floors below doesn't count — not in hospital. The ward you're on is your diagnosis. A cure goes floor-by-floor, down, down — until you're out. Or the years can pass, up, up, into forever. At the end of the long corridor leading to the locked wards, two attendants — they travel in pairs there, — are closing the door on a yell.

I wake.

Margaret's screaming — 'I can't stand them. Get it away.' Braced in the window, she has drawn her feet up on the arm of the easy chair.

The cat is in the rafters. Crouched. Above eye level, they double in size. Tawny, it stalks toward her, transfixed by her screams.

'Don't lean, Margaret; don't lean —' I am screaming too.

But she already has. The cat springs to the empty sill.

When I get near the pad it's a dawn fresh with leaves, like the city can still come up with when it wants to. Cooling toward summer's end, and so early even the garbage looks innocent. Orange peels and other natural throwaways, instead of filth. In this part of town no police-car has come yet for a body, tacking a notice on the boarded-up front door — not up here yet, not today.

When I sneaked down the stairs, how long after I don't know, it was still dark. As I sat in the empty house, white day seeped in from the storefront. It became light enough to see Margaret's stash in a corner. One blanket-heap looks like another to most people; they wouldn't know it was hers. A black blouse she traveled in hung on the wash line. Alphonse's extra tee-shirt was gone from there, but down at the end was his flannel shirt, hung waiting for winter; he must've forgotten it when he was cleared out — or not had time. Would he be back for the shirt? Should I take it, on the chance I would see him again? Would I ever? I couldn't decide. Be too neat, and you might suffer the consequences.

When the light is normal, I leave. Behind me, the Club

looks like one of those storerooms where some dumb occupational therapy has failed. But I know better. Here I am in a locked house, but I know a way out.

When I go out through the shed there's another decision to make. Who can be sure that a club with no membership will really die? So I did what we always did. I threw the bolts, one after the other, leaving them in the trial-and-error positions that most anyone could solve.

I hike all the way up from the Village to the barrio. Not that I am to blame for what happened to her. But when one of us dies like that, everybody ought to take a little punishment.

I'm out of practice though. Walking is our way of staying in the fog. Now my head is too clear for that. And I haven't even taken my pill.

One block to go, I meet up with Angel. He looks good these days; he's in a ball team that plays in Central Park. *Madre de Dios*, he says; I guess I don't look so good to him. 'Watch it —' he says before he runs off. 'You got company.'

What's Mickens doing, tracking me down before she's due? On the new bi-monthly schedule she'd put me on. Hinting that with her heavy case-load I can't expect her to give me the one-to-one attention. And I know I'll have to deal with her about the desk. Why's she breathing down my neck? Then it hits me. She must have lined up a job. Wait 'til she sees her prospect. Smears from that stairway, a nail-hole in the sock. Dust-patches on elbows and knees. Cobwebs in the hair. Or droppings from the rafters.

Then it strikes me. I'm in luck. Rest of the block, I drag my feet, rehearsing. Oh I'm ready, Miz M. Secretarial skills maybe a mite out-of-date. But I can get along in Spanish, for some firm needs that. Or maybe some nice office needs a go-for, for sandwiches. These days I button my blouses right, and both are washable — maybe a receptionist?

This early, the Avenue is still a family place. Off-Track betting office not open yet, no men ganging around in front of our bar. Somebody's on our stoop though, slumped. Worn out by us already? She didn't seem the type.

But hey. But — hey. This is not the SW. Or not any more.

Don't turn around, please. Stay where you left me. Don't. She already has. It's Daisy Gold.

I knew just what to do. Why wouldn't I of all people?

'Daisy. Daisy,' I say low. 'Daisy.' Just that. Her name.

I know what else she'll want though. A haven. Even if for starters she refuses it. A duck-blind, where the creature behind it is the duck. Even so, you have to test whether it'll come where it wants to. I can't help that what I say is what attendants say too. 'Come along.'

Even if you want to, sometimes you run. But she comes quietly.

Four flights, poorly lit. You don't see much, but it's a long time to smell a person. I never did any dope. But the body don't distinguish. Any way you choose not to clean it, it'll respond. Months on the road get ingrained; Gold's not there yet. Her flesh is only sad sour from being ignored, first by other people maybe, then by her. Girls in a dorm get that way — the shy, depressed ones. But the gym sweat can cover it, and the monthly rut.

On the outside, a person long there can smell like a bear

has moved in next to you. Even in the Club, one such person can fill a whole corner with vegetable evil. But that kind of stink is still part of the going world.

Gold is on stoppage. Dusty hair fades into her dim sweater, with a little human leakage at the armpits. Some rose petals, if you dry them they only go bad, like the past they come from. On the ward, that's all taken care of either way. I don't see her there yet.

On the road, certain body-hints are like measurements. A guy can knock a guy, saying he pees soda-water, meaning not as yellow as a jock. The blood odor can link women temporarily. And it is well known, even counted a blessing, that street routine can make the sex machinery slack off. You hunker down into what you are.

Gold's not there yet.

At the top, last floor, is my door. She stands in front of it, legs apart, like she's about to fall. 'A wreath. A white one. That's for a dead child.'

'Carmen Lopez picked a load of wreaths off the garbage truck.' Shouting at the sanitation men didn't they know enough to sort out the goodies for people to keep? Coming up the stoop afterward with two, three, like bracelets on her arm, one around her neck and on her head a wreath crown. 'We all got them, the whole house. Carmen says a wreath is a protection. And they're not all-white. They have red velvet wound in.'

I take out my new key.

Gold says 'You have a double lock now.' She begged me to, when I first got here, but I held back.

'Yeah, Lopez again. He's gunning for high class super. I'm his Master's thesis. He'll get in the union yet.' Then the Lopez's will leave. But before that, I could be gone.

The lock sticks, but I push in. She falls into the desk chair just in time. . . . I know that allgone shuddering, not connected to any muscle you can name. A tremble that a medic may identify, if he thinks you're worth explaining to, as 'indiscriminate.' The long words that intern used peeled out of my brain like on a string. 'Fear can pool in the limbs like blood, Miss —.' He'd stolen a glance at the name-choices on the chart. 'Call me Carol,' I'd said. . . .

He was right about the fear. It lies ready, like blood. But I am maybe wrong about Gold. She can still cry.

'They took the kids away from me,' she says. Her hands come down from her face and settle in her lap, tremoring. She squeezes them to a stop. 'The worst is, I wanted them to.'

It's hot up here; my room is the oven of the house. She shrugs off her jacket, the same plaid one as always, and lets it fall. I pick it up; the floor is always powdery.

'Let it lie,' she says. 'It could use a spot or two.'

The jacket is dead clean, and flat out of the wringer. Like it no longer wants a body in it. This is the way the clothes you go in with come back to you when you leave.

'It's been disinfected, huh?' Now I am shivering.

'It's been in the vat, yes. Of community wrath.'

We are both whispering.

'They said you were in retreat. That Mickens; she did.'

'Who's she?'

She doesn't remember?

'The new worker.'

'That was kind of her.'

I am out of talk. Ordinary talk-fest — I'm beginning to

be able to. But when an emotion comes up, I have to wait. Funny, that it was Gold herself suggested how to handle that. Count to twenty, she'd said — or to whatever the traffic will bear. So I do twenty-five.

'She's no substitute.' I hack out then. 'Not for you.'

'That's kind of you.' She chokes. 'Can I have some water?'

I keep it cold in an old milk bottle I bought at the thrift. There's more food in the fridge now because of the Club — little goodies I bring there. It's worth it to see maybe the dancer's face light up with a yearn. And so as not to push for thanks, I'd have to eat along with them.

Gold stands in front of the fridge like before a shrine. Everything is in perfect rows there. I'm not squeaky clean. But it is. 'Still not —' she whispers.

'Not what?'

'Casual.'

'I keep telling you. Don't ask me to be what I can't.'

'Why not? That's what they asked of me.'

Shame colors her face. When people first come out they are too delicate; they don't want to be asked anything. But where's she been?

'Up the Hudson, were you, Gold? You never sent me that card.'

'I couldn't.'

'Rockland State, was it? They do drug rehabs.'

She goes so quiet. With such a look. Must be hard for her profession. When it crosses over to being us.

'That what Mickens told you?'

'Come on, Gold. When does a worker really tell you anything?'

Not fair. She did, sometimes.

She's fisted up. So have I. I put my fist against hers, giving it a little push. 'Besides —.'

'Besides what, Carol?'

Almost the old voice. Maybe they put her in jail after all. Most people would prefer that. 'Else — why would you come back here?'

She is drinking the water. She puts the glass on the table. Lopez has bolstered the table's gimpy leg. She sees the desk, still upended with the bike on it, but Angel has slung a great blue-glass parking-chain on the handlebars, the kind you wear around your neck for decoration when you're riding. It all looks like I'm using the bike. She sees the new window-blind. 'I was in emergency — Bellevue. I did take pills, a lot of them. But only once. They pumped me out. When the nuns at the retreat wouldn't take me, the hospital made me stay on. Last week — they let me go.'

So that's why she doesn't look streetwise yet; only no longer housebred. I know the whole route. 'Where'd they put you?'

Laugh — and that's only a joke. Answer on the level, and it's routine.

'My mother-in-law wouldn't take me back either. My husband's family home, in New Rochelle. Two years ago, when he got a job teaching out there, we went to live with her. Temporarily. When he left me for someone else, the kids and I had to stay on; my take-home wouldn't cover a move. Now she wants the kids. Their father is alone again. He's moving back in with her. He teaches their same school; maybe it's best for them. Keep them out of the inner city, where I'd have to be; maybe he and his mother are right.'

She's already folded her hands. Body posture. On the ward you learn to recognize it. Underneath all the social work.

'New Rochelle don't have drugs, Gold? Angel here don't drug.'

Don't, doesn't. She used to nag me my street lingo was an affectation. Now she doesn't even notice.

'I make a fuss, he and my mother-in-law are set to declare me incompetent. And where could I take the kids right now on my own? Up there, they have their own room. I no longer even have furniture.'

'Thrift shops. Except for the beds. By law, they can't resell those.' I like sleeping on the floor. But since we exterminate Carmen has lent me a cot. Anyway, soon I'll have a sleeping-bag.

'Carol. I don't even have where.'

'You're — not on the street?'

She draws back, like a bird. 'In a parish house, in the Bronx. They have a program.'

A rehab program. I've gone on those. 'That's good.' It's what you say. And sometimes you can touch a tamed bird, if you move slow. I do, just the back of her hand. 'You're on interim, hey.' I smile, to show I recall the lingo. Interim relief was what I was on when I first came on her load.

She takes so long to answer I wonder what medication they've put her on.

'Carol. My first job after I took my degree, the hardest thing to do in a city court was to separate mother from child. Any mother. My first load, I had a crazy, her half-grown kids still in diapers, fed on sour milk, never out in the air, the house a sty. In court — she was Mary, mother of

God. Now it's all turned round. Child abuse — one hint of it. And my mother-in-law and he will hint.'

'Abuse? Those kids? They didn't even know you were there.'

Shouldn't have said that. You can't always say what you think. When you're on the mend — the docs all say to me — that'll be the hardest for you. Tact — it's not really a lie. Means you're making the break, Carol, from just being only you.

'Maybe I wasn't there enough for them.'

'You? With how you do for people. They didn't appreci-ate.' I know they didn't. Pure brats.

'They were jealous of that. My husband too. He said he didn't want a woman with misery always on her mind. That I couldn't turn off, when I got home.'

Home. Homes can twist people. Some tribes, maybe they're the smart ones, they make a different camp every night. The load of being stock-still inside a house is too terrible.

'But you didn't turn us off, Gold. Here you are.'

'Not that way. The office — they put me on leave. They say I'm burned out. Indefinite leave.'

'But you're here, Gold; you're back.' She's looking at me funny. 'So why? You going to come see us for free?'

She looks so gone I say, 'Hey. Joke.' She used to say that was why she had hopes for me, that I could joke. That we two could. But now she's transferred it all to me?

'I came into the city for a hearing, Carol. On me. At the office. Severance pay-to-come — and thank you very much. "You had too heavy a case-load, Gold; it can happen to the best of us."' She wipes her mouth with the back of her hand. 'Too nice to say the real load was me.'

I get up to walk. Even inside, I have to. The pad has more excuses to now. I can make tea. I can shift the blind.

'And then they console me how good I was at the job. How well some of you worked out. "There's that case you had forever, Gold. Remarkable."'

I keep walking.

'So I came by, Carol. Unprofessional of me. But anybody can use a little upbeat. So I came by. To sit on your stoop. And have a peek at my success.'

Do I want to be that? To anyone?

I shift the blind. Pull a cord, and the outside pays you a call.

'Yeah, your pad looks great, Carol,' she says behind me.

Even before I turn I pick up that nasty tone of hers. I never minded; it kind of braced me. That she would take the trouble.

When I do turn, she's scrunched up on the desk chair. Who does she remind me of? Head between the shoulders, ready to spit. 'Yeah, the pad. But does that mean you yourself have to look as if you've been to-hell-and-gone? Like you've slipped back?'

I had honestly forgot.

I touch myself, the smear on my tee-shirt where I leaned on the sill, the all-over dust. The dirt-bobbles the rafters must have shed on my hair. 'Oh Jesus God. . . . Look Daisy. This is not the way I'm being anymore.' How can I say it? 'I been going to a kind of club; it's been good. People I can hang out with. Reasons to eat. I even help out. But last night, they had — an accident. Bad. Nobody was to blame. But when the police came, I hid, that's all. In a dirty place. The rest of the members had lit out. And I walked home. Where you met me.'

I go on my knees to her. 'Don't be disappointed. Don't. Listen — you always wanted me to have a mirror, right, but I wouldn't? . . . Wait.'

The full-length mirror's in the ell too. Don't use it much, only when I feel I can afford to. It's good value, four dollars, got at my usual. No frame, just leans against a corner. A mirror with the silver backing so scratched there are empty streaks in it. But you can still see a smile in it. How long since you last did that, facing yourself, Carol? . . . Now use the shower Ramon Lopez fixed you, even if it spills into the sink. Out with the clean tee and the dungarees. Brush the hair hard. And listen, Carol. Be-ee ca-a-sual.

When I come back — well, I emerge. A fashion plate. Earrings even. Angel gave me. They almost match the barette.

I see she is not disappointed. Very offhand, I open the refrigerator and take my pill-of-the-day. That reminds her. I see that the pill she takes from her box is over-the-counter. Take more of that kind and you would just throw up.

She watches me watch her take it; I can't help myself.

I make the tea.

Sleeping on the floor of this old tenement is like sleeping on the ground. Basic thoughts creep toward me from the sidewalks down below, and up through the old lead water-pipes that no Lopez can fix. I saw New York ground-dirt once — when our eighth-grade class from Dedham visited, at a time when the last empty spaces in midtown were being 'improved.' In the construction sites a giant gamboge mud oozed from the deep of the planet, swelling toward the curbside vans lined up to hold it in, thinning to a yellow glaze on avenues long ago paved. Teacher said iron oxide caused the color, but we were used to neat brown garden earth and knew we were catching a glimpse of the planet's true turd.

Nowadays any such wounded sites are quickly fenced in, with whimsical crescents cut in the solid planking for passersby to peer through — but only after the foundations are in. No one sees the city's underpinning any more except the pit-workers, whose hard hats maybe hold down the iron thoughts reddening their necks. I sympathize with whoever is that close to the ground.

Gold sleeps in the ell, on the cot. Day after she arrived we phoned the mission in the Bronx, to report. First she talked to them, citing her search for a job down here. Then I. I was the 'cousin' housing her, the Dedham accent returning cool and New England to my tongue. When we finished I put a quarter in the box the Lopez's keep on the kitchen table for any neighbor's use of the phone, then added the second quarter I always insist on: 'It's for the overhead.' A word that Carmen doesn't take to; maybe she considers it anti-tropical. This time she waits until Gold, at her suggestion, goes off to do her clothes at the new launderette three stores down from the bar, then nudges me aside, though there is no one else in the apartment. 'Your friend, she's how old?' She insists on calling Gold my friend.

'I don't know — maybe forty?'

It still amazes me that Carmen is only a year older than me. She says she has the jump on me 'only in the body,' while I have been 'happened to' in the mind. Not that she rules this out for herself. She has given Lopez an ultimatum. When she is thirty, things being as usual with him, she will kill that woman in the bar.

Now she says 'Forty, s-s-s?' between her teeth. 'And nobody clapping — si?'

So that night, using my sink, we do Gold's hair. A soft female light comes through the blind. Angel sticks his head in the door, mocking us — 'Yah-h-h.' Such a stink — *zal hedor* — should he phone the gas company? When we are done Carmen claps her hands in front of Gold like she did in front of the plaster virgin she'd found in an ashcan, after she repainted it. Gold is standing as still as that statue, which is now in the Lopez's bedroom, with Carmen's headbands stacked on it. Carmen pats Gold's cheek. 'Now your hair is the same as your name.'

Carmen is a circus I have come to love. Where I have been taken into the scene behind the acts. Before she let me use the floor to sleep on again she made me sweep it, and wash with her latest discovery, oil soap. She held up the bottle, worshiping. Together we have repaired my year. I say, 'Tell Angel to come, later tonight. For the bike.'

I see she knows what that means. She's looking at my new possession, which for want of anywhere else to put it, I have slung on the gorilla cage. A one-person backpack which can unfold to serve as an outdoor shelter. First designed according to the newspapers, by a minister in Philadelphia, it is reputed to have saved many a life-in-the-cold. Thousands are said to be now in use. People who still live inside tend to avert their eyes from the user carrying one; it is a badge. A few stare in envy. Not Carmen.

'Found it at the thrift,' I say in awe. 'Brand-new.' Everything in life ends up at that shop. There's a moral lesson in every bin. I touch her cheek. 'No bugs.' She touches mine.

Tenement people are used to partings. It's then you can embrace.

'You no come back, Carol? You no can stay?'

What can I answer? My talent is otherwise. I bury my face in her shoulder. My hands grasp hers. I leave the barette in them.

By the time Angel comes, Daisy is back, and sleeping again. Sleep is her tent just now, but she is a house person. I shall be leaving her mine.

Angel lifts the bike down, cradling it. I unwind the glittering blue glass chain from the handlebars and put it around his neck. 'Don't go for too many marathons.'

He has something for me, from his mother. One of the maté gourds with its silver spoon, and a sack of maté.

I say, 'I'll send you a card.'

Now that the bike is gone, the freed desk looks at-the-ready. Like it's upended only at night, to give the sleeper on the cot more elbow-room. Like it's waiting, like any good desk, for me to practice my secretarial skills on it, including some not too classic Spanish. From the opposite wall, the rolled-up backpack answers it. . . .

In Dedham, September was the month we brought out the Hudson Bay blankets; in the mornings their stripings glowed like grates. Once a week we burned one of the lumps of cannel coal which were — as I had learned to say after the aunts each Sunday — 'As big as Titus's heart' — he being the owner of the coal-and-wood yard who every New Years sent over the quarter ton we stretched throughout the year.

Titus's great-grandfather, helped to come North by the abolitionists, the aunt's great-grandfather among them, ended his days in that man's household service, as what was known in the turreted mansions of that era as 'the useful man' — his tasks, where other servants were of course kept, being to carry and sweep for them, attend the furnace and polish the brass only, the silver being the butler's or housekeeper's chore. All duties of lower degree, but in no sense a slave's. Titus's father had established the coal-yard. Titus's own son, who went to Howard University and died in a war, attended high school with my aunts; in the pile of year-books he stands in the class picture between the two of them. He too perhaps had a heart.

A night-wind is moving the blind. We face the east here also, though city chill is not the same as in a house with enough windows for the decades to rattle through, and a staircase wide enough for all that had blown in. City steam swells and steeps you in your own juices, rather than truly warms. Cannel coal burned cleaner than the low-grade bits which served the one wing of the house that we kept open in winter, though any that came to us from Titus's yard was first washed down. When the old man died my aunts, two fiercely single women who had learned from manuals how to solder burst pipe and rewire cables the mice had gnawed, took to washing the coal themselves. I — the useful child, helping. The aunt who taught in the daytime roused me for school; the one who taught in the evenings greeted my return. The air in that house was pure — like an ethic one didn't know one had. I didn't know they were saving for more than the college I mightn't get a scholarship to. For the trust. . . .

Time for my pill. I'll miss the refrigerator, which whenever I open it spoons out its own mite of encouragement. My Miss Tidy, waiting every day to be refilled, it belongs to a stationary future. A backpack is always urging you on. When I go, I'll stick the note already in my pocket on the fridge door. 'I'm off, Gold. For what you did for me there is no substitute. Keep on the room here if you want to. For yourself, not for me. Carmen will tell you where to pay the rent. Good luck. I'll send you a card.' Once the note was written up I saw I should have said Daisy instead of Gold, but let it be.

I take my pill. The past — the pills bury it. Else why do those on the ward, both the meek and the violent, try to refuse them, until forced? A pill buries the self that you are, that others must make manageable. Docile, one feels guilty for not being faithful to those depths.

Gold sleeps on, heavily. A 'good' SW is instructed not to 'identify' with the 'clients.' That is their lingo. But Gold is now merely the SW of herself. Before she slept we had a long gab, from cot to floor, floor to cot. I am in Angel's Boy Scout sleeping-bag, which his mother pressed on me the night Gold came; it smells of boy, and woodsmoke. Gold, bending down at me, smells of her new hair. 'You never did tell us —' she says. 'How you were orphaned. Why you had to live with your aunts.'

In my childhood, half the people in town knew some of it. Or thought they knew all of it. But once you turn yourself in, you are mostly a footnote. The facts are there, but in a public facility nobody much notices them. Still later on, from transfer to transfer, from a detention set-up to a medical one, public to private, the case-record fattens, the facts all but disappear. And the names — I had so many. But in any record, your conduct — the most recent — is what counts.

'No. I never did say.' I did tell the private hospital the trust could only half pay for what was owed. But their records are never revealed.

'I know your father died in a war, Carol. I never told you, did I — that so did mine?'

'Oh?' The SW's aren't supposed to tell you, about themselves.

'But about your mother, how she died. . . an army nurse, is all the record says. Let go, because of her relationship with a non-commissioned officer. When he was killed, his family's long-time former employers took the child in.'

So they did. The town thought the aunts were misguided, if charitable. Or perhaps that, with no money except what they earned, I too would be indentured to the big ruin of a house that must be saved. Perhaps Titus, staring at me like an owl each time he came to deliver the coal, thought that too. When asked how his wife did he always answered the same. 'Poorly. Ever since Hezekiah was los'.' Though from well before the son was lost she had been known to be odd, finally retiring early from the library. I remember her, a light-skinned lady, a little mumbly, who no longer worked at the front desk. In the town there were a great many I would remember, with whom I was never to connect.

'I knew about my father, of course. I would have had to.' I see Gold's eyelids flicker; she agrees, staring down at my face. 'About my mother, I was only half-told. And not until I was half-grown. They thought it best.'

. . . That summer before I went off to college, Titus came for what was to be the last time before he died. By then I knew who he must be to me, but it was too late for either of us to remark upon it. 'College?' he said to my aunts '— that's good. We none of us knew how much you had toward it, short of what's needed for the house. But now she has the scholarship.' The house was a monster, yet also half ancestor to him as well; he was in agreement that it had to be kept. Once the horse died I had grown indifferent to the old pile and its haze-filled barns, as the aunts knew. To my mind, I had no further stake in it. That was why I was told.

Until then, my mother had been a cipher. I could sneak a look at the man whose by-blow I had been admitted to be, in the line of dead soldier's faces at the American Legion Hall. On Independence Day I sometimes had. And once on Memorial Day, when the parade ganging up to go to the cemetery had again opened up a hall off limits to kids except at events. That time I had even asked if I could help sell the poppies always sold on that day. 'In Flanders Field, where poppies grow' — the poem was in our reader. Though that was not the war the face on the Legion's photograph had fallen in, it seemed the thing to do. But the marshal I asked said, 'Only veterans can sell them poppies, young lady. Got to wear one of those khaki hats, so's people know.' But then he reached over to a table for a bunch of those red cotton flowers and gave me one, for free. Maybe, looking at me had made a connection.

But of my mother — dead in childbirth, or vanished after? — no pictures, not even a name. 'His family was willing for us to adopt you,' was all the aunts ever said. 'And we sure wanted you. Now let's rustle up the peanut butter sandwiches. And have us a game.'

In senior high, by which time, in order to qualify for the normal legalities I was required to present a birth certificate on my own, it was revealed that an 'infant' had been born in a small town just inside the U.S. at the Canadian border, delivered by midwife to one Carol Smith, American, not otherwise described, the infant being christened the same. 'Father not identified.' Signed illegibly, in the midwife's hand.

Color was not discussed in my aunts' house, but mine was taken for granted by those who saw me there: a member of the town's servant clan. When *Noblesse oblige* was murmured in my presence by a chance guest from one of the other turreted houses, and I asked later what that meant, Rosanna, the day aunt, rallied with, 'To keep one's obligations is noble,' while Adelaide, who taught music to her evening classes, drummed on the table to the tune of *La Roi d'Yvetot*. As for me, no sooner did I show signs of knowing my lowly position in that household, than an extra blast of their love would knock me off my perch. I felt like the only surviving fish in the grand bowl in the sitting-room, swimming hither-thither to keep its place.

By my eighteenth birthday the house plainly needed young shoulders: roof-tiles whirling away in a nor'easter, foundation sagging in the warm. Neither aunt was now well; one might not last my college years, although this I was not told. Once graduated though, if I could teach? 'Any subject of your choice,' Adelaide said — 'Though I would not suggest music,' Rosanna said. 'And I would suggest — by day.'

The voices blend forever, over the tea napkins and special cakes — pink-icing'd squares I didn't know were *petits fours* — that had meant decision-making ever since I could recall. 'And if you could aim to teach in a college, for which we are told you have the capacity — what a tribute to your ancestors that would be.'

To Titus, and the sad, lavender-cheeked librarian? And my dim handsome father, not pictured anywhere in the house except in drawings I had done and kept hidden, or in pre-dream I narrated to myself?

The aunts knew my every expression, from the games always laid out for us in the bay. I have since been told, and I believe it, that this gaming was their own childlike expression of love.

'Oh — the Oldfields?' one said, the other adding 'Of course. But not only them.'

Then who? What game is this?

The tea steams from the pot; we owned a Salton hot-tray given one year to steady savers at the bank.

'My dearest.'

'Dearest dear.'

I no longer try to piece out which of the aunts said which.

'To those ancestors —' both say, pointing, napkins in hand. Their faces flush, like when either of them wins at chinese checkers maybe, or even dominoes — but how can two win a game at the same time? 'To those, dear, up there, on the wall.'

Their tribe crowds the sitting-room's floss-flecked paper; I know every face, bearded or lace-capped, painted by an artist or photographed, and their legends as well. I know what a busk is and a peruke, and who brought home the ivories, all but two long since sold. The abolitionist minister, circled by four dead wives? The baggy Congressman who had deserted William Jennings Bryant and the free coinage of silver, just in time? — I know them all, the heritage of this house. Only, now they come down from the wall to me, gold frames, speckled ones, mourning banded ones, and the two silhouettes I cherish because no one knows who they are. One by one they are brought down and put in my hands, these ancestors. They are also mine.

'Daisy — you still asleep?'

No, she is awake. 'The rain.' Pit-a-pat, autumn coming. Top of the fridge, the radio-clock glows. It's any time, past time, I don't want to know the time; tomorrow I'll be gone.

'I'll tell you who my mother was,' I say. 'One of the aunts. But they would never say which one.'

The Shelter-Pak — its official name — is in the hall outside my half-open door. When you live with a backpack you are always looking for a clean place to set it down. The hall's scrubbed linoleum is a palace rest-stop, compared to what that one will endure. For I'll have a domestic life as much as any householder. Only of a different order. The search for running water being prime. After that the question of where you can lay your head. I have no grand theory on the adventures of the road. Except that in desert or oases, California or Niagara, the ground-rat knows early and best what the country's coming to.

It helps to leave with an errand. Outside, it's not light yet. Too early for those here who will be going out for milk

— and coming back in. I can't see the note on the fridge, but it is there. On her pallet, once mine, Daisy lies face down, her hair gleaming in the dim ray cast from the hall bulb; we got the color just right. Accepted — when Carmen brought her a mirror — with a weak smile.

My last night's revelation sank into her like the dye. In former days she'd have cried out, like someone who'd found a lost key. In my own mind I continue speaking to her all the night through. Or to the eternal someone: grateful, that neither of them replies.

This is a new silence for me. In a head with a dialogue solely its own. The aunts have taken their enigma into the shadows behind me. My parents, whoever they were, have played out their variations. Gold has a hole in her where the children once were; it may never heal. I have no hole in me any more — its rim working like a mouth that wants a breast, its core of air sucking me toward the fatherless. My case is different; I was the child. Time will be my triumph. Whatever it brings.

I stand in front of the mirror. Full-length, yes, a bargain. You have an instinct for those, Carol — Gold said to me once. So I do. Comes with having a bargain for a face, neither ghostly white as the lady librarian's nor so Blue Coal dark as the sergeant's in the Legion Hall. The short haircut is becoming; it was a bargain too, in a barbers' training-school, where I paid nothing. Except for my dues, which were internal.

The girl student who gravitated to me, like a young witch riding the shears she was pointing, had almost the same skin as me. All down the line of barber's chairs people's heads were turning into spiky cubes, or other propositions out of Euclid. The carrot-head next to me was being shaved to the crown, except for one sprout. I am like on a ward, but this time I am laughing.

My operator touches my cheekbone, then her own. She has almost the same hair too, curly but smooth, straight but not dead straight. 'Man, are we going to make us kicky,' she says, sleeking a hand on her own coif, that sits like a bell halfway up her nape. 'Will you have the same? Look great on you. And easy care. Grows into a pigtail, if you can't come in here regular. Or a bun.'

After she was done, an attendant moved to scoop up behind my chair. The whorl of hair that went into the carpet sweeper looked like the long-outmoded head of a college girl. 'What made you finally do it?' the operator said. 'I kind of like to know.' We smile at each other, sisterly. 'I had this great barette,' I said. 'I wanted to give it away. I cut my hair so I could.'

Goodbye Daisy Gold. Though in a way we're still linked. Both of us on the receiving end now, you on the severance pay and whatever welfare you can luck into later, me still on the stipend the street calls 'the disability.' Both of us bound to whatever offices that so dispense. You to the courts, for judgment — I to the clinics, and the streets. The mails may make things simpler in your case. So I give you this house. Easy-chair.

This woman, in this mirror — who knows what she might yet be? Or how bright are her errands?

The gorilla-cage is bare now except for what's hung there, still neat under its plastic. Alphonse's shirt.

The street ahead should look more crooked. Seen from behind, it somehow looks straighter, even before she's there. Has the long bus ride put her off balance, as it used to? She knows it has not. The spacey side-to-side she once spent her days in is a trance she can scarcely recall. Shoulder to waist, ankle to knee, she is now aligned as most people are. Though in the street itself an outline is missing. Some indication always expected, even at dusk — chimney-stacks? Somewhere along.

As she rounds the corner she almost bumps into a barrow stacked with pots of yellow flowers. Mungo is standing on the sidewalk in front of it. Hand to forehead under his visor cap, he stares like those Indian scouts who used to be painted looking down into a canyon from their mountain top. What Mungo is looking at is only a vacant lot. A long, narrow expanse of ground, rubbled with crushed stone. Almost neatly. Some giant machine has patterned it.

Her sight is as clear as a falcon's must be. Or like after eye-drops. She may have perfect confidence in it. Those slates there, ranged up from the walk's edge like a stile to nowhere; those were the front steps. In front of her is a huge parallelogram of air.

The Cat Club is gone.

'They came in the night —' Mungo said, as if continuing a conversation. 'Cop on duty says. Did the same last year, to a building same block as our church. Where I'm sexton. Complete wrecker's crew. Gone like the wind.' An embossed tin box is in his palm. Opening it, and lifting his mustache, he inserts a pinch up each nostril. 'Tax relief. Or they sell the site.' He sneezes; his eyes tearing. 'Only the snuff,' he says.

She recalls how he used to say that, at intervals. All those habits that houses have — where now is the cat? Where's everybody, anybody? She knows the whereabouts of one. 'There was a notice on the door. After an accident.'

'Don't fancy that crew came in by any door. Or left by one.' He sends her a sidelong glance, almost proud. 'And I have a heap of business with doors.'

'Doors?'

'Aye. From the Seamen's Institute. Lived there. Until they got rid of the building, and us. Same bloody wind.'

She's inching into the shock, slowly. His big red face is a help. 'You sell flowers too?'

'Distribute them. After the church weddings. Young couple, this time. So it was plants. Three dozen of 'em. Hospital couldn't handle. Other outlets closed for weekend. So come here.' Suddenly he poked a finger at her. 'Three dozen of 'em. Count!'

She sees too close his gelid, distracted eye. Nothing dangerous. But does as she is bid. Yellow rosettes on stiff stems, not dead yet.

'Count.'

They have no smell. 'Thirty-six.' When she raised her head she saw what was at the far corner of the lot.

'Three dozen,' Mungo said with satisfaction. 'No mismanagement. Hey, hold back — don't walk in there. There's glass everywhere.'

She'd forgotten how cogent in some matters the Cat Club's non-members could be. Or when abroad, in their pursuits. The walkers knowing *down-to-the-ground* as it were, what is possible, ignorable or threatening, underfoot. The can-collectors, who know all the classifications of tins — as well as the stores that by law have to accept deposits — and for how much.

'I've got new shoes' she says. 'Stabilizers.'

'You'll ruin them.'

'I got to have one last look at it. The shed.'

'Ah, in that case. Well, I have on me workaday boots.'

The rubble ahead of them, tinted by the rising sun and glimmering with points of glass and wave-crests of metal, looks more of an expanse than a city lot.

'That's what keeps a chap at sea,' Mungo says. 'Your last view is no change from your first.'

They pick their way slowly, his hand on her elbow. His two pairs of boots classify him, just as Alphonse's 'other' shirt, now in the outer slot of her pack, classified him. As being a step above those who have only what is on their backs. And only the one source of cash.

'Minding a church —,' she says '—what a nice job.'

'A dispensation.' He lifts a small, evil sliver of metal from their path. 'Nights only. I watch until it's light. Days, I'm on the docks — if there's nothing for the barrow. Or on the ferry — if luck presents.'

Does he mean — if he can pay?

'Is it an open church, or a closed?'

A splinter of glass has lodged in the heel of Mungo's left boot. Bending, he pries it out. 'Open for services only. And Sunday soup. Otherwise closed, with only me there. All the riffraff that's around — that would doss down in the sanctuary? Can't do else.'

She wonders whether he stays for the soup.

The long shard he tosses out of their path is amber. From the storefront window's border. She decides not to mention this. They are almost at the shed.

'Wonder how come they left it,' Mungo says.

A voice answers from around the shed's side. 'Daylight. They had to scramble.'

It's Jerry Guido, the cop on the beat. Who as all of them know, volunteered to walk his territory instead of riding in a police car. Who even the teenage hoods go to, in a jam. 'That fuckin' moneybags. She must of figured the courts won't bother her for the demolishing, just because she's in Florida.' He comes round the side of the shed. 'And how are you, my Aussie friend?'

'No she wasn't. She was here, in her mink. The morning of the accident.'

When a cop alerts, even in chat, his hand always goes to where his gun is stashed. 'And who are you? And what do you know about the accident?'

Whatever is wrong with her chemistry — for of course she's been warned there may be something — it's also common knowledge that people like her share one of the stigmata of childhood for which they are neither cherished or thanked. Their tongues will not lie. Even if they take a daily pill.

Fortunately, Jerry now recognizes her. 'Why it's you, is it? Alphonse's Miss Boston Special. Hey there. Looka you.' He whistles. 'Got yourself a job, maybe? At the Rainbow Room?'

It's the haircut. And starting out. With the men at the bar maybe watching. She has on all her 'other' wardrobe. The shirt, the belt, the dungies. And Angel's earrings.

But when he sees the tell-tale backpack there's that shift in his face. When it recognizes the outside. 'Don't get me wrong —' he says. What he means is — he had her wrong. 'But where are you two heading?'

'She has to see the shed.' Mungo speaks as if this is some faith he won't question.

'Does she now. And why?'

Mungo turns to her. 'Why?'

When both the outside people and the inside ones want to know your reasons, their own whys become starkly clearer. Mungo's asking only because wherever he is, he travels in circles. Answering docilely to those who hand out dispensations. And always a little at sea.

Jerry asks because he has the eye-crinkles that come from kindliness, but also a holster somewhere.

She says, 'I want to keep a memory.'

Mungo swings his head uncomfortably. He's wearing a round collar back-to-front — his minister's discard? — which he has fastened with paper-clips. The cop purses his mouth. If she mystifies both parties, that's nothing new.

'I don't think maybe you ought to go in there,' the cop says softly.

'Somebody's killed the cat?' She could almost see it, hanging there as once the aunts' cat had been found, strung

~80~

up in the barn. *No significance* the aunts had murmured to one another. A word she had added to her hoard.

'That moocher?' Jerry says. 'He's already in the window of the woman who gives readings. She's always had her eye on him. Maybe he'll assist.'

Cops never spread their arms. Jerry spreads his gut though, to relax him and you; he was once cited by the department for being too fat. It's still a gut. 'Well, folks — going off duty. We'll have the lot fenced in by tomorrow.' He stares at the airy space above, into which the clouds are sneaking as if long prevented. 'Betcha the neighbors aren't organizing any protest.' He gives her a long look. 'See you got yourself one of those.' He flicks the Shelter-Pak. 'Hmm. Up to you. Anyways, take care.' He shrugs. 'Upta you.' On the way past Mungo's barrow he seizes a pot, calling back: 'For the wife.'

'He never respects my inventory,' Mungo says.

She says, looking past him, 'I know who's in the shed.'

The bolts are still there, but swing loose on their fittings, as if one of the destroying crew had said at the last minute, 'Nah, not worth it,' and had let the shed be. Or else somebody, tripping the set-up of bolts and knocker for one last time, had then wrenched it half out of the weathered wood.

'It's still a door,' Mungo says, and pushes in.

At first she thinks the body there is dead, — shoved up against the wall with its knees sunk to its chin and left there, by the decamping crew. Or by Jerry Guido, who had really gone to meet the squad car. But then one eye opens owlish. Then the other. 'Don't come near, whoever you are. 'I up-chucked. Forgot I was on like an antibuse.' His voice is tired but still competent, the way it always was, separate from any bottle in his hand. An actor's voice, no whopper of a baritone, but the thin, dry kind, that tickles one's ear.

Both eyes close, open, focus. 'Carol. *Carol*.'

She smiles.

One scarecrow jerk, then another. He stands. 'What did you do to yourself?'

'What did you?'

'I said. Fell off the wagon.' The shapely head hangs. Its haircut is still sharp. 'After nearly a year.'

'Fell off?' Mungo cracks. 'Weigh up, pal. You were never on. Tossed — from one night to the other. Bottle in your britches, dawn to dusk.'

The long harlequin face lights up. 'So I managed it then?'

Mungo's cheeks puff. 'Manage?'

'Thought you knew I was playing the fool. An old Aussie like you. You ever sniffed at those bottles, you'd have known it was tea.' He turned to her. 'I know I fooled you. I was acting. Acting it out. Like it helped — see?'

Acting it out — she knows that phrase. That's what she had done — they said, the docs on the ward. Maybe she's still doing it? Stage acting is a whale's distance apart. But she daren't say. 'Tea, Alphonse? That's what they use onstage, isn't it?'

He sees what she's up to. 'Thanks.'

'I'm a good smeller. You don't smell as if you barfed.'

'Barfed?' A college word, new to him. 'Oh. I did it in the bar. Washed up, some. Came back here. And passed out.'

'Because of — that?' She points. In the open shed, a pyramid of two-by-fours and chunks of cornice rears like an unsigned work of art.

'The club? No, I knew its days were numbered. That's what made it so special. Never dreamed it would go like this though. Or like with that poor woman, Margaret.' His voice has deepened. It mustn't be that he can't act. He can't stop.

'No — I was celebrating,' he says softly. 'Because — I got a job.'

When somebody comes out with that it's like a lens lifting, if only for them. But over their shoulder you too see out of the dog-gray, into the light.

Of course it's a division too. She's remembering how that is. When maybe you and the jobbie are on stools in the diner, side by side. When whoever's behind the counter offers a coffee, and don't offer you. So you scrounge an extra paper napkin, in reply. The steam that runs down a diner's window on a winter morning, it's not important to most. Coming in from the real outside, it's like a hearth. Your nose weeps for joy.

'A job, a job,' Mungo gobbles. 'Better look sharp.' He lashed out an arm — as he always had when he gave you something — and dug in his puttees. 'Here.' A bottle of his fizz. Then bowing in embarrassment like always, he backed out the door. Only to stick his head in again, the mustache quivering. 'Stop calling me Aussie if you please. I'm from New Zealand. Auckland.' The door closed.

Alphonse had finished the fizz. 'You off somewhere?'

'Maybe to Philadelphia? Maybe I can get a job giving out those new packs they have?' She has just thought of that.

'Neat.' He touches the Shelter-Pak, almost as if he's touching her. 'Always thought you had a pad.'

Will she lie? Not worth it, ever again. 'I do. Did. Not now. Giving it up.' She watches him brush himself off. The chinos are still okay. The tee's armhole gapes. 'I always thought — you had one too.'

'Buddy of mine, in Jersey, just across the Tube. I want to sit for their kids, I can stay. Not too often. They don't have the cash to goof off much.' He slides the empty fizz bottle into his pants pocket like he needs it there. 'Sometimes I did stay at the Y.'

Already, even in the torn, stained turtleneck, he looks as if he could. She wonders what the job is. On that thin-limbed body with its lurking sadness what role will be draped?

'That bar I went, Carol — it's where that go-go girl — remember her? She gave me a coupon for it once. Free drink, lunchtime only. And topless girls. Way down Ninth Avenue. She wasn't there. But I stayed.'

'You swing?'

'No. No I never. Lived with a girl once; she was on the vino too. But now — it's like I'm on the antibuse for that too. Like until I get straight for sure.'

That figures. Even if it makes her feel the weight of the Shelter-Pak. She can't put it down, not on all that broken glass.

'And you?' He says. 'What about you, Carol?'

'I swung — But not now.'

'I figured.'

He checks his watch, a round one with a simple face. He told anybody at the club who noticed it that it was a Canal Street rip-off. It's not junky-fancy. And the strap is leather. More like a graduation present from too long ago.

Shouldn't she be making off now? But everyone needs some dispensation. He always liked the way she said his name.

'Alphonse?'

'Yes, Carol?'

'I brought your other shirt.'

Outside Mungo has set the flowerpots with the stiff-standing blossoms at exact intervals that form a diamond pattern over the entire plot before them. The rubble holds the pots firm. If it were springtime those blossoms could be arunculus, but it is autumn and she a wanderer, who now cannot be expected to know what plants are. Those hold their heads high in the breeze though, as if everyone is saying their name.

Alphonse's 'job' is to be a three-time walk-on — as a con man in a street card-game, a bagel-seller and a rube in a Western hat — in an off-off-Broadway production still in rehearsal, that has a big last-act crowd scene, and a low budget. But he may have a chance to replace the understudy of the second male lead.

'The role is a drunk,' he says, as they sip coffee, looking out on New York Bay from the huge palm garden of the World Trade Center. 'Good part.' 'But the actor doing it just got great reviews in a film. Gossip is he'll move.' And the understudy, Alphonse's friend, will shift up. 'That's how I got the tip. He knows me from the AA.' 'An actors' association?' 'No — Alcoholics Anonymous.'

He likes to look at her as if she is the more innocent. 'It's a big chance.' His voice deepens whenever he mentions what she thinks of as being onstage and he calls 'the theater.' She sees what a prospect can do — how it hones down the gross details into one gaunt meaning. How it silvers a path.

Two days and nights had gone by since she had last seen him, parting from him at the curb. Mungo's barrow had been just rounding the far corner. 'Odd guy —' Alphonse had said. At the Cat Club, where all were odd, he wouldn't have said that. 'I'm off, then.' When he'd asked to meet her down here in a couple of days time, surprised that she hadn't seen this dramatic place, she herself had felt odd — at planning anything that far ahead — but had agreed. As for knowing the city, its new haunts and plazas, that indeed is her obligation. Over the summer she'd grown rusty at it. Behind the two of them, the crooked street had already realigned itself. He hadn't asked her where she might be off to, with her pack. Standing on the leftover slate steps, she'd waved goodbye at him. Yet she has kept the appointment.

'This Palm Garden plaza's in the news,' he says now, swilling his coffee with vigor. 'As "a democratic anomaly."'

The last two words ring like bells from a distant convent. If she lets them into her brain, where words like that had used to rear like fists, they will stretch her mind, the way the tailor's wooden form had stretched the hat of Milan straw bought for her when she was ten, and every year enlarged. What can she do with such a phrase, in her daily round? He has brought the newspaper with the article in it; he's enlarging himself, for the job. She sees the phrase like a storefront that sells foreign wares.

The Garden is wonderful. High as a church, silly with de luxe shops at the sides, and cleansed by the view of the river that comes from the sea. Children of all races sprinkle the stiff rows of metal seats like poppies, in the bright cheapy jackets that could be bought at any mall; their folks, seen when the tots run to them, are not the sort who would buy at the shops here. Outside the great central window, figures stroll the walk as if the painter behind all this has unfrozen them. Tourists chat, lifting their chins. It hurts her to observe these levels; she is used to being solely in one. The barrio had had none too challenging. She hadn't been for years in the streets of perfection over East. Here, she feels uneasily, the people, all of them, are being challenged by the decor. 'Where's that word again?'

He puts her finger on the newsprint headline. 'Anomaly.'

'I still have trouble,' she says. 'Observing.'

He nods, not yet thinking that strange. They both will be receding from the Cat Club, she thinks. He in his way, she in hers. She tries to read the newspaper column, but shakes her head. 'You may need glasses —' he says. 'You better check.' She knows he doesn't believe that. Maybe he's being kind. If so — she wants to tell him, it's all right with her.

'There's this controversy, you see —' he says. 'On whether the buildings around this plaza are allowed to keep the odd people out. Or whether the city must demand that they can stay. Even in the daytime, they're being shoo'ed. Nobody'll say who's doing it. Maybe the city itself is taking advantage, this here says.' He taps the news-sheet. His nails have always been nice. 'Now that winter's near, it's coming to a head.'

'The dirty people,' she says. Sorry though, when he turns red. One can't act that. Or not so quick.

'I'm not distancing myself, Carol. And I could lose the job.'

Sneakily, they scan the rows of chairs, the tables like their own, the long aisle leading to the stores on the garden's rim, the bright wind-protected vision up front.

There. In the second row of chairs. A middle-aged man with a woolen cap; at first glance he might be anybody, even a ringer for the waiter at the Greek restaurant, dawdling maybe before time to go on shift. But the collar of his lumberjack is badly frayed, and the body in it has no outline; you wear the extra blanket; she knows that trick. And the bag on his lap is too plump for groceries. But his feet are decently on the floor, and he is staring rigidly eyes front, as if the view is his defense. No guards anywhere, that she can see. Police? Yes, there's one lounging near the Restroom's sign. And there, not too far from him, in the last row of chairs, a girl is sleeping, her feet stretched on a second chair, a bundle in front of her on the elegant tile-stone floor. All in a not too dusty black, she might pass. Some yards behind her, one of the huge bordering vases rocketing with flower-and-fern displays gives her thin figure the background a model might have, in pose.

As they watch, the cop comes over to her, ambling. He taps her outflung arm at the elbow, his own arm drawing quickly back. When the girl rouses he stands respectfully. Leaving her plenty time to sit up, blink awake. Then he taps the sole of her shoe, signaling her to keep her feet on the ground, that chairs here are for sitting only.

The girl has an ordinary face. Half a dozen stories might attach to it. A wee old though even for a senior down to the city for the fall break, just off a train and the friends she's staying with still at work yet. Or saving hotel rent for another kind of splurge. Now that her feet are on the floor though, the posture that made her a model is gone. She nods to the cop, as if he has corrected her manners. Then smiles at him. She has no front teeth.

When the cop walks on down the row of chairs there's a kid jumping on one of them, but he saunters on.

After it's over, she finds that she and Alphonse have gripped hands.

They loosen them. She looks down at herself. Still all right, the tan sweater fresh from the launderette, the shoes more than okay. And the blessed haircut, that she had only to shake into order, like a debutante. 'She shouldn't have smiled at him,' she says.

They scan one another. Dented some, both of them, worn some. She too thin, he too puffy for that fine profile. But no more than any in the true world might be, if temporarily off track? Teeth fine. And together in the public eye a couple, if a little scuffed? Each other's protection, to a degree?

'Two-thirty curtain —' he says, on a big inhale. 'Want anything more?'

They haven't eaten here, or together. There are limits to their kind of couple. He had bought her a coffee, then she him. 'No. But I'll just run off to the restroom.' As she hoists her pack she sees he is troubled; does he think she won't come back? She has done that, to others. 'I need something in it,' she says. Women in his family back there in turkeyland, she guesses, as his eyes veil; he thinks he knows what. He is wrong.

What she wants is to check the mirror, to see for sure whether two nights spent on the outside aren't already showing. Once on the street, the details begin to blur. Now that she can't cook for herself, sensible food will be a problem; you can't get grains and cheap chicken liver when you're on the run. But for a plus, the food search legitimizes the wandering. The pack holds vitamins, a water-bottle, a flash, and what for the street is a princess's wardrobe — one complete change, down to the skin. She's had to sacrifice the bathrobe — leaving it for Gold. Bathrobes are babyland, dorm, Sunday fireplace, Claudette Colbert in a log-cabin, old weekend movie — the pure fluff and sweet of the uncorrupted inside.

As she enters the restroom, the policeman eyes the Pak.

Inside — no time for the bodywash she gives herself in sections, in the toilet stall of any washroom she hits that is empty enough and has paper towels. She grabs a couple, wets them, ignoring two women at the sink, and once inside the stall, blots her inner thighs. If you have to wear dungies, a crotch is a woman's cross.

First night out she had dossed down in the Park, dangerous but gracious; you could dream poems there and hear grass music. But washing was out. The second night she had slept out on the gay dock, the family dock being under repair. A boy she asked said, 'Oh doll, where have you been; the public baths are closed, the *pubic* bath, dear. They left us one on trial for a bit — but you know — life goes on.' So it was the city shelter, which he wouldn't advise. 'I'm dying for a shower myself.' Summers, he used the swimming pools; there are winter ones, but not that time of night — and strict at any time. He sighed. 'These days, no funny business. No business at all.' He squinted at her. If he got the idea she might be slumming, he and his pals could run her off. But she passed muster, maybe by her matching squint. 'Tell you what,' he said. There was a guy in a basement off Christopher street who rented his shower for sex, but he wouldn't bother her. When she agreed to go, a boy stretched out at his left rose to accompany them. Threading through the night's crowd on the dock, some awake and busy, some catching a few winks with their worldly goods under them, she glimpsed several packs like hers. The two boys with her, both in the many-pocketed sharpshooter khaki jackets that the stalls sold in this district, had none.

In the basement, an older man and a younger had been playing checkers on a card table. At a mumble from the two boys she was shown the shower, off to the side. Clean enough, with a brown-tiled floor drain and a bar of soap, but the backpack couldn't come in with her. Already she had felt the lion urge to guard it that would entrap her, hamper her, even doom her, in the life ahead. Hanging it on a hook outside the stall, she left the folding door open a crack and showered minimally. Sure enough, as she was drying off with her own towel, she saw the Pak move. Opening the door, she stood there bare-breasted, then lunged for their stealing hands. One of the boys screamed; she had raked his forearm with her strong nails. 'What's going on here?' the older man at the table said, rising. He took it in at once. 'Scram, chippies. And don't come back.' When she was dressed and asked how much, he said, 'My pleasure,' and seeing her glance at the board, 'You play? Go ahead. He always beats me.' She'd won from the younger man in a few moves. Both men laughed. There was no sun in the room but the checker board trembled with focused light. A breezy camaraderie stirred at her cheeks. This was one of the moments worth the wandering. 'You off somewhere?' the two said as she shouldered the pack. She nodded, encouraged that they took her for somebody with a destination. 'Come back any time,' they said. 'Any time you hit town. Pot of soup on the stove, generally.' She saw it upended now, cleansed and drying.

The younger man held the door for her. Up the areaway steps and she hit the slow circuit of male cruisers for which the street was known: men of all ages, beauties and wrecks, down-and-outers and paying gents, carrying their urges in steady line and past all diseases, a line like one saw in early religious paintings, of either paradise or hell. The night above her and them was that bell of blue which colors New York as it gets colder. Back of the moving line, in part of the painting, the two men in their basement pad were a comfortable vision, pursuing their decent, accepting, feline life.

In the restroom mirror she tosses her head at herself. The ungainly jacket, too warm yet for now, has to be worn. In her household she is the only clothes tree. Tan shirt, rumpled but not soiled yet, and a hip choice for the coffee-with-cream face above it. The fingernails filed now to curved points, like women in the barrio. But the haircut was what kept her from sliding over the line. When she exited, she smiled at the cop.

Alphonse was not at their table. Maybe his will to pull over to the right side of the fence has nailed him. Or maybe he was ashamed of loving without sex. Then she saw him — coming from the men's room — on his face a waiting look that made it clear she had a continuity for him, and she was shamed. Her thoughts were changing, rubbing against one another like knives in a drawer, when not set all one way.

As she came up to him a second cop approached the man in the woolen cap. The man had sagged down, one foot feeling for a haven on the chair next to him. He was dead for sleep but fighting that. Wanting to be where it was safe, and where he could pee respectably. He pulled himself upright. She knew how that was. Bravo.

The cop passed on, not threatening, but measuredly.

'That's what you call "patrol,"' she whispered — 'isn't it?'

The two policemen had joined up, staring vacantly over the scattered crowd. And shifting their feet, side to side. Though of course there was no comparison. 'He's not such a bad guy, that second cop,' she said. 'He looks — puzzled.'

'You're too easy,' Alphonse said. 'Sometimes I think this city should be running in blood.'

'Oh, no. You haven't been — in the slammer.'

'Haven't been where?' He always heard how you said things. But there were some she had never said.

The two cops had seen they were being observed. Four persons, when you came down to it, staring across the checker board.

'Come on —' Alphonse said. 'And give me that pack.' Slinging it on his back he took her by the elbow and walked her up to the cops.

'Would you be knowing the best way to the City Center now, Officer?' he said, jaunty, with a slight Irish burr.

'Well now —' the first one said. He sounded relieved. 'Would you be wanting the City Center? Or the center of the city?' Both men smiled at Alphonse. His accent was almost the same as theirs.

'Hoo — the hall. We're ahf to see a plee.' Alphonse was in his element. She prayed he wouldn't ham it too far.

'And to meet up again with the tour,' he said.

'Aha —' they said. He had explained her.

Directions were given benevolently, metropolitan to foreigner. 'Longer to the subway from here, lad. Shorter by bus.' She kept her lips tight. Who knows where his tour pal might be from?

As they were off, the first officer touched the Pak. 'Neat. Get it here?'

'All over Belfast,' Alphonse said.

When they were yards away she turned around to take in the luxurious plaza, the view, the soaring palms, the arching roof. And the restroom. 'Great —' she said. 'But it's having trouble being a public space, isn't it.'

How could I have forgotten the way a theater smells?

Sweat — from gestures long gone. Tragedy's gunpowder, blown away. Matinee candy. In this former union hall, postered with faded campaigns, even the dust electioneers.

As Alphonse proudly leads me through the unattended stage door, toward wings cluttered with ladders and paste-buckets, and down into the auditorium, I am treading the avant-garde of a Boston light-years back. We munched that daytime candy in the student evenings, rattling the stale slot machines like pledges to the new politics. Any performance, free or on the cheap, was our guildhall.

A stage is a place born to show insurrection. Only send across it a crowd like the one up there: in motley, its garments calculatedly ragged, its gestures on the cusp of anguish and the edge of violence, yet falling plumb.

'Carol, you're shivering,' Alphonse says. He pats the hand clawed in my lap. 'Take it easy, huh? It's only a rehearsal. And the crowd is all friends.'

I can smell them also. Up there on stage and in the rows

behind us. Memory is a smell. Memory is a crowd. Memory is a rehearsal. A whine of the slot machines, as they pay off. A tread of sneakered feet, stealing toward the armored heart, kicking at the drug-sealed brain. Memory is an underground minefield. On tiptoe, I'm treading it. . . .

. . . I'm seeing revolution as a nest of college girls had once seen it. They are nothing like the calico-skirted, flower-scattering princesses of ideology who had floated the cara-vans of the mid-century, later lulling their breast-fed babies with plainsong, while on a diet of bulgar wheat, Molotov cocktails and LSD. When Peace was the bomb.

Four dormitory radicals, only as pinko as their shorts and tee-shirts, they are sorority sisters linked by a daisy-chain of steel. Rich girls, spoiled for their lot by a humane education, they will act solely in response to what they are. Daughters respectively of an Illinois industrialist; a banker once a conscientious objector, who had fled a war-time USA to Montreal, made money there, and now lived both places; a titled member of the inner council of the government of the island of Bermuda; and of a New York attorney for 'lost' causes and his activist wife — they themselves have no dogma beyond what they will do. They're of course the same girlfriends who house-guest each other at poolsides in Evanston, Westmount, Paget, and Bridgehampton. Along with their follower, the 'Bos-ton environmentalist', veteran of two rallies and one long march — me. They admire me for having done it all on foot.

I see them — us — at a long wooden table in the basement of a brownstone in Greenwich Village, the house of a boyfriend whose parents were in Europe. The basement was once the servants' kitchen, from which meals were carried upstairs to the dining room; now it is the 'family room.' The long table has been swept clean of picture puzzles — the expensive kind, each with two hundred fifty pieces as sharp as cameos, and is piled with bomb parts. Our trouble is — or my four friends' trouble is — that though no one of them knows everything about bomb-making, each of them knows something. No matter, they are in practice session. I can feel again that electric atmosphere. They are feeling revolution. I can see all four, as sharply as if memory had never lapsed.

On the left is Doris Brody from Evanston, a brownie dumpling of a girl who believes her life there is a bore. 'They're sweet, my folks, but like marshmallow, though our food is much fancier. No — like the upholstery in Cadillacs. They gave us kids everything but real ethics; we did nothing for the world. Not bad people so you could see, nothing satanic. Just co-omfortable.' She moos the word. 'We live in the suburbs of life. Lots of pillows.'

Then comes Emmy Sklar the banker's daughter, skinny bird from commuting between three houses and back-and-forth over a border. When she invited me to the Westmount house where she was born, her favorite, she and I were the only ones who turned up, and the *bonne* served us our holiday meal. 'My father collects pre-Nazi German art about the masses. Though we never met any of those. My mother kept the Käthe Kollwitz drawings on Park Avenue, to show where we stand.' And the Hampton house was great for benefits. Her mother died, though, of leukemia. Now her father collects Klimts — 'Sexy Austrian dames, with bodies like waterfalls,' and at first had a mistress who

looked like one, then married again, not her. 'My step-
mother, I have nothing against her, except I can't be in the
same house with her.' When Emmy chokes, is it sentiment
or revulsion? 'She's a ringer for my mom.' And her own
analyst is advising that if she has no boyfriends it's because
she can't choose what kind to have. Monied guys, like the
only ones she meets, or bruisers from the bottomline South
Fork bars, who scare her blue. 'Better be red —' she says, her
tiny fingers manipulating the wiring into what must be its
proper destination. 'A bomb's surer than most things. And
you don't need a collection.'

Carey Plumford. At the table she never said much. I see
her stretch, strawberry blonde in daisy-print bathing suit,
never bikinis, neat sports-girl from the elite of Bermuda.
Never wore make-up, toenails like a baby's. In the hay with
boys since she was twelve. Papa, a Sir somebody, suspected
nothing. '"Dear girl," he calls me. But my mother, she
drinks so you don't see it, slow but sure. And alcohol makes
one wise. She always sneaked me in to see American movies; Dadda forbade me them.' And raised the roof when she
wanted college in the U.S.

I see that roof again. Long, low, sub-British in the not quite
tropics, it had needed raising. Solid conservative new, the
house could have subbed for Triminghams's, the traditional
shop for tourist goods: blue-and-white Wedgwood ashtrays,
silver boarding-school style bracelets. Carey laughed when I
told her that. 'We're related to them.' She would be the one
who flaunted me at all the pools down there. And took me to
visit the family of her former nurse. They had no pool but
were the most polite. Their manners to me rustled like tissue
paper. Though Carey had worn a skirt, she was out of favor

with them. Her last boyfriend before she left the island had been black, like them. 'That's how I got away.'

'I'm not sure I approve of why you're here, Carey,' Laura, daughter of the dissident lawyer and the activist says sourly. 'Your politics consists of giving your father apoplexy. Not that it doesn't make me jealous; I can never do that. My dad represents every leftist in the book. Though my mother, the peacenik, is the real radical. I was fed ethics before I could speak. And met the masses, even if we had to go to rallies to make contact.' Laura was the one who knew where to steal all but one of the needed materials — like at her former school's chem-lab in the Village, where science was taught pragmatically. And it was she who claimed to know best how to make a bomb. But if she had nothing from which to rebel, why was she here? 'I'm my parents' best protégé. But they don't do enough acting out.' And she is kind of spaced-out by Carey. Nothing lezzie — Laura's boyfriend from sixth-grade, whose parents own the house we meet at, is the one male allowed in — but like goody-goodies are some-times entranced by sexpots. 'So we better keep you for show, Carey doll. You're so healthy. No analyst even.' The other three have had some psychiatry as routinely as going to dancing school. 'And you're our prize Wasp.'

Carey could afford to laugh; she got top marks like we all did, though she said it was only due to her Brit school habits. And I felt the most comfortable with her; she was the one who didn't make me feel like their prize. Do I need to say for what? Though in a way we were all on show.

I am beginning to remember it all now. How, down the table somebody's hands are always pushing in, each pair of hands eager to have a part in this object intended to collide with what its owner has been bred to. They are so bad at it, I can't take it seriously. Calipers and tongs, cotton waddings and a kitchen clock with its innards all over the table, each time we come. Surely the air down here makes them clumsier, reassuringly slow. Under the table is still the unopened bundle from over the border, delivered early, the one component to be kept to the last.

'Here it is, chums — the canister sinister!' our Canadian liaison had said, taking a wrapped oval from her backpack, which she had worn forward, and depositing it carefully. 'Of course, it may contain only bicarb of soda.' Since then she had disappeared into her own Quebec operation. 'Dear God —' she'd said, surveying the litter of manuals at every chair, 'you'll be at this "til the Pope turns Protestant,"' and at the basement door— for they'd tolerated me only as doorkeeper and gofer — she'd whispered: 'Might as well have poured that stuff down a drain — they'll never never. *Bonne chance!* Ta!'

Half wanting to leave with her, I'd gone back inside.

All three heads are haloed in golden Saturday afternoon light. They are interweaving wires that will make sense and idealism interact chemically. Across the street, in the brownstone opposite, antique lace curtains hang ready for the petard, ignorant of the commune — and bless them. This here is only the parcheesi game that rich girls play.

But was I sent for sandwiches?. . .

'Production's on the cheap, but getting a cast together was no problem,' Alphonse is saying. 'Not for this play. Now that half of Europe's in flames again.' He hands me a flyer.

'Director fresh from Russia. . . . Look at that crowd, must be forty of them. On this peanut stage. And how he handles them. New arrivals too, some his friends. They work now as hairdressers, vendors, anything. This is their spare time.' He is meanwhile saluting people across the aisle. 'Of course, there's an Equity cast as well.'

On the flyer the play is called *The Heart Of Europe*.

On the outside, one may scrounge a newspaper now and then, from a bin. Back at the pad there was only the Spanish daily taken by the bar. Angel, clearing my trash, had noted my lack. A sports fan, he picked up his copies from park benches. 'I could bring you.' I had declined. Politics was a clock I could do without. It pretends to take you inside of what will be happening to you anyway, willy-nilly. Or nevertheless.

'What flames?' I ask. 'Which particular ones?'

By his sad shrug he knows my lack. 'No dialogue. Dance drama, sort of. Mime. Now and then some fife-and-drum.'

'I see.' Like at a rally. Nobody really has to say what everybody's already for. On the flyer's cast-listing I see there are no heroes or heroines either. Just a long column of names, a rag-bag of all the world — or maybe just the city's boroughs. And all identified only by their props, as in Coffin, Carousel, Three Men and A Steeple, Drum Corps, Hospital Ward, Green Table, File Room — Secret Police, Kitchen Crew, Business Office, and even a simple: Wall. Sometimes there is a doubling up. The six Coffins are also the Carousel. Orphans and Widows are also Anniversary Ball.

'Crowd's the real hero, see?' Alphonse says. 'This play comes straight out of the velvet revolution.'

I know better than to show myself the fool again by

asking which one that was. Still — I think to myself — I know dirty-sweaty-more about crowds than this fairy tale.

'So it did.' A tall, stocky man looms over us. 'And already out-of-date. Hi, Phonsie. Hear you're working in this too. Aren't we the lucky stiffs. Or are we?'

'Keep on saying. This is my friend Carol.'

'Hi, Carol. I'm Wall.'

When I sneak a look at the flyer, which lists Wall as played by Martyn Brice — who is also listed as one of the two under *Adapted by* — both laugh. 'Good part,' Wall says. 'I gave myself it. I'm in the whole last scene — I don't speak, but make the best prime noises trying. To get people to pull me down. Klas — that's our mad director — wanted me to shave my noggin as well, but I said, "Not if I'm to sprout flowers at the end." Where I do fall apart, all on my own. Breaks people up.'

'Like. . . . Bottom —' I say, without thinking.

Alphonse turns to look at me. Surely he knows who Bottom is? Though he'd said he never played Shakespeare. 'In — you know. . . .' I can hear my brain creak, almost. The words come slowly. '*Midsummer Night's* . . . .'

'*Dream.*' Wall has a good low baritone. I can imagine the noises it might make. Hollow, as such a wall would be. Yet there.

'I suffer from memory loss,' I say.

'Do you now. Mine's a silly harpist. Always at the cadenzas.' He has a nice smile, the kind that can accept the flat statements which some persons can't avoid making. And offering one of his own.

I am grateful. 'You're right not to shave your head. Noggin.'

'Except maybe for God,' Alphonse says. 'Like at the monks' school I went to. And got kicked out of. Thank God.'

'The Jesuits? You never let on.' But it figures. And where he and I had been, who shared?

Now he's cocking an ear, away from us. An intercom is on, low and constant. Until now I hadn't noticed. What does register with me is still up for grabs. I see Alphonse knows. He pats my shoulder. 'It calls us by number, the cast is so huge.'

'And changes daily,' the tall guy says. He's older than us, but not by much. Forty maybe? The sandy thatch he won't shave has gray in it. 'They run it off a computer. Even in a big scene everybody knows his place.'

'Forty-eight —' Alphonse says. 'Is that me?' He slips a stub from his breast-pocket. The shirt is the one I brought him. 'No.' He doesn't say what number he is. I think now that he's seen me this far he wants to leave me. For good. He's done what he can for me. From now on I'll only remind him of the other life. He's now on a job that isn't only himself.

'I don't need a number —' the tall guy says. 'I only come in at the end. So I know when.' He turns to me. I don't want to think of him by name yet, I don't know why. Such a vigorous presence he has, yet such a pallor. So easy, like he's been in the sun all his life. Yet can't tan. 'I'm no rebel, alas. But I like what you said about heads.'

'She knows a lot about them.' Alphonse is like poised, ready to split.

A rebel? Is that what's coming out of my pores? So that anybody who meets me can feel it? Something is.

'So why don't we meet after the show? . . . We three.' That last is added on.

Alphonse is taking a folded piece of paper from that shirt pocket. Maybe his whole future is there. 'Here, Carol. The Jersey address. They're moving next month to Parsippany. They'll always know.'

Where he is, he means. That's the sum of knowledge maybe, for him and me. Not who we are, but where. And he doesn't want to whistle me off. They can't believe that you might want to be, because when you begin to feel — there's no knowing. I better make it clear. 'You have a room there? That's great.' I lean forward to put my cheek against his. Never have. Now I can. 'So long.'

'You have a place you can stay, Carol? I always thought you did.'

'I did. Don't worry. I always have a place.' I pat the Shelter-Pak.

Does the other guy get this? Alphonse isn't sure. Does he want him to? 'No, Martyn, you're no rebel,' he says. 'He's an understander, Carol. He's the one got me in AA. And not in the city. Out-of-town. "For you, Upstate boy," he said, "the alcoholics shouldn't be that anonymous." Heh, heh.'

I see that Alphonse has the start of a jowl. Is that what a job brings out in you? No more Picasso boy. 'I think I hear your number,' I say.

This Martyn gives me a look. 'So do I.'

Once Alphonse scoots off I say: 'We didn't hear any number.'

'We don't *know* his number.'

'Should we be laughing?' We aren't quite. I need these cues.

He shakes his head. A good one, as heads go. More of a broad front-face than a profile. 'Alphonse isn't laughable. But we can laugh.'

'He know you were in the play?'

'May have. Casting news gets around. I teach theater, my country's mostly. Came here with a troupe I managed. Like to keep my hand in.'

So he isn't AA too. Not the one who got Alphonse the job.

I peer at the stage, which is empty now. 'He was no wild turkey, Alphonse. But a friend.'

'A friend.'

'We were members of the same club. Though — he was never quite in good standing.' I see I've puzzled him. 'Not people on the bottle, no. Just a place to hang out.'

'He was once a student in the class next door to mine. I used him once, in a play I did. Saw his work later, now and then. Spotty as it was. Lost sight of him, until today.'

'So he wasn't —?' Swingers' language. My tongue curls toward it but is too out of habit.

'Setting us up?' That smile. 'No. But the dinner offer still holds.'

Noggins? Mine is like opening, at a feverish rate. Careful. If this is memory, the pod bursting, all the brain's integers on the march — then there's no pill for it in my bag. 'I'm kind of full up on understanders.'

'I'm not a professional.'

'I've had a lot of those.' Walking in sand, this feels like. But toward. Not in retreat.

'Carol —' he says. 'Carol.' How does he know to say it over and over?

The lights are going down, up, down. There's no curtain. The stage has filled again with people still in the dark. 'Come to think —' the voice opposite says, 'maybe he was. Setting us up. Once he saw us together.'

'Why?' I haven't said that spontaneously — since I don't know when. And for a minute he's silent. He's taking advantage somehow of the dimming off-and-on-again light, I do know that.

'I used Alphonse in that play, because we needed somebody who was white.' It's then he takes my hands, both of them, like to cushion a blow.

A blow that would hit us both. 'Your country — you said.' I almost know.

'South Africa, yes. I'm what they call a colored. I saw you didn't know. Some of us are whiter than white. If a bit buttery. Or sallow. Even if we don't want to pass, in another country we do. When that happens for too long, I go back.'

The stage is rumbling now with the passage of people still in the dark. Soon they'll be showing their color, their shape. A good play is a slow revelation. But I owe him one now.

'Have to go,' he whispers. 'I wear a lot of silly stuff for the part. . . . We won't get through 'till after eleven maybe. If you can't wait, tell me where to call.'

Tell me where to call. It tolls like a bell. Hurts. Like a string pulled. Totting up what I owe the world. Or what it doesn't owe me.

'I can't,' I say. 'I live on the streets.'

Even in the dim I can see how he's looking at me, feel it. 'I know, I know,' I whisper. 'Just now — I'm passing. But I'm a homeless.'

That stops most onlookers. Like the barrier at a railway siding, shunting your tramp vehicle from the traffic rushing on. But he's not ordinary.

'Bed and board?' he says. 'Surely that could be found for the likes of you. But that's not what you're saying, is it? That's not the kind of homeless you are.'

'No —' I whisper. 'I'm a professional.'

Is he going to touch me?

He touches my pack. 'If I take up with one of these — maybe I won't have to go home. Or not yet.' His lips compress, whiter than his face. 'Have to get ready. Will you stay to watch? If not —.' Pressing a card in my hand, he scuttles down the aisle, vaults to the stage, which is thronged now, and is swallowed up, as if his leap is part of the action.

As we are, down here in the audience. Up there, the play is speaking for us. War and peace, homeland and rapine — the stage is gradually strewn with their properties. People carry their housing on their backs. Soldiers in shakos bark ditties on their faith, jigging across stage to their own falsetto, or falling wounded. Prostitutes slide their scarlet between the bandages. Children rise jack-in-the-box from their coffins and subside. All human character, or as much as a hall can handle, troops on, eddies into mime and dances off again. Only to repeat the message: all human character, human property, nullifies. Movement alone must suffice. At least in the first act.

The play might have been invented for me to watch while the flanges of memory turn, serving me up on my own camera, as sharp as on anyone's. Or keener, for having half-slept. I see a prison yard, painted Day-Glo orange for sun, a metal screening above us allowing in air. Our moving line — round and around, squaring off at the corners, is for others to watch. Yet a one-time, blocked Eden that no flicking of the television button would ever find for me later, endless in the day-room of the hospitalized. . . .

I am breathing so hard that my left-hand neighbor, bending curls that brush me, whispers: 'Are you okay?' An anxious girl-angel, at twenty still benevolent.

'Oh sure —' I breathe, 'just feeling lyric — y'know? And a little crazee—' and receive a me-too nod. That was quick of me. Who have been so slow, so — immovable? And far better to say what I had, than if I had croaked: 'And a little — sane.'

Onstage there's a parade of personages I can assign to parts of my own saga. That old man, toting an eternal log of wood, hod of coal — he's Titus, saying to the aunts with a shake of his grizzle: 'She don't know squat about herself, do she.' He sets the gift log in the grate. The gift coal is already down cellar. I am twelve years old and hiding in the store-closet, so near I can hear his joints creak as he straightens up. 'And Missies — who's to pay for this?' He meant for the coal, I say to myself later — he only meant for the coal. But he meant, Who's to pay for her — the unacknowledged story? Me.

The aunts could never bear to owe anybody. They left the house to Titus, a man by then in his nineties. In the wills of those who live by heritage does time always stand still? They left me, their fancy scholarship girl, the trust. The two of them dying hand to hand, in my junior year, of the same woman's complaint they had ignored. We played parcheesi in the hospital.

And so, my senior year, at Christmas and Easter and many weekends, I became the unfancy visitor — to those four girls. Carey, met in the college infirmary, both of us there on suspicion of anorexia, confided grimly: 'I'm not eating for two.' She had just had an abortion. 'You too?' I told her of what had been ripped away, leaving me in a town that had never been mine. 'Don't ever go back,' she said, and took me home to Bermuda with her for Thanksgiving.

. . .The flesh of well-to-do girl radicals will grow any variant cause; to be down in the melée is their bloom. When I met the other three, Laura, who spat her feminist rage at her boyfriend; Doris, who ate her way through her pity for the poor; Emmy, whose recurrent breakdowns, neatly divided between three residences, seemed only to reinforce her beauty and her backbone as well — I could not further define their politics. As for Minna, their fringe adviser, an older woman who had picked them up at a college workcamp in the Catskills — she was working-class. Of her, Doris, the dumb bunny who too often put her finger right on it, said solemnly: 'That's her career.' And Minna's hold on them. 'I don't want to owe anybody,' I said to Carey, on the brink of all the swimming pools. She said, 'Rats: we all owe you. You're our token; you know that.' I was beginning to. 'I almost appreciate it,' I said. 'Back home it was kind of personal.' And the Memorial Day poppies were never really mine. . . .

Onstage.

One corner is a field where humped-over figures inter-change as the crops they are carrying do: cotton, corn, sugar cane. A line of soldiers advances, their red uniforms and beavers the staples of military dream. From the opposite corner, girls in off-shoulder Mexican blouses pelt the soldiers with flowers as they pass. What era is this, what decade? What agriculture, what war? Are those girls flower children of the nineteen-sixties or camp followers to Napoleon? Or village girls on the Marne, First World War? And who are that other trio who scuttle into a cardboard foxhole: one in a Foreign Legion kepi, one in a cavalry wide-brim, and one in a helmet of pilot-blue? From the wings stage-right a kite whizzes, kamikaze. The actors' faces are all colors, all nations, and in a portable landscape. All the houses on the roadside are hovels carried on the back. Dust rises and settles after them. Shouts fade, but the singing is steady. Shots ring out, a faraway put-put, the fifing skreeks, but the feet, civilian feet, march drumbeat toward the final detonation. And the single flag.

And I know what I am seeing. Whoever patched this charade-parade from all the props of history, there's always some dramatist who will, scarring some in the audience, leaving the majority unscathed — but passing the flag of insurrection along.

My contribution would be small. I gave up memory. I ceded a mind. And lost a decade. Swaying from side to side, in one place.

But as the curtain now rises and dips, struggles aloft and wrinkles to the floor, a poor scrim that can't hide a stage emptying of all its images of revolution, my own images rise there. Again that table, three of the girls seated there — and a fourth, me, ten years ago, exiting in silent turmoil through a basement door. . . .

Next to me in our theater seats the twenty-year-old stretches, sighing. 'Intermission. Wouldn't think they could top this, would you.'

I say, 'Not unless they set off a bomb.'

She says, 'You in the cast, huh?'

I shake my head. 'Not this time.'

She's not stupid. 'Ah, you're not that old. You could even join us.'

'Join?'

'Word gets around,' she whispers. 'Me and some other guys, we want to be part of it. We're gonna crash the stage, Act Two.' Her eyes sparkle. 'Right from the audience.'

I recall that old ploy. We thought it was new. Activists swarming up from the audience. Of course you have to choose your play. We four went to a couple like that, but sat tight. We were not vicarious.

'See you —' my neighbor says, edging past me. 'Gotta tinkle.'

Up on the blank stage, as I sit enthralled, the specific scene is played. . . .

We are still in practice session, although end-of-semester dispersal is near. All these sessions are so much the same that we might be situated in eternity. At one end of the table a depression-era movie, idly recommended by a history professor, is running. Once more those milling crowds, so skeletal of face they must be real people, pour across landscapes only dreamed of. Steeltowns flare. Slag-heaps loom. Sometimes the other girls will cast a glance at the screen, more often not. Down the table, somebody is always fitting together or dismantling with utmost care those components that on demolition day will cause dogma and deed to interreact chemically.

Dora, whose fat fingers limit her at this work, hates the industrial documentaries but moons long over the mountain folk. 'All starving people look alike.' Then sighs. 'So do fatties.'

I watch all the movies. I am not allowed to participate in the handiwork. They will only let me sort parts, classify the smallest in a drawer cadged from an old printing press, and hand these out as called for. I rock from one expert to the other, like a hairdresser's assistant rhythmically handing out the rollers. Ever so often they order me out: 'Carol — don't you need to go?' In the bathroom I fight off the undertow of doubt pushing at me. Do they know enough history to be making it? Or if simple passion is enough, do my giddy, often winsome friends have the right circumstance for it? They never argue what they're doing here. Yet their tongues are so sharp.

When I said, joining up, that I wouldn't want to hurt anybody, they closed arms round me beguilingly, eyes moist. 'We're after monuments, not persons.' So I was satisfied; their ethic and mine was the same. But they only see persons psychologically; that's their standard. 'Of course Carol would say that —' is their attitude. 'She's been hurt.'

So far, the bomb target is undeclared. Actually — undecided. On this their talk is quite free.

When I get back from the toilet, Laura is nimbly fitting in the tiny key-shaped metal piece I had last handed her. She's a lefty. The engagement diamond on her fourth finger glitters oddly as she works. She catches me staring at the weird collage she's making. 'You're not supposed to look too hard,' she says, crosspatch. 'We don't want to incriminate you.'

'She means — if we're caught, you won't know anything much,' Carey says, her eyes as bright blue as the harbor she comes from.

'Caught?' Emmy says. The more dangerously thin she gets the more feisty. 'Why do you always harp on that?'

'Because she wants to be caught,' Laura says. 'So's her relationship with Dadda will be complete.'

Carey says, 'Lolly.' That's a Wasp nickname Laura loves to be called by. Carey's face is too meek. . . . Like when her father forbade her to see *La Dolce Vita*, which was playing the island again. 'I can't speak for your friend here —' he had said, so-o polite. My whole visit, he never addressed me by name.

'Mmm, sweetie.' Laura is now using a tweezer to insert a coil so hairline I'm just assuming it's there. 'Hand me that little tab, Carol. Over there, dammit. I can't let go.'

I am about to hand her the tab when Carey says in the softest voice: 'Laura — do you tell your analyst about the bomb?'

The word detonates. Laura has almost let go what she daren't. 'The installation' is the term they normally use.

The boyfriend says, 'You dumb bitches. I wish I had never. Maybe you better ask yourselves not where we're to go, but when.'

Until then I had seen little of Minna. Minna was our labor unionist, already out of the City College, 'Not a paying one like you gals.' No clothes you'd notice, a dull accent; wherever she sits there's like a space of gray. And grayish words. But there's a crown on her head all can see. She's done this kind of operation before.

Getting up, she comes around to Laura. 'I'll hold it for you. To do the rest.'

In slow motion, the hands interchange, then withdraw. I can hear us breathing.

Minna says: 'So what are we waiting for?' Like a bell has struck.

The boyfriend speaks. 'I gotta phone my parents.' It is his house.

The table stares at him.

'Just to be sure they're not coming in today.' But he looks about to throw up.

Laura blows him a kiss. We wait. That thing on the table — while we wait it seems to grow.

When he hangs up he says, 'Somebody on the street

already phoned them. Noticing the blinds were drawn. They know we always leave it like it's occupied. . . . You heard what I told my folks.'

We had. 'I'll go by and check,' he'd said. As if he wasn't calling from their own house.

Looking back, I recall the glance that the four of them: Laura, Doris, Emmy, even Carey, exchange. So that's what you do when you join up in a lie. You smile.

I take no credit for not joining in. Clearly they find me wanting in tact. Or wanting in the ability to calculate ahead? Or do I want to be a no-show? It feels like that. Under their stern eyes I go to the bathroom on my own.

When I come back, I can feel the tenseness in the room. They are a team. Minna, in the background until now is smiling at me — why? 'I'm starving —' she says chummy to the others, 'aren't you all?'

I can still hear their chorus — the boyfriend's bleat coming in last.

They want me to go for sandwiches.

'But not to that usual place,' says Dora, always depend-able on food. 'There's that new dairy-deli over on Sixth. Bring me a pastrami.'

'Club sandwich for me.' Laura.

'Deli's don't do club,' Dora says. 'Or don't call it that. Ask for a double chicken, heavy on the mayo, and with tomato, on white.'

Emmy, on some elite diet of her own, says nothing.

Carey says slowly, 'Nix on any of that for me.' She leans toward me winsomely. 'I have a yen for Chinese. Chow mein. Spring roll. In the next block after the deli, that place. Bring me some, hmm. And take your time, Carol.'

'Thought you were all starving,' I grumble. 'And you know what — I'm sick of being the gofer. Why'nt one of you go?' But in the end, I can't resist Carey. 'Okay-y. Join you in Chinese.'

They are so quiet. Like the bottom has fallen out of all conversation. Then I see that the table is bare. In a heap at the door, their backpacks. Under the table, the bundle stashed there is gone.

'You're moving the project on?' I say. 'Where?'

I am still on probation in that respect. They don't trust my allegiance to the cause. Whatever their cause is. Although they've never told where they intend to plant that thing, I have heard talk. Laura is for the Empire State Building. Doris wants the Rainbow Room, as a symbol of the bourgeois. 'Your bourgeoisie —' Carey shot back. Carey is against the Hague and the U.N. — all diplomats. I have no idea what she is for.

The boyfriend speaks up. 'We're sunk, we don't get out of here. Laura will tell you my mother checks the house top to bottom the minute she comes home. Just plant it pronto, will you. Wherever it's meant to go.'

And they are not going to let me know where.

Minna gets up, stretching. 'Off your butts, keeds. I've got a union meeting. Come on Carol, I'll walk out with you. Here's the dough.' She is humming that tune she always does . . . .'The *In*-ter *national hmm* mm — shall *bee* the *hyoo*-man race.' But when we get outside she gives me the high sign, and walks the other way. . . .

The bell has rung for intermission being over. Through the

open doors, at the rear of the empty hall, the audience can be seen, still smoking and chatting outside.

But up there, on that blank stage, there's no stopping me.

I am on my way back obediently loaded, chow mein whiffing in my nostrils from its cartons, sandwiches crackling in my arm. I have performed my errand well. Police cars and sirens sound, half a block away. I hear it, that city madrigal. With a rush of energy that carries me around the corner, I answer it.

How can a house-front, blown half-in, blast a mind? Or across the street, lace curtains, stirring through shattered glass, obscure life's recall? In the cop's arm, heavy on mine, is the destiny I require. He says, 'Everybody got out. They got away. You come from there, eh?'

In the buckled façade the basement window is wide. They flee me. They have fled.

'You the maid?' the cop says. 'That who you were?'

In the case record that weighed down Daisy Gold's handbag is my answer, excavated first for authority — prison; then for me — hospital. Until now I myself could not recall it.

'No, I'm one of them. I belong.'

. . . In the police precinct afterward, where I am made to sit for hours, I feed myself. The club sandwich that is Laura makes me gag, but I chew on. Ham-and-cheese on wheat — Doris, the Jewish girl who loves ham — that goes down easier. Carey's chow mein I save for last. With each mouthful something in my head shuts down. Then a matron takes me to the john and I retch up, but only the food. The rest of me is gone. . . .

Nothing in the record mentioned that meal. Now I remember, on my own. Memory laps me, that bath in which the brain lives. Mind stretches, as elastic as anyone's.

I am responsible.

And intermission is over in this theater. I prefer not to see Alphonse, in whatever roles he will assume. I regret not seeing Martyn as Wall, but maybe we'll reconnect. I can even imagine that. But first, as the SW's kept telling me, I have to get my act together. That's their style, why not adopt it? I'm so happy to be back that I don't mind remembering everything — which is more than many in my case would say. Or even ordinary persons? Is it now my ambition to become one of those? That I can't yet predict. Maybe that's Act Three.

Whether I'm still 'counter-culture' — as the program says of this play, or just prime obstinate, will have to evolve. I'm hopeful. Maybe I have just swallowed unawares the great big pill that most call reality.

As I stroll out of the theater, the rest of the crowd are just strolling in.

Outside the hall, at the dingy entrance serving as lobby and stage door, there's a solitary bench. I sit on it in the ebbing day. Down these old commercial blocks the hairy air is lion-colored, with tinsel sparks at the warehouse cornices. This is that other sunset the city gets no credit for. One the skyscrapers will never see. A slanting magic, folk art comfortable. Like I'm in the bowl of a worn but gilded spoon.

Now to the night's conundrum. Where to bed down?

— 'If that's freedom of choice, Carol,' the last doctor I was with said, after the hospital finally agreed to release me to no permanent address — 'isn't that a dead-end form of it?' I liked Dr. Camacho, whom the patients called 'Dr. Cee.' He looked like the governor of a zoo who had chosen to sit with the animals. At least part of the time.

Dead-end? 'Not if you're in a hospital.'

Or worse, the halfway house. Where at night you lie in bed — very good beds they have, far too suitable for dreams; and think — I'm halfway to what? Gender? The road not taken? Some forever home it will take an anti-choking maneuver to haul me out of? — So you lie there, neither fish nor fowl, or like the riddle says: Are you half empty or half full?

'What's it like for you, Carol, on what you call the "outside?"'

Most doctors in his line have one tone for when they state something, another for when they ask, but Dr. Cee's tone is always the same.

'In summer, it can be more — like playful. You're making your own moves. Like the men at chess in that little den of a house in the park. You can brood.'

He says something under his breath I don't catch. 'And in winter?'

'In winter, to be outside is a moral obligation.' Thinking

of it, I stand straighter. 'To hang on with those who. . . who are in the wrong.'

'Like how? You mean — with the law?'

Not always. Not only. 'Like — they're on the wrong side of things generally. Like they have more of nothing. And more coming.'

He doesn't say anything. Like they do.

'Yet who am I to side with them, Dr. Cee? A person who inherited. A girl with a trust.'

'If it's any satisfaction, the trust is about exhausted.'

It's neither one way or the other to me. All the money goes to the hospital. Perhaps that's partly why they're now letting me go. So much is 'partly,' in a mental hospital. I don't blame him.

'I worry about you,' he says. 'Because physically you're strong enough now. But ten years from now, five, what'll you be? Like we see them get to be? Broken down, toothless. A hag. Or worse.'

I've seen them. But he doesn't understand. They're not them. They're us.

'There's other ways of — of living,' he says. 'Than just to — to signify. And don't tell me Jesus did just that.'

When I say, 'Who?' — like I don't know who that is — he laughs. 'Just another activist.'

I trusted Dr. Camacho. He never urged me to have more tact.

'I know why you all give us pills,' I lashed out at him once. 'It's so you won't have to listen that much to what we say.'

'Not all day —' he'd said, nodding. 'It's not bearable. Because it may be the truth.'

After that he let me come to him without the day's medication. Which was hard, because there's more of yourself to give pain. But when I referred to myself as schizzy he got sore. 'You have empathy. For whom is after all your business. Not ours. You're not disoriented. Rather, you suffer from a constant, even exquisite sense of where you in fact are. Which may give you philosophical trouble. That's after all not our concern.' This small dark-haired man with a nervous moustache, he's never talked to me before on this level. And the next thing he says to me, his tone does change. 'You don't hear voices, Carol. Not even your own.'

And when that has sunk in he says those words that clang like an echo I'd always been hearing.

'It's like you weren't sure of having been born,' Dr. Cee said.

No anecdotes of my babyhood exist. Nor pictures — for who was to be sent them? The aunts showed us three off sufficiently at the bay window. End of my schoolyear, on prize day, they came, blushing seasonally over my good grades. On the streets I went to and fro, instructed not to mingle. Rarely visited, we did not reciprocate. It was as if we had made a pact with the town.

'And that blast you were barred from made you even less sure, eh? Better to remove yourself.'

Then why does he so love my aliases?

'Who cares how personality breaks out, Carol. It's like you're asking us to share a joke — that you do exist.'

I want to laugh with him now, wishing I could share this hour with him, and the hours to follow. How after ten blocks or so one begins to tingle with the walking pleasure, not all of it in the feet — or in the body alone. So many secret haunts for our sort in this city, on all levels of secrecy, of course: in some you will find company, if never quite of your own kind. Which nobody expects. Meanwhile, people have rosters of places known only to themselves, confided only if buddyship briefly strikes, or drugs or drink.

In ten blocks or so, I can arrive at that Ukrainian Hall which is no longer in business, but can be sneaked into. Or if I crave more space and am willing to shake a leg for it, I can push on to the area just before you get to West Street. There, in that quarter of mostly vanished meat wholesalers, the old cornices offer good broad rain shield, and the laddered fire escapes a river view. At times a graveyard quiet may afflict, or the slightest smell of animal blood. Yet hit the area on a balmy night and it may be a ballroom for a drag queen frolic. They have lovely manners, even if you're a woman.

Anyway, it's a menu. And for free.

— Last time I saw Dr. Cee the medical board was to be sitting on 'releases,' mine among others. When I enter his office, on mental tiptoe though I stride, he raises his arms in hurrah. 'It was iffy, yes. But they're hoping to let you go.'

'Every release is iffy,' I say. 'You never can be sure whether they think you're sensible or they're giving you up.'

'Ah, Carol. You have a tongue. But I'll miss it.'

So I spare him a mention of that third qualification for a release which can zap you the quickest: money. Something about the Hippocratic oath changes, when you are expected to pay for it.

'And the ward will miss you.'

Often on a ward there'll be a patient who becomes advocate for the others. On mine I'd become that. 'Only because I hear too much,' I told him. 'I don't unload somewhere, I'll break.'

'Just remember what I told you.'

'You've told me so much.'

He looks hurt, so I say: 'Tell me again.'

'Carol, you do hear. You empathize.' Schizoids don't, or not that much, he repeats. They rebel, because they fear. They can be violent, or retreat. 'And violently intelligent. But with people — they're hard to unplug.'

I don't go for all of that, I tell him. Not from what I've heard on the ward. 'I think: sane or mad, or intermediate like I've been — everybody has spells of everything.'

They don't like to hear the word 'mad;' they have so many more complicated words for it. So he just shakes his head. 'You'll find danger.' He comes down hard on the 'find.' 'So watch out for yourself, hah? And drop me a card now and then.' He hands me a packet. 'Don't open it now. Only postcards.' We shake. He grips me by the shoulders and almost hugs; it's a lenient hospital. 'And I'll remember what you've told me too, Carol. It's a deal.'

I'd used to stare at the sky outside his window, while we talked. He never called me on it; he knew I was trying to get my colors back. But this last time he can't resist asking what color the sky is that day. Actually it is the same gray I always see, like they say a dog does. But I say: 'The sky outside a locked window is always criminally blue.'

I am still on my bench. In the walking world it takes no time at all for a bench to become one's own, and this is rarely disputed among us, although in Central Park's upper Babyland the nannies may glare. Meanwhile, the crowd in the theater has dispersed, easing out past me, chatting its judgments, in the furtive decibel that audiences do. They have their destinations, what is mine?

Perhaps I should send the hospital board, which was so reluctant to release me to nowhere, a list of my addresses since? Dozens of them, no doubt showing my own patterns on a mythical pedometer, from that arch under a bridge not Brooklyn's, to the niche behind that construction hut on Roosevelt Drive. I am an architect's reference book of ignored ruins, boarded-up row houses, forgotten monuments. But a bench is for the interval anybody might snatch; seated on it I'm a common profile. I never sleep on a bench.

Maybe I should go Mungo's route? Seek the salvation of a church? Not to nestle inside or to take its communion, but to bed down against its wall, through which there would surely be some seepage of the good? But the trouble with churches, even those too poor to have garden borders, is that some volunteer sexton can always be found to sweep sternly clean all niches and porches, and of course lock the door. If they knew the biblical needs of those like me, perhaps they would not sweep.

... Once, when I was in the halfway house and coming back after curfew found the door locked, and unanswered as well, which they had warned me of, I had found such a church. In the mist from the harbor I could just see its steeple — not too grand. At its base, a rundown stone border, no hedge. But in the rear, dusty but not garbagy, just the cul-de-sac for my kind. Some past sojourner had even left a coned smut of ashes from a fire.

When I woke, a man with a round collar was bending over me. 'Will you have coffee inside?' he said, 'or would you prefer it out here?' My neck was stiff from resting on my backpack, but I could still stretch it. 'The steeple is grander than I thought,' I said, in apology. 'It considers itself a cathedral,' the priest said, smiling. 'With accommodation for all.' I said I would come in for the coffee, but not stay. And what do you know — it was he who said 'Thank you'. . . .

But this is another city. And I'm out of touch. Having a pad will do that to you. Or a hang-out — even one that had no membership.

What I'll have to cope with now is that I do have my memory back. A headful, heavy with chartings and allusions. And with a need to see how things will turn out. I *remember*. How half of memory is the urge to tally destiny. However humble that girl back there was, she had a taste for dynamite. Wow . . . . Page Ms. Mickens. Ms. Bryna Mickens. I even remember your first name. On your bracelet, in gold. I had aliases once, a whole charm-bracelet of them. Wind-chimes, that's all they were. Telling me of lands I hadn't come from. And when it was time to blow.

Hello, Mickens. I'm Carol Smith.

I am still lounging there, as a stage door allows, and smiling at how I handled that, when this freak emerges. Blushy red-powdered cheeks, eye pencil, tufts of papery grass and flower buds in the hair. A gray running-suit.

'Go on — ' I say. In the genteel voice of Dedham, yes. I mustn't be ready yet for what-the-fuck. 'It's Wall.'

It grins. Underneath is Martyn. 'What d'ya know. Stage-door Jane. Am I to take this as a compliment?'

I blush. In depression one doesn't; there's not much empathy even for oneself. 'I left before you came on. It all came back to me.'

'Yeah, it does affect people that way. A good play.' He scratches his neck, picking a plastic flower from it. 'But backstage, the sinks are jammed. All two of them. No dressing rooms. Half the production is from the Warsaw underground. They're not on to union rules.'

Neither am I yet. I'm not in the union I was. I've lost the street-savvy. I'm not able to slouch off. I never could snarl, though sometimes I could confront. And he's looking at me that easy way, hands on hips. 'I had a kind of revelation, I guess. I mean — recovery.' Trippy tongue, Carol. But yes, that's what you had.

'Jesus. Didn't know it was that good a play.' Bending over, he pulls a long, floaty clump from his head. Waves it at a cop just then passing us at the curb. The cop waves back.

'That the cop on the beat?'

'One of them. Why?'

To laugh like I am. To laugh, any old way. At seeing a cop wave friendly-like to a painted man pulling out his hair. 'I'm just seeing the advantages of art.'

He flips me a salute. I watch while he cleans the blacking from his face. He'll get any remark I throw off. And easy does it; he seems to have no guardedness, no need of that. How are these people made? And he gives off like sex doesn't have to be involved; I don't have to think of that.

Like with most persons now you have to identify your gender at the outset — even if you've never had a doubt about it. Indicating what satisfactions you pursue. And whether or not you would pursue those with the man or woman or gay you're talking to. Even on the ward, that shadow play went on, if only verbally. Until, down the drug-clotted hours, we lost all the structure of our lives except the ego we were burdened with.

I have to stand still in all this clarity. And what do you know? — I can.

He has picked off the last greenery from his head. 'Should've had a wig. But they couldn't spend.'

'You can stand in the street with daisies sticking onto your scalp and not mind?' I say. 'That's because you're not a freak inside.'

'My country doesn't think so.' He slaps his forehead. 'What time is it?' His wristwatch is blurred with scratches; it has been places. 'Past four. Gotta get a paper. News I expect. No news-stand around here.' I can see he doesn't want to leave me here. 'Want to walk along?'

Does he guess I'm a walker? Wouldn't put it past him. 'Okay.'

He points us north. It's Deadsville down here: boarded-up shops not even broken into. Sunday, but no church anywhere. And not a soul but us.

As we head off I'm wondering what kind of news he's waiting for.

'Home,' he says, as if I'd asked aloud. 'I've got a mother, a half-brother down there.'

'I rallied once for South Africa. Anti-apartheid, I mean.' The scent of packed bodies washes over me like a vinaigrette.

Left of me, back there, a man's upflung arm. On the dais a sea of heads sway, as a speaker snarls a quote in what must be Afrikaans. Right of me, a woman protrudes her tongue.

' Boston. Yes, that helped,' he says.

'How —? Ah, you've caught my accent.'

We slog on.

'My mother's been anti all her long life. My brother, a police chief, a rabid separatist. But, dammit all if they haven't become allies, now that we're legally free of the old scourge. Neither of them willing to concede that we are.'

'Free?' I find I have no gesture for it. 'Free? Since when?'

On his face, wiped clean now, I see the years I have lost.

'Not soon enough.' He takes my hand, swinging it. 'You been in stir, eh. So was I once, when I was young. But nothing could be kept from us. We had the drums.'

He has dropped my hand. But we are still walking. 'I was young. But I wasn't in that long.'

We walk on.

'I took you for maybe color-blind,' he says. 'Or trying to be.'

'Shouldn't we be?' I toss out. 'Like a church?'

'When the whole world is. Not until.'

'My two aunts brought me up white. Best they could do.'

'Which side were they?'

'Side?' I say. A patch of rouge still on his nose twitches. I see he's amused. 'Oh, they were white all right. It was a wartime thing. So was I.'

'Orphan, eh. They adopt you?'

'Oh no. One of them was my mother. They just never told which.'

The big surprise about a memory returned is how it wants to pour. As if that itself is the blessing. Else how could I be smiling? Of course part of that is having a person to tell it to, natural. 'They kept us apart from both sides. So people wouldn't do it to them first.'

He stops us on the curb. Passes his hands near to my cheeks, one to a side. But doesn't touch. Like a magician? Or a dermatologist? Or as a man might do if you are his first of your kind. 'Be any way you want, Carol. You deserve it.'

I can't quite believe this, but it's balm to hear. 'You get that much charge out of being what you are?'

He winces. 'Only way to go on being it.'

'Sorry.'

'Deserved.' He rubs his face. His palm comes off pink. He grins. 'But it's a real relief sometimes, being a Wall.'

And there, way down the block, is a news-stand. The street we're coming to is a main artery, four-lane and buzzing double-time, like an old movie. Not the kind for me. When we get there I better leave, but not without telling him what I should. We are walking slower anyway.

'When you're on a mental ward, Martyn, there is no news. None that affects you. That's when I lost the habit. And when you get out — that's the big news.' I sneak a look. No change in that blunt profile. 'Alphonse tell you about me?'

'Nope.' He turns his full face to me. 'You're telling me yourself.'

So I am. So I am. 'Want to know what I was in for?'

He shrugs. 'This is now.'

So it is. 'Thanks.'

All of a sudden I would like to make him laugh. 'Back in

the slammer where I was first, there was more variety, at least on the women's side. The hookers took a real interest in "Family Court," that program. But the real draw were the serial killers. The general opinion was that women don't get an equal chance at it.'

He laughs all right. What I haven't counted on is that so do I.

At the stand I say: 'I'll buy one too. It'll be a start.'

'It'll be a weight. The Sundays always are.'

'I can use it, wherever I bed down.'

He lets that pass.

But what do you know, the Paki in charge of the stand shakes his head.

'No more *Times*?' Martyn asks. The Paki, an older man, signals No, turning his back. He and a younger man start closing up the stand.

'Hey, wait —' I say. 'They're not sold out. They've just already tied up the leftovers for pickup, and don't want to bother to untie. I've often seen the trucks coming by.' And sure enough, near the curb back of the stand are the bundled papers.

When Martyn points, they shrug.

'Bet you —' Martyn says to me. Leaning close to the older man, he says something in what must be their language. The older gives the younger a look. The younger goes to untie, pulling out one copy. When Martyn pays up with a fiver they have to unearth the money box. All without a word. They begin again to close up.

'What did you say to them?' I whisper.

When he grins, his eyes close halfway. 'It wasn't from the Koran.'

When you can whisper with a person it expands you. 'News-stands used to be places where you could ask direction. Or even be greeted, if you were a daily customer. There was one like that in the barrio, my old neighborhood.' Where the bar owner bought the Spanish paper every afternoon, below my window. 'But these people, they never talk, never smile. Yet they own nearly all the kiosks.'

'They're separated from their country. They don't yet think of this one as theirs.'

The sun is behind Martyn's profile, raised like a person who doesn't whisper but will accept one.

I manage a voice. 'Maybe they've had amnesia too.'

He knows what I'm telling him. When he answers, it's to the bundle of newsprint under his arm. 'Morning rehearsals are a bitch. Screw up the whole day, fuck it. . . . Join me in a spot of tea?'

That breaks me up, the style of it.

'Your place or mine?' he says.

'I don't have a place.'

'You have the whole city.'

To have someone say that. Like it's in the Koran. 'In that case, yours is okay.'

When he dumps the newspaper on me I think he's backing off after all. But he's only running after a cab .

Years since I've been in one. It feels tight. I have so much to relearn. At least I know how to walk.

'Where we were standing —' he says. 'Canal Street. Asia city, all the way East. Wristwatch stalls, where you can buy a fake Cartier or Gucci self-winder, last you a year. For ten, twelve bucks. Give it a shake, and it'll last you another.'

'I've never walked East much. From now on, maybe I will.'

We exchange the proud smiles of New York know-it-alls.

We stop somewhere in the Twenties. I've no compass for wheels.

'This is the wholesale fur district,' he says. 'Lost a little steam during the animal protests. But up a few blocks, on Seventh, the flower sector has shrunk too. Don't know why.'

'The city's like an iceberg herd. Keel one over and who knows what'll come up for air. A robot maybe, screaming "Raise the Rent."'

'You do sound — professional.'

'Only on a street.' Put me behind a window-pane and I'm a ball of fluff — but I'm not saying. We're entering a small commercial building, four-story, down-at-the-heel.

'Top floor,' he says. 'No lift. The shaft is crumbling. Place belongs to an estate. Statutory rent. Started out as my office. But they let you bunk here, don't hassle. Haven't used it much lately. Been on the road.'

I haven't climbed stairs since the pad and the Cat Club. The pills, they'll only keep you in the present, and no future to count on. I have stopped taking them. — 'You can stop,' the doc said in parting, 'when you feel able. But I warn you, only if you put something else in the drug's place. A routine, say.' He spares me the four-letter word the SW's keep flinging you, like you're on mental welfare —W-o-r-k.

These stairs may not be residential but they are nothing like the Cat Club's either. They're in the normal world. They're working stairs. It helps to climb them. The fifth floor is the top. Only one flat up here,' he says. The lock responds to his key. The door swings open. Some doors push in. *Open sesame* is what you should feel, not a stifling. I don't feel either. This room is Martyn's. Martyn's life.

Twenty by thirty, say, and barely furnished. Like the ante-room of some village doctor with a practice not in need of too many chairs. One armchair, which can chat with its neighbor, a captain's seat, two other bony spares. The left-hand wall is solid bulletin board covered with clippings and photos, down to the dado of filing cabinets below. When he turns on a fan the clips flutter like messages, incoming but ignored.

Center wall, broken by a hallway door, has a cubby-holed refrigerator, sink and grill. But the main feature of the room is that the right-hand corner has been sectioned off floor-to-ceiling, with that semi-transparent glass. 'My office.'

Ten by ten or so; the door must be at the side. One of the two front windows must be within. Even now the enclosure gleams faintly with reflections from buildings opposite; by daylight or summer sun it must dazzle. In front of its long wall is a line of —?

'Drums. I managed a tribal song-and-dance troupe from home. We lived here during their two-year run.'

Any drum is primitive. But these, of umber and tan stretched skin in varying tones and sizes, must be what he has said: tribal. One or two would be tall enough to reach a man's thigh. Several are paired: to be slapped alternately? Or with the heel of the hand? No drumsticks are visible.

'Bathroom?'

'Down the hall.'

I go.

The hall is lined with bedrolls, neatly hung but hard to creep by. I see that one of them is actually like what I am toting, a Shelter-Pak. The bathroom is ordinary, to anyone but me, to whom all-white tile is votive now. On the wall opposite the toilet is a two-foot-long framed photograph, a family picture? — a household? People lined up in front of a low house or barn in a stunted landscape, the whole thing mostly sepia brown. I haven't time to examine either the costumes or the faces. What I covet is a bath, but must pass the tub by.

When I come out he has the kettle aboil and a brass tray-on-legs set between two of the chairs. 'Crowded, when the troupe was here, but jolly too, once we settled the food. Found an African cafe that would cater too, across town, and a grocery on lower Ninth. Once in a while we cooked. You can get anything edible in this town except maybe grilled larks. And those too, if you know somebody in Little Italy with a cousin who regularly plies the airlines. The hotels and motels wouldn't take us — they said because of the noise. Though I've known practicing bag-pipers to be quartered.' He chuckles. 'A kilt is top entrée almost anywhere in the States.' A good host, he's talking to ease me. What I hear is that on another level this man knows the city as well as one who walks.

'How many was the troupe?'

'Six, usually. Eight was too many. Sometimes only four, if some had to go back for family reasons. But they could fill a stage. And they've not gone quiet. My country will be needing new songs.'

I am projected back into that youthful climate where nations were seen to need song. And were sung to. So it still goes on . . . . He has been at the newspaper, scattered now on the floor. I see the floor is gouged, where the singers might have banged it with their — staves? Several such troupes had played the Boston political arenas.

The tea is strong. In prison one slurped, dug at a nostril, felt the back teeth with a fingertip, smoothed the mouth with the flat of a hand. On the ward, one might see worse. On tea-break, a new patient, a bride whose husband had discovered she was a klepto, had come to the table wearing a feces moustache. But I have kept my home manners, whether for good or bad. Look how Carol eats, Carmen had said to Angel. Sure, twelve years old, you're a man — but here they don't shovel it.

Tea is drinkable memory all by itself. . . .

This dark plain tea is the kind brewed on sail-boats by the fathers of the families who once a summer invited the town's Girl Scouts for a day on the water. I wasn't a Scout, but some extra were invited. Our patron, a big blond man in whites, wore one of those white duck hats with a brim too small for him, as did many of the men. The joke was — and the mothers on board gaily made it one — that outfitted by the aunts too eagerly plundering our attic for a hat to keep me from sunburn, I was wearing one too. . . .

'Male tea —' I say, with a glance at a theater poster center of the bulletins, on which a trio of men, bare except for a clout of fringed cloth tied over their sex, squat wide-kneed over their drums.

I amuse him. 'Do you always say the right wrong thing?'

'How do you mean?'

'Like what you said about my noggin.'

And does he always ask the right questions?

'I don't yet have a firm "always." It's still shaking down. From before.'

'Before —' he says, musing. Not asking. That's why I can answer.

'Before my break. Since then, until now, oh I had the facts. I was told them, over and over. But not the feelings that went with them. Or much else.'

He's staring so hard and steady he's drawing it out of me. He must have been good with the troupe. Drawing them all the way from Africa. Barefooted, to these streets.

'It was like the case-record they attached to me was more theirs than mine.'

'Carol —' he says, and I twinge to it.

'That's me. I made them name the record Carol Carol.' I am looking back at that day now. 'In hope.'

'I'd a nickname when I came out of jug,' he says. 'Political. You carry it like a flag. Useful, when a man is on the run. Though I was never that.'

. . . 'You have to settle what you're running from,' Dr. Cee said. . . . And I said, 'Couldn't I be running toward?'. . .

'I walk —' I say now. 'But I could never carry myself like a flag.'

'No, that's not been your style.'

'How could you know that?'

He's messing with the newspaper on the floor. One section has had its top page cut out of. He tears the date border from that page and stows it in a pocket. 'Because I saw you once, and never forgot you. You and I never met. But I saw you. Before.'

In the slammer? On the ward?

I only mouth those, but he shakes his head. He hasn't

one of those mythic faces you're supposed to remember best. Or be caught by. Like are in old pottery, or growing out of the stone ruins, or in an artistic photograph. His face is blunted by what's been pushed at it. Or by hard thoughts from behind. No wonder the part he played had been given him. 'But I can't have seen you, Martyn.'

'I was in your Cambridge once. The Boston one.'

'The rally? Where they showed the films of the townships? That's the one I went to.'

He rocks a bit, like he's back there. I would recognize that rally rhythm anywhere. Like you're rocking in time with the convictions all around you. Like you're with inner song. I cover my mouth with my hand.

'You were with a yellow-haired girl I did meet,' he says. 'And two or three others I didn't. None of them spoke. Nor you. I watched you stay in the background.'

'You were Carey's guy, then? We knew she was going to meet him there.'

'No. That was Dabney, British-style black from one of the island governments. He pointed you out. He said, "She's the way these girls are showing cause." But then his girl pipes up: "She's the only one of our cell who's not an amateur. But she doesn't know." And then I lost track of them, Dabney and her, in that crowd. Never saw him again.'

'Neither did she.' Poor Carey, grinding her teeth against my shoulder later, not a sob out of her. 'I wanted that kid of his, but he wouldn't marry it. He said girls like me were dangerous to the cause.' And when she'd said to him, 'What cause am I a danger to? Could its name possibly be Dabney?' he'd given her the big stare, and lit out. . . . 'I was in danger, all right,' she said to me. And sat up, smoothing her hips with a movie star smile. 'Abortions thin you,' she said. 'Let's go swimming somewhere!' —

'I lost track of her too,' I say. 'I must have wanted to.'

He sees me looking down at the cut-out news page. 'Bad blood now, in some of the townships I worked with. Before freedom, many in the worst places weren't paying their rents. Because what they were getting wasn't worth living in. Now the banks won't give mortgages in those townships, using non-payment as excuse. Bah! Freedom is owning. As anybody knows.'

Not to me. I don't know my total self yet. But surely it's not an owning one.

'You don't agree?'

'You going back for that — for just a mess of mortgages?'

He laughs. 'After a revolution, you cope with civil life.'

The dark brew we're sipping gives me impudence. And sitting in a civilized chair is such a help to argument. The two basic needs being sated, if temporarily. 'When I was a student, any American sympathizer could like own a piece of some revolution, from afar. I went for that. It made me feel more American.' I choke on that last. I'm getting back my background. 'But then a revolution would be shut down. Or be over. And the newspapers would point us to another one.'

'One needs to be on local ground. Which reminds me.' Rummaging on a shelf, he brings out some crackers. 'Peek & Frean's. Ate bushels of them when I was at school in England. But they taste bland across the water. Sorry.'

'Why, we had those at home. For company that just might happen.' If not, we ate them at Christmas. They'd tasted abstract, as food often did in that house so separate from the gatherings. I take one of these to remind me. It does. 'I am on local ground—' I flash at him. Saying that heartens me. 'I'll keep this for the road.' There's a place for such stores in my pack. My fingers fumble; they hint at what I may be leaving. But I have made a pact with the bag. 'Thanks for the tea. And the walk.' Can he tell which I value most?

'We have a bag like that here. What's it called again?'

'Shelter-Pak.'

'A well-wisher gave it to one of our men, to take home with him. But it wasn't the cold he would need most to be sheltered from. And toting it would mark him, even for some of his own kind. Besides, going from place to place in our countryside, he would stay with kin. Or some who felt kinship. If a man is on the run, say. Hospitality might even empty a house for such a traveler. Or fill it suddenly, so that a newcomer can't be targeted.'

I can see the houses, or huts, crowded with sudden kin. All over the land, a sudden gathering. 'Were you — a target?'

His eyebrows go up, thick ones that had needed no extra tufting. 'Not long enough.' He stares at his hands.

'Sorry. I've been told I have no tact.'

'That has its uses.' He's looking at the drums. All appear to be of natural skins, stretched over varying woods. Some are identical in size and fringe decoration. One pair, not as high as the rest, has a design on each drumhead, a face with slashed cheeks. No need for drumsticks. They would be played with the heel of the hand then, and slapped. Even with elbows. All usable anatomy.

'They're all handmade,' he says. 'Two of the troupe made their own; the others generally took pride in using instruments widespread. Which, as they said, any man could have. And when they played, each took pride in the difference. Even the critics noticed. Like a chamber ensemble, they said. Those who carry the progression, and those who are the solo wanderers. But when I told that to my singerdrummers they laughed. "If the song does its work who cares?" they said. "And the work is all the same."'

He sees my question before I say it; that's always lightsome — when people do.

'Their "work?" To move people. "The feeling that moves the feet," they called it. And they really did, you know. Their emotion was their politics. Audiences saw that. What they did abroad really counted.'

'Then why did they go back?' It burst from me. 'When they were doing such a pure thing?'

'Pure?' The word drops like a spat candy, although his face is still kind. 'That's a — our usage. For them the elemental has never split.'

Ah then. They would have to go back. I see it.

'On the circuit, here and in Europe — barefoot most of the time, which they insisted on. They finally said they wanted to return to their families. Very politely, because this I couldn't argue. But really they were tired, very tired, of being just theater. They wouldn't be that at home. But to me — who'd enticed them here, they couldn't say.'

'Because you're the — the theater person?'

He smiles. 'Good phrase. Yes, I wrote their songs or arranged them, and the little dance-dramas we found we could do. . . . Know what "business" means in the theater?

Not money — though I took care of that. It means what actors do other than speaking: props, interaction, the physical movement of the play. I'm no playwright, though I can wordsmith, a bit. I can carpenter a song. Put a time clock on the drumbeat. Push the presentation along. I'm the "business" chap. But that alone wasn't why they held back from me.'

He wants me to ask. Compelled by his talking to me this way, I can. 'Why, then?'

'Because we had been brothers. But I wasn't going home.'

I get up from my chair.

'More tea?' he says quickly. He wants me to stay. I don't want the tea, but I can be polite. 'Thanks.'

While he puts the kettle on I go to the window that's not boxed in, and look down. I know the garment district. Street is empty now. By morning it'll be a bramble of people. I like to walk through that gutteral, hearing the know-how that unites the smart, anxious girls, the fat men clamping cigars — a street fair. 'He's bankrupt,' you hear. 'Him — he's flush.' I press against the window-pane. The dank feel and smell reassures me. The outside is there. 'You've got a lamppost down there. How lucky.' The New York ones are too elegant, like out of an old movie. Gangs used to bust them. I saw one uprooted once. But now they don't bother; they're used to them. This one has a solitary glow.

'The men liked it. At this time of night especially.'

I am still here, yet half outside. 'If there were somebody leaning against it, it could be a painting.'

I hear his chuckle from behind me. 'You're the painter.'

'I'm no artist. Even in occupational therapy, the hospital, they couldn't make me be.'

'There are artists who have no art.'

'That crap —' I say without turning. The word slips from me. I feel the old elastic quick-sass between the ears. 'You mean I have the temperament. Without the goods.'

— No, I don't mean, Dr. Camacho said. I mean — you're trying to make art of your life. When you should be living it. —

'Can't say what you're doing in that line,' Martyn says from behind me. But it's clear you're doing something. . . . Excuse me.' He goes down the hall.

He's getting too close. I have to head him off.

— 'No, you can't draw, or sing —' Dr. Camacho said. Says. 'And though you have a flair for language, many do. Historians, say. And occasionally — doctors.' He coughs, waits. I don't speak. 'Carol,' he says. He knows how that affects me. 'Carol, what you have is the single vision. Carried too far. Saints have it. You have the tenacity of a nun. But you're not a saint. And a hospital tries to humanize, Carol. You're just afraid of the doubleness of the world.'—

All I answered was: 'I hate the word "flair."' '

You have to head them all off.

'Excuse me,' I say when he returns. 'I hear old dialogues.' But when I wheel around the drums confront me. Their owners have returned to the family. 'You have a family there, Martyn?'

The water is boiling on the tiny range. He pours some into the pot and serves up. 'I had a wife. She was an Anglo but she could pass for a colored. Old Cornish stock from the silver mines, maybe with Romany mixed in. We met in Britain. She joked Africa was the first place she felt warm. Now she's back in England, married again, and has the

family we couldn't settle to. I still hear from her. Once a year.'
He too is looking into a distance. 'She's a New Ager now.
Those couples who live in caravans, trippers on other peoples' land? Christmas, she'll send me some address I can
reply to. Plus pics of the children we didn't have. Products of
the caravan life she mistook mine for. . . . That fill you in?'

'Quite.' I say it with a Brit accent. He smiles, but before I
can smile back for a joke shared, he says: 'On the road — a
professional — you ever want a family? Or say, if it happened to you?'

He's not asking if I screw. Or would with him. He asks
straight, this Wall.

'I would have to learn, first. How to be in a family.'

'Just having one seems to do that for most.'

When a Wall is bitter, you're reminded it's a man. 'You
were very fond of her.'

He nods.

'The aunts who brought me up — I was fond too. But I'd
have been fonder of the mother one, had she ever said. She
never did.'

'You are half-and-half.' His tone takes it for granted. 'So
am I. My mother was the Brit. But braver than yours. She
kept me by her.'

'Oh — they kept me by.' It trails out, expressing the way
I'd felt exactly. So when he grips my hands I let him.

'Oh, Carol. Unidentified?'

Confiding is simpler than therapy. You nod.

He drops my hands carefully. 'I was kept, and acknowledged. It was given out — not by us, by the other Anglos,
that our Indian doctor had sired me. But our black servants
knew it was one of their own kin. And so did the commu-

~144~

nity. My mother carried a gun everywhere. My father couldn't, being still, on and off — in the household. She was pressured to say she'd been raped. So they could dispose of him. Instead, she made it known we were a family in a way — she and the young school teacher who was our majordomo's grandson. And me. My father was sent back to Joburg, where he'd been educated. He was shot in our garden, on a visit to the house. When I was two.'

'Who by?'

'The grandfather.'

'Her father.'

'Oh no. His own. Though it is probable her Brit husband supplied the gun. So honor was done. Since our majordomo kept his job. And so I grew.'

Violence hushes me. I'm in awe of it. In the slammer I knew enough to get out of the way. But the hospital had to dose me extra to stop the shivering, if I witnessed any. They tell you it's because you really want to do damage too.

'My dialogues took place in our garden,' he says. 'Every shadow spoke.'

We sit in silence. The kind you can share with a person suitable for conversation.

There are few shadows in this room, except maybe around the line of drums against the glass wall. The room is unlived in. That smell of bread-and-blood currents which people exude has faded out. 'I like lived-in places. Not that I have to meet the people involved. That's peculiar of me, isn't it, Martyn?' His name comes so naturally.

Most people would evade. He nods. 'And when you're so easy to meet.'

'I never think of meeting, or being met.'

'That's why.'

'No, it's depression. They said.'

He gives them the raspberry. That glorious rudeness.

'I used to whistle —' I say low. 'But not through my teeth.'

'You can admit that out loud, Carol. All the examiners are asleep.'

Except him?

'I met my grandfather —' I say. 'I never let on I knew who he was. He delivered our coal.'

We're sitting up straight in the two bony armless chairs. His face is clean now except for the blond stubble. I see the wet start in his eyes. Mine begin to fill as well. 'Funny —' I say. 'I never bawled over that before.'

'Go ahead. Here's my shoulder — if you'll allow.'

It's only a wall to lean against, as the tears in my throat granulate. 'I never cry —' I say, as my gullet fills with slush. My neck cracks forward. Under my forehead his shirt is smooth. Am I bawling for having been inside of places for so long — or for getting out? 'Why'm I spilling my guts?' I bawl. 'My father won the Purple Heart.'

As the sludge of tears racks me, the wall grows arms. When we stand up we're bracing each other.

'Posthumous?' he says.

'Um.'

'So you never knew him either.'

'Oh no. There was a picture of him. In the American Legion Hall.'

Under our feet the newspapers have rucked up. I bend to smooth them.

'That's all right, don't. I got what I needed.'

'I should go, then. It's getting light.'

'To walk? Little early for that.'

'There're no rules for it.' The strap of the Shelter-Pak tangles, the bag's only fault. Broad as a belt, the harness takes fiddling to get comfortable in.

'That thing your badge, Carol? Or your cross?'

It does weigh. 'Maybe it's my saviour.'

He doesn't laugh. 'Like my glass enclosure. Look at it.'

It's merely that translucent paning common to basement windows, in a pattern of hexagons if you look close. But light is light.

'Salesman who subleased me had a refrigerated closet there. For his mink samples. So I tore out the beaverboard, put in glass you could imagine distance beyond. Only an illusion. But the troupe needed it. Western rooms are hard on them.'

'So are they on Westerners.'

He ducks his chin to that. 'But you had a pad.'

'Part time. Too much of the time.'

He kicks the *Times* across the floor. 'I'll have to be off tomorrow, on any plane I can get. And you, scatting off in this vast city, God knows where. The place is yours, if you'll use it. As a favor.'

'Favor?'

'To a part-time friend. No obligation.'

The bag lies there like a wily octopus, the multiple catch on it glinting like an eye. 'I'm just sorting things out. My obligations.'

He flails his arms. 'Water my plants.'

The one window-sill is bare. The billboard clippings hang motionless, waiting for tomorrow's breeze. The drums wait. 'Oh Martyn. You have no plants.'

Why am I smiling? And he the grim one.

'Park that heavy jacket you're wearing then. Until you really need it.' He toes the backpack. 'Give this guard dog of yours a night's rest. Throw yourself on the mercy of the city, if you must. Just keep this, will you? And use it? Once in a while?' He throws a keychain on the table. Scowls at it as if it might rat on him. 'Truth is — I can't bear to lose sight of you.'

A rich voice; as an actor he can't help that. But pushing no lie. And to be answered truly.

'Being kept in sight by one person — is not on my agenda. That's what people in houses do.'

'Hah. So that's your vocation? Walking the open road, watched only by God?'

'God's not on the agenda.'

'Somebody has to be. A life that's not watched — counts for what?'

'It's my routine. Or will be. And maybe that will count. And if there are enough of us out there, strong enough to be seen — then people will watch.'

Down in the street below, traffic is beginning to whir. Trucks will be bringing in the furs, guards swaggering as they open vault doors. The fruit vendor will be opening his cart. Not that they will much regard my sort. But we will be passing.

'Hah. Knew there was something. But people get used to — people like that. In the end, you'll be the only one watching. Watching yourself.'

'Maybe. But better than tossing a bomb was.'

When you say your secret you have the impression that for a minute the world stops. It doesn't, of course. Even I know that much about the audience.

'So that's it —' Martyn is repeating, hushed. 'So that's what they got you for.'

'No. I meant to be — in on it. But when it happened, I wasn't there.'

He groans. 'So then?'

'So then I was nowhere. I cracked up.'

'Nowhere.' He looks beat. 'I've been there.'

'You?'

'I didn't — crack. But I've an idea what it's like.'

'How come?' This is how we used to ask each other, on the ward.

'My country turned upside down, remember?'

The news sheets on the floor are crushed, but still powerful. 'There's years of those I'll have to bone up on.'

'Well, you won't find me in too many of those accounts. Not personally. I meant to be. But I wasn't.'

'You helped sing the songs.'

'So my mother counsels. And of course, I helped her. . . .You remind me of her, somewhat.'

'I — remind you — of her?'

'Not in looks. She began as a tall, spiky blond. And still has the manner. . . . No, in the way you're both always — running for Parliament.' His smile is mischievous. 'She is actually, once again. That's one reason why I'm going back for a spell. To see her through.'

'Me? Running for a parliament? You're out of your skull.'

'Think about it. . . . Meanwhile, you don't have to sleep here, if it goes against principle. Drop in. Stationer's down the block keeps my daily paper for me. Bone up.' He grins. 'Feed the cat.'

'No thanks. I had a bad cat experience. More than one.'

I'm remembering the cats the neighbor boy hung in the aunts' barn. I look up at him. Height determines how far a person must stretch, or bow. The aunts were exactly of a height; it helped them blend. 'Not all memory is a joy to recover, is it? But when you're given it back in a lump you get all of it.'

He shakes his head, but not as if I puzzle him. 'Agreed. But I'd like to do more than remember you.'

'I'll remember you, Martyn.'

'How would you remember me, or anybody much? It's not in your scheme.'

'That way! That you credit me with a scheme. Even though —'

'Though what?'

'You mayn't approve.'

'That's not me you'd be remembering, Carol Smith. That's still you.'

Those steady eyes shame me. Gray — I'll not forget those. 'What you just said; I'll hear that. I'll hear how we talked. And how, when we didn't — we were still company.'

'Were? That what the doctors taught you? To stash everything in the past?'

'For me the present was a long time coming. Hard to believe I would have one. And when I got into it . . . I mangled it. Swinging like mad. Like being with somebody would tell me the time of day.'

He grasps my hands. 'I see you, Carol.'

'You and me — it's like we're flirting with our minds. Not just with sex.'

'No.' He squeezes my hands, drops them. 'I mean — yes.'

'I don't even know your gender for sure.'

His mouth moves like hypnotized. 'Not to worry.'

'It's just that these days it's polite — not to assume.'

'Excuse me then, if I've taken you being female for granted.'

'Oh, that's okay, you'd be right. Even when I was brainwashed, I always knew I was straight.'

He bursts out laughing. Covers his face with his hands a minute, then shakes himself like a dog. 'It does seem about the only point you don't question. But I'm not pressing it. I'd like to see you when I get back; that's a fact. But there'd be no strings to your making use of this joint. Or in letting me keep track of you. So once in a while we could have a gas? Or a cup of tea?'

Not having a present tense is scary. So I nod.

'Good. So let's seal it with a non-gender hug.'

Over his shoulder I see the morning gleam. Even at the gentle distance he keeps, I know when a body fits mine. There weren't that many. Any? Once. A boy in a halfway house. Where we didn't dare enough. — 'What we crave most is the arms,' that boy said.

Martyn holds me in his. Like in a core. You can be haunted by that, when it stops.

And he does. The arms fall. The mobile face you would never think could freeze to a mask — how severe. 'That routine you mentioned. Nothing binding. Like to the launderette? Like for a shower here, now the public baths are closed?'

'Or, I could do your roaches,' I say, dreamy. 'Though that's not a daily routine.'

'All the other tenants are in fur. The building fumigates. Daily — for all I know.'

'D—?' And then I get it. 'So that's what you mean. I smell.'

Whatever we could be to each other hangs in the balance.

'You look great. That's what fools people. Maybe fools you. I don't identify the odor, won't try. Or say whether you should be wooed from it. Or if it's bona fide, in some book I'm not privy to. But yes, Carol, you do. You smell.'

I bolt from him. But not before I yell, 'It's not as if either of us is busting to lust.'

Through the bathroom door do I hear my confounded name, on a whiff of laughter not mean. There's something homey about laughter heard through a door. Under the longest shower the old contraption here must ever have been put to, my skin turns to cheese. I'm thinking: He isn't trying to humiliate me. Nor will he waste time curing me.

At last I'm through. Nothing beats argument like necessity. He has no big towel. I can't bear to put on again the clothes dropped on the bathroom floor. I have to get to the Shelter-Pak for that change of clothes I carry. But is this the time to scoot out nude? The toilet seat is warm wood. He's given me such a bundle to think on. Or to banish from my aching head. What a headful I have. Like I'm wearing a tight new hat. Some headaches maybe provide energy.

It takes me a while to hear the quiet out there.

The bathroom door creaks from all that steam. I creep down the hall, past the hung bedrolls. The table where we had tea is bare. There's nobody in the chairs. In the glass enclosure, now thermally bright, something inside casts a shadow — maybe a salesman's trunk?

No breath disturbs. He's cleared out.

Headache gone — says that ever attentive coroner the body provides. Replaced by empty hole in chest.

Piece of white paper on the Shelter-Pak. Envelope. I hear my cry.

> Back in a month or so. Mother's address and number next to hall telephone. Further info on bulletin boards. Stationer's down the block stockpiles newspapers for me. Pick up, if interested in the world. Buy a plant and water it. If interested in me.
>
> Martyn

But it is the address on the envelope that rivets me.

> Carol Smith, Footsoldier
> Parliament of the World.

I hear the fur district below, the snap and chortle of the trucks, the low weave of footsteps, the business shrill-and-mutter that starts a commercial day. Plus the unrecorded passersby who are the staple of the city. And the fixtures. On the corner already perhaps, the animal-protester, her hair a furry tangle. On the standpipes in winter, or in summer stretched out under an air conditioner's exhaust, some anonymous body, clothed in stuffs no one district supplies.

Time to go down there. Up Carol, and to your business. That agenda for which there are no printed forms. That routine which has no office. That Parliament which has only one party — the Outs?

How easily you've judged me, Martyn. A song-and-dance man would have to be tops at summing up.

I am still here. The glassed-in cubicle is now a realm of light cast from the window it must conceal. On its front panel, behind the drums, is a decal of a continent whose shape I recognize. Pasted there so that once a song is unfurled, or a bedroll, a troupe can dream that on the other side of the glass is Africa?

Maybe once the sun was gone, they lit a lamp behind it. Or one would come on, from within?

Inside the enclosure there are shadows. Boxes maybe, into which I shouldn't pry. Empty boxes, the prop shadows that a man of action might save. Or only the salesman's air-conditioners. Around the side of the enclosure the glass panel has a knob. The panel rolls easily.

It's an office. Two windows, each with air-conditioners at the base. The office fittings are old and frail. A desk as narrow as an ironing board, on it dusty supplies of the sort purchased but unused: paper envelopes, a jar of ball-pens, an empty spring-binder, some clips. It's an on-again, off-again assortment I recognize. I even know that old-model computer on its rickety metal stand, that beat-up adjustable typing chair with a hole in its gray weft.

In front of me are all my secretarial skills.

I back out of the enclosure but leave the sliding side-panel ajar. The dusty computer screen draws me in again like a magnet. I wipe it off and sit down to it. After a kind of prayer to the gods of chance, I plug in. It works. The tufted gap in the chair seat gooses me like a familiar overseer.

This is a volunteer's office. Whatever the cause it serves. 'Inner city,' the 'aged,' the 'juvenile?' — the vocabulary is roughly the same. New diseases, old insurrections — on behalf of the rights of the wronged.

Summertime, the scholarship student was the only paid staff. 'So good of you —' the polite one-day-a-week patron women would murmur as I typed, printed out, and usually instructed, pressing the levers, shifting the innards, cartridges, software, on their roster of second-hand machines. Sometimes a young deb in for the afternoon swung her bob at me — 'Won-derful.' . . . So good of us to have her, their glances said.

Winters, I had a second job, scuttling between the college's admissions office and the Dean's. The paneling was boardroom, the machines improved, and the typist's chair an Italian import that cupped one's bottom like a pair of hands.

But the apogee was my last year in college, when I worked for a pair of professors who lived together, an American of the English department, and a French historian: 'Thee Renaissance, c'est moi.' There I learned words like 'apogee.' As well as what a 'variorum' edition was — the

American's speciality, and how to breathe carefully on the Frenchman's illuminated manuscripts.

The pair had lived in their Beacon Hill house so long, and had subjected it to so much word bombardment, that in the evenings, when I was sometimes invited to supper after my stint, the walls of the small residence, wedged between two larger ones, would seem to all but disappear. While as we ate, ideas sent up in chat between them whistled over my head like arrows meant to pierce the old window-screens and be let loose upon the world. Yet there was no garden. At Christmas, my presents from them were inscribed: To Our Amanuensis, and in parenthesis (Look it up!), so I did. Finding in one source that I was a servitor who copied by hand (Latin, *a manu*), which was no longer true, but in another that I was a 'devoted' person — which I was.

The scarf, from the American, was an illumination I could touch. The Frenchman's small check bought me a thrift shop bathing-suit — for they were not rich. The 'study' I worked in, arranged for the line of students who must have preceded me, held equipment nearly antique. Yet the old copier — Xerox? — was just there, where this printer is. There are no atlases here. They had a globe, its blue nineteen-thirties surface never updated. But at my right is the same dictionary I used when the American's longhand was too cramped for me to make out.

There are no books here though, beyond an encyclopedia. Theirs, hooding the air in brown, parchment, and gold could not be lent. Instead, centered in constant hints from the variorum of what could be learned — and could be read in odd hours — I absorbed. But never told anyone. Though now and then, a reference escaped. — 'How is it, Carey, that your guest knows what the Nicene Creed is and you don't?' says Sir Somebody, her Dad. . . . — 'We know you did student billings at the Dean's office, course catalogues. Those professors report, "When she left us, she was literate." . . . And I suspect you've some Spanish from the barrio. All of which translates fine, employment wise,' said Daisy Gold.

So that old terror confronts me. Not of those little tap-tappings, the 'skills.' But of the wide flooding-in they can release. Pills don't bury the frottage in a brain that has a story to tell. Or the tremor in the fingertips which have discovered the words for it.

A variorum. A 'classical edition, with quotes from suitable commentators' — of me. The keyboard appears serviceable.

I stand in front of it, the nude volunteer. I have forgotten my nakedness. I reach for the dictionary, to look up the word: Parliament.

By night or day, as I sit at this desk, the pair from Beacon Hill fly over me like geese, honking Work! Work! To follow routine is easier when you have more than one. I spend the weeknights out, coming here on Wednesdays and Fridays, Martyn's newspaper, picked up at the stationer's, assuring me which is which. On Saturday I sleep over here, leaving on Sunday, after doing the wash. Wednesdays and Sundays I bathe.

The desk is my church. Where I hear only my own sermons. My words are not arrows. This old word processor cannot listen as it records. But it takes the pressure off.

Crediting any voice it's fed, it's the only schizoid here.

Maybe a mind like mine, furnished so old-fashionedly and recovering itself on the same terms, will soon be among the last to worry over what is sanity. Or to insist on any such baseline. This morning I found two flyers pushed under the front door. One from a computer outlet, notifying Martyn that a year had gone by since he had had his serviced, and offering him bargain membership on a new network in cyberspace. The other, a take-out menu from a Chinese restaurant.

I see us all chatting in cubicles, our hair electronically on end. All of us ordering our food in. Our body wastes being sucked from us on networks so ethereally worldwide that no sanitary arrangements will be necessary. While the battered outdoors, a relic of the twentieth century, is regretted by few. And my own dilemma exists no longer, everyone being comfortably outside — at home.

I joke because I must. The single vision — will I end up losing it? 'And who is it most begrudges Carol Smith the norm?' Dr. Cee asked me once. He and I answered in unison: 'Carol Smith.'

Martyn's mail, directed to that same stationer, is presumably kept, or sent on. When I pick up the paper I do not ask. The store-owner, one more Paki or East Indian in the city's scheme, is usually attending to the day's lottery ticket purchasers. He hands me what he knows I come for, his head averted to the luck-seekers and his and their mutual business: grab the ticket, here's your change. He sells luck, news, cigs, mags, and soft porn; everybody wants some of his wares. I have the feeling that his life is all scheme. Perhaps we are colleagues in reverse, he in flight from streets that have rejected him.

I store the newspapers in a pile, under the bulletin boards, appropriately opposite the drums. All in them sounds as Before. Hard to believe they are reporting Now. Yet no surprise. I read first as if through the wrong end of opera glasses, in whose smaller lenses tiny people are still rolling their planet toward Utopia. Reverse to the broad end, and the magnified print swims up and over my head, nearly drowning me in its omnivorous wave. But I suspect this is usual. So the ideologies return, like college barflies I once jogged elbows with.

But today is Sunday, which Martyn's subscription does not include. Once inside, the gleaming bathroom is my icon; I become its acolyte, my handmaiden the suave brown wooden toilet seat. Wrapped in the buff towel I carry in my pack, I don't quite match any of this, but in the mirror the sun, slanting up from Furtown in seventh-day quiet, turns us all into an art nouveau print.

Behind me, in the mirror, that picture of a family or families assembled in front of what could be a longhouse or a stockade, keeps me company. I have the feeling the air in the picture is hot. The sepia tone may be partly responsible for the skin tones. Dark to light, the faces have accepted that variorum. Man, woman, to child, down the line-up the impression given is that they have learned this posture or have been taught it. The house or barn behind them is the power. But is it theirs? Or are they its helpers? Clothing nondescript but neat, the men's white, whether Western or not, the women head-scarfed or bare.

If I stare long enough I become part of the photograph.

Where is the garden? Was it there the shot rang out?

Later I'm dried and dressed. A woman seated at a desk that though narrow is not up-ended, avoided. Her past at last wrested from behind the muted landscape of the pill-country. Her flesh newly cleansed — for the offices of all the norms?

'And how do you view those norms?' Dr. Cee is saying.

'The norm is a honeybear,' I told him. 'Ever at my elbow. Waiting to be fed. Amiable. With claws.'

'Carol, restrain your images,' he said. 'If you ever want to get out of here.'

So I say, docilely: 'The norm is a decent little dog, Doctor. I have it well on leash.' And it sees only gray. But this I kept mum.

But now, am I learning? I see even by the morning paper what the normal message is. Restrain. Confine. Police the crime.

It is dangerous, what I'm doing. This keyboard, this smallish screen so palely lit, as if by the ghost of confiscated paper, this jiggery-pokery software whose parts, no matter how jumbled on the table, will explode only on a print-path targeting a brain — I know what they're offering me. Alternatives.

Next, unless wary, I'll be living by the calendar. Giving each of these entries a date.

It was Saturday night. Top o' the week for all the prom kids in colleges in all the boroughs. For the high school goonies shifting their platform sneakers and twenty-inch hairdos on line for the Hard Rock Cafe and Planet Hollywood. For the prossies on lower Park, poking their silky-shiny breastpoints at passing motorists. For the oldie couples fox-trotting for a fee at Dance-night, Lincoln Center. And tired mom-poppas in McDonald's, wiping off the baby's milk-moustache.

And for me, to sleep over here.

What I wanted, like anybody, was to celebrate — even if I didn't know what. To kick responsibility in its doughy, daily face. And to stay Out, as late as possible, from this glassy prism where all the colors of the world seemed to have churned themselves. What's with the color spectrum that once you have it again, the eye can't limit that wily profusion everywhere? Like at the disability office, where I still must check in. Once, the clients and their garments were dun, their dependency drizzling down on them like rain. Now their civil rights have exploded into opera, jun-gle-striped; the aisles crawl with pink-and-brown babies, inching into what one has to hope is a top life.

It takes grit to face the multiple. That's why they put you on pills, and put the hospitals out of town. To simple things down.

Bottom line — I find myself hankering for that old quagmire — pill-land. Bury the head?

Pervasive underneath all my days is the image of the person whose quarters these are. I've studied the wall-clips until I could recite them, charting Martyn's and his troupe's circuit home and abroad, and much of the formal circum-stances of his life, historical and pictorial. And no — his mother doesn't look like me. But Martyn, the understander, is still about, still occupying this room. And the best side of that may be the worst. Still gentle if compelling in my memory, he doesn't try to corner me. What woos me is that he never will.

Stop the pills cold turkey, and the body doesn't yet know why, craves a little sweetening. *Hack hack*, a legal drug can say, as you swallow it, alerting the nurses and your body too. A whole ward, dulling its crazy-quilt anguishes all at the same time in order to save staff, can sound like a gaggle of fowl. But if you are remanded, you steal away, stiff-legged, with the belly-ache they tell you is sanity.

On the ward the scuttlebutt was that when off pills, sex was the best substitute. But too many like me had gone cold turkey on that too. You are counseled then to marshal other satisfactions. Yardages of fudge. Or those lessons in martial arts. Or go shopping in safe pairs on your weekly passes, even though one of you might be reported on return: 'He asked to see what they had in space suits.'

Or the dose is yours again, if you beg; or bribe.

I couldn't believe my body wanted to go back to that hypnotic balancing act. But addiction is a nostalgia of the flesh.

So I sit here in my glass cage, thinking — for what? It's more than being house-sick; maybe I'm even getting over that. What is it that would allay this hollow in the throat? This rictus in the jaw, like before you wail?

Then it comes to me. Perhaps it's the window that does it, with this Sunday quiet seeping in. Where I would like to be is sitting in a bay window, through which a breeze is rustling the pieces on the card table. What I would like to do is to be playing a game.

The door around the corner from Christopher Street was still open. That pair who lived there must still peddle those showers. What a neat way to earn.

I peer in. The room looks the same, with those broad armchairs nobody could carry off. Pillows, the same taupe as the shadows. Floor was once battened down basement earth; maybe still is, under that linoleum, a sawtoothed pattern you blink away from and come back to. And there's the card table in front of that cozy pot-belly stove. No fire behind its bull's eye pane. Wasn't then, either. I haven't hit the season for it maybe. But, 'Come back,' they said. 'Anytime.'

Just then the same older man shuffles in from a door in the rear. And now I remind me. I have stepped on a buzzer just inside the entry. When I shift my feet the buzz stops.

'Want a shower, do you,' he says. 'Singles only. No sharing allowed.' Then he halts. 'You been here before?'

'Yeah. You said I could come back.'

'Right. You know how it works then. Go ahead. There's soap.'

'Thanks. I have a pad. Temporary.'

'Ain't they all. You just hit town?'

'Not really. I just kind of thought — you said stop back any time. And I'd like to. For a game.'

His hand goes to his teeth, rubbing them. 'Hey. I know you. You're that girl.'

I nod.

'You beat him. I recall.'

Then I see the table. His eyes direct me to it. Bare. 'Where's the checker board?'

He goes through those well-known minor motions. Toss of the head. Mouth turned in. Good-looking guy for maybe sixty, but moused up some since I last saw. 'It died.'

'Died? Oh you mean — yeah, they do wear out.' Like the parcheesi board we had to coddle, it was so cracked. But you can surely replace a checker board? 'Ah, you lost the habit.'

He's not answering. People can get petulant about a game. — 'Can't stand that Chinese puzzle with the missing triangles made out of construction paper. Can't stand it. Not one more time,' my music aunt huffed, tucking it well back in the cupboard under the window-seat, where it stayed. 'Makes you lose the rhythm,' she'd said.—

'No, it's there in the drawer,' the man said. 'Just went dead. After him.'

'He's dead? Oh, I'm sorry. And he was still so —'

'Not that young. But younger, yes. Months ago. And here I am. "Healthy as a rat" —he said.' And I could almost hear the other one. 'Yop, I am. Eee-eye—o—Negative.'

He sits down. 'Have a visit.'

I sit on one of the armchairs.

'You're admiring the floor,' he says after awhile. 'People do. He laid that pattern. Fourteen years ago. After we knew we were going to stay.'

After another pause I say: 'When do you light the stove?'

'Never.' He half smiles. 'Has no stovepipe. He just liked the look of it.' He speaks slow, like doing it singly is still new. 'Fools 'em all.' I see that pleases him. 'I remember how you beat him. He talked about it for days.' By now he's on his feet, fiddling at a counter. 'Coffee?' In a couple of minutes he serves it, from a tray on the pot-belly. The espresso is neat, with a thick cuff of foam.

On one wall is a wastebasket in a hoop of iron, so you don't have to bend down. My chair has a side-pocket with mail in it. 'You have lots of nice arrangements. Nice to look at.'

'And for comfort. All his,' he says, following where I look. 'That's why I keep on with the shower. Don't need the income. I've a pension. And he was always doing it for free. Did it for the company that came in, he said. And because he never had showers as a kid.'

He's talking better. In between he stares at the black-and-tan zigzag floor. 'Started it when the public baths were banned.' Glancing at me, eyebrows raised, to see if I know what that meant. Smiling when he sees I do. 'You're not gay though? No. I remember those two characters who brought you in. Took you for a patsy. They were wrong. . . . They're gone.'

'Scrammed?'

He shakes his head. 'Gone.' It echoes. Like from a battle.

I say, 'Let's have a game.'

'Me? He could always beat me. And you beat him in three moves. I can remember him saying it.'

'This'll take longer. Like when you're thinking of alternatives. Like — this game, it's for me. That's why I came.'

He's interested, like maybe nothing new has happened to him.

The board comes out of a drawer. Same old beauty, old-style crimson and shiny black, the counters grooved deep, and cool to the touch. He says: 'Gadroon-edged.'

I take the red counters, laying them along the board. Leaving him the black. Finally, he sets his up. We sit.

After a while, when neither of us moves, he says: 'What are those alternatives of yours?'

Why did I choose the red? We hadn't tossed for it. Or for the first play. 'The red — I guess that's me up to a certain time.' My hand hovers over that line up.

'And the black?'

'Where it stopped. Or I did.'

'How come?'

'I told somebody I was twenty-eight. Only last year. I thought I was. Because I'd stopped there. Out of circulation. And later — just not calculating.' But that's over. 'I'm thirty-six.'

'Nothing like a dame,' he says. 'But you still look very good.'

'Wasn't vanity. Or else, so down deep —'

'Hah — I know that kind. He was in his twenties, me in my late forties, when we bumped into each other. "I'll always be younger," he said.' He spreads his hands. 'And now he is. Always will be.'

'I remember that ring you're wearing.' Darting across the table at me with its gold-flecked, flamy eye. 'That was his, wasn't it?'

'I'm not for rings on a man. But he asked me to. So I do. "Twist it," he said, "and I'll be there. You won't get rid of me."'

'Never seen a stone like it.'

'Fire opal. Not sure it's real. He went for the red. Sure enough did that. . . . So, the black's me, huh; you saw that. Somebody had to be, around him.'

'We're not playing for him.'

'I can't play for you, gal. Besides, I'd lose. Whyn't you play against yourself? Seen people do that. Not him. He never would.'

'You played a lot?'

'Only when he wanted to win at something. Because I supplied the bread.'

'Oh?'

'Salesman, church supplies. I had the whole top field, city wide. Votive statues, priests' albs; you name it. No greeting card calendars, none of that small stuff. Maybe a breviary now and then. No, I stocked the big stuff. Ciboriums — you know what they are?' He sees I don't. 'For the reservation of the Eucharist' — he almost chants it. 'Thuribles — he said the catalogue was like a church service, when I recited it. And what do you know, he asked to be buried from one of my customers. That church they call "Smoky Mary's." Pounds of incense they must use, yet not a soul coughs. Beautiful. And they'll bury those from that line around the corner here, even. By special dispensation. Bar none.'

'That line. I walk past it sometimes.' All types, like in a play. Male prossies mixed with yearners. Habitués of the sex fix. 'Still going. People watching say they can't believe it, given the times. But I can. For some it would be because

there would be no place else. But for some it would be —
because you join the street.'

'For the principle of the thing, hah. He said that. He
joined that line openly in the end. I knew he'd been sneaking around the corner for years. Joined it with a bandage on
his bare skull and walking with two canes. "They still pick
me —" he said.' He bends over his row of counters.

The checker board is still neatly aligned. I could hate it
for that.

'Wasn't so long ago you were here, gal,' he went quick.
"Beaten by a dame," he said, "— how'd she ever get so
good?"'

'Taught by dames,' I say. Not to make anything of that.
'They would play against each other. Only in demonstra-
tion. Not to win. They were teaching me.' And they did.
That I was the game.

'So play. Be the red, be the black. I'll be kibitzer.'

'Star salesman?' I can hear that push. 'Thanks, no. I
better go.' I make like consulting my wrist, where a watch
used to be. Had the days of the week on it as well. Gave it
to the boy in the halfway house; laid it on his bed, he asleep
when I scrammed. 'It's Sunday, by now.'

'Got somebody, huh?'

'No.' All of a sudden, bending over the board, I move a
red. 'I used to swing.' Stretching across the board, I move a
black. 'Now — I don't even date.' I look at the two chips,
positioned blind. 'Only right now with a — I dunno. Not a
diary really. But those years I lost, I got recorded by other
people up to here. Now it's my turn.'

'Hah. You the manifesto type, huh? The Village wouldn't
be the Village without you.'

I can laugh. 'Come on. You yourself keep an open door.'

'With a buzzer under the mat.' He lies back in his chair, squinting at me. 'Can't tell what you're carrying the torch for, but you sure are. But it wouldn't be just for dames or guys — right?' He looks me over. 'And something tells me — let me walk on eggs here — that it's not — just for skin?'

'No. Walk on. But I don't know how to say it, really. Except that it's not a military campaign.'

'They all get to be. Anybody who isn't like yours truly gets to be a gook. Like in that war.'

'Your friend. He favor the streets?'

'Him? Not on your life. He wanted to rise. Wanted us to. And we did. Some. Classy dinners, travel. Little jobs he got to have; he had his crowd. At the end, true, he wanted to be out there, on line. He'd get ripped off now and then.' He looked down at the big ring. 'That's when he gave me it.'

The dead guy hadn't played that well. All stylish moves, like he was fencing. At checkers! 'It took me more moves to beat him than he said,' I say. 'He was pretty good.' I get up to go.

'You remembered us, dolly. That's nice.'

'Yes —' I say, 'I remember.'

'We were never in the closet, God knows. Except uptown, at my job. Last time he went on the line he said, "Go with me. It's not just for pickups I go anymore. It's like you say your stuff is. Votive." He could tell I thought he was shitting me. But he was almost blind. I went.' He's smoothing the checkers into their bag. '"If somebody latches onto me, Joe, let him," he says to me. "Compassionate visit, Joe. They get us home." So we walk out there. Seen it, haven't you?'

I have to nod. The men, boys, walk round and round the

block. Getting picked off. Getting left out. Maybe you're votive. Maybe you're not.

The checkers are in the bag. He pulls the string tight. 'I walk with him on that goddamn line, thinking maybe he's just showing off what he's still got at home. But then, somebody latches on to me, by God. And Lee feels for my wrist and says, "You fool, you must have worn that watch he's after. Go on home."'

He's folding up the checker board. 'So, not much later, two of them bring him in. Right through that door, they dump him. And one of them steps on the buzzer. "It's a plant!" he yells, and they scram. . . . I shouldn't tell a woman this.'

'Go on.' I feel like a Dr. Cee.

'So he says, weak as a kitten, "We never got to do anything, Joe — be compassionate. Long time no see.". . . I was in health, you see. So we hadn't. He says, "You're my pickup now. And I knew you weren't wearing your watch."'

He claps the board together hard. 'And at four am that morning he goes to the hospital. Lee.'

So that's their names: Lee. And Joe.

'Here.' He hands me the board and the sack of chips. 'Thanks for the game.'

Clutching both board and chips my hands are full, a warning sensation. 'Gosh. I forgot my Shelter-Pak.'

'Oh boy. In the station? Too bad. Lots of those around now. But they cost.'

I feel in my slacks pocket. Martyn's keys. I'd been taking just those when on short errands from the pad. They look at you funny otherwise, in the food stores. 'No — it's okay. I left it where I'm — where I work.'

'Work.' He brightens. 'I'd like to go back now. But they have somebody.' He gets me a shopping bag. 'Here. You got car-fare?'

'It's only to the fur district. I'll walk.'

'Fur —' he says. 'You're not — standing on those corners — at night?'

'Me?'

'Used to be boys there. No cops.' His mouth tics. 'Long ago. Excuse it.'

'No, the girls are over on Fourth. Real beauties. High-class.' Long silk legs, and in winter, fur coats blown wide. 'No, on our block there's only the anti-fur activist. She stays late. But I don't think she tricks. Except maybe for the animals.'

I've made him laugh. Good crowns on his teeth. I see him easy among the church purchasers, in a white shirt and bible-black tie.

'So, one of your old pals put you up, eh? Maybe a guy?'

'Just a friend. He's in Africa.' I like mentioning that. A friend, a pad, a favor given. It grounds me. Which even the confirmed floater can now and then crave. It brings me out of the cold. But should I want to be?

The shopping bag he's brought is gray with a white cross on its front. 'So what did you commit? To have to do time for so long. Riots? Get dragged from the White House lawn? Hunger strike?'

I shrug.

'So it's over. Like when I finished my military service. And you don't know what you did it for either, do you.'

'Keep your shopping bag,' I say.

'Ah, come on.' He's stashing in some green.

'Don't do that. No.'

'Tide you over. Or maybe you're already on the welfare.'

Disability — I have the disability. Once I could say that like a password. Why's it sticking in my craw?

'I have a — family trust.'

When I raise my eyes his face has got it, that stare. When people look too long. 'So that's it. I should have known. But you're — so together, otherwise.' He touches my shoulder, a finger brush, like he might get a shock. 'Maybe you do have that pad; maybe you don't. You haven't been to the shelters yet; I can tell. I won't ask what you do. You hang out that area though, there used to be security guards; they could be rough.' He's talking fast now — the way he would've to Lee, when they first met? 'Case you get stuck, there's a priest runs a damn decent soup kitchen. Near that Lime-light disco, used to be a church I supplied.' When he hunches up the fringe of hair on his nape shows dyed. 'Maybe it still is a church, daytimes.'

He refolds the shopping sack and presses it on me.

I take it. 'I'll remember you guys.' I see that's thanked him. 'And the board is a doozy.' I smooth it. 'Just to carry it gives me an air of distinction. Like if I had an Italian bike.'

To weave that in gives me a real sensation, like I'm linking the bad times, mending them into the now. Cold turkey is not that good for the now.

He thinks I'm being funny? So why not be?

'Maybe I'll start a checkers club.'

He shakes his head at me. Like when the hospital aides guided some of us on practice trips downtown, and passersby at first took us for girls on an outing from some private

school. 'Must have been a charmer, when you were —
twenty-eight. Or younger.'

'Uh uh. In college, I was the one got charmed.'

'Knocked up?'

'Group charmed.'

'Hah. See a lot of that, down here. Can turn you a loner,
on the rebound.'

'Loner?' I scan the musty arrangements, this waiting-
game he still plays. On the one memory, hoarded. While
outside, out that door, on line or not, the city's monuments
at least join up with you as you meet them. The pavement
strides under you. The heads populate the air. 'Maybe. But
in company.'

In a pause like that, in such a house, I swear you can hear
the pillows mewl.

'I have company —' he says. The words shake, like a
rattle he keeps handy. 'You don't have another person's load
in your life — you don't have a life.'

I ease toward that door always kept ajar. I can see Lee's
reason for it.

'Free shower, any time —' he calls after me. 'Only if you
don't have the crabs.'

So you can only qualify here if you're not lousy to begin
with.

As I edge further, he calls like an echo: 'What's your
na-ame?'

I see his misery. Lead a too personal life and your woe
will be custom-designed.

I can't think of any of my names I would want to leave
here. In this halfway house, where the stove that should
warm has no pipe.

Quick, ankle it over the sill.
'I'll send you a card.'

This is a Friday dusk. Everybody on the avenue knows that; so do I. Offices are letting out as daily, but there's an edge to the voices saying, 'Good Night.' A weekend flurry is in the air, even for those who have no weekends. I am walking back to my office. The calendar, whether I keep to it or violate it, has been seeping into my bones.

Also — have I begun to cherish events that face me toward others? Or even to initiate those? The accidental graze, for which one apologizes? The weather-chat? The smile at a child? I have taken the subway — countermanding the walking code. To a man who boarded a bus without the proper change, I was the first to offer. I have entered shops only to dally. My infringements have been endless, given the logic I had been living under. Yet I feel less and less reprobate.

On exiting Joe and Lee's I had an impulse to turn down Christopher Street and join that line. I knew better than to do so. To impose what I am not on what they are — as they might see it? That warmth, that solidarity, that intermittent agony, was not for me. Nor the sex. And Christopher Street was not on my way. Yet I had the impulse — toward.

In the hospital, we were all wary of that recommended reaching out. On my ward of eight to twelve youngish men and women, everyone sensed when a member was 'going off of sick' as it were — that is, relearning the manners of health, or able to assume those sufficiently. Those patients, as they left, were seen as traitors to the madnesses or mental injuries that whelmed the rest of us, and which also were the hospital's raison d'etre and research glory. The cured were seen as mercenaries for the norm.

And we could clock the terms of the cure, in our deviantly uncanny way. We knew what health was in the way a man with one leg observes a man with two.

— 'What's going on in me is like an inner tuning,' my room-mate, shortly to be released, confided. 'It's like in your body, your head, there is a pattern violin. And each day, you tighten the strings. Then play.' Of course we were a mildly non-delusionary, non-violent ward, mostly obsessives of familial despair. Or broken world-crockery, like yours truly.

'Madness is bad melodrama,' my actress room-mate says scornfully. 'It's no wonder we can each see each other's, but not our own.' Health— or cure, crept up on you, a delicate accretion that you had best keep mum about. For since it was never totally positive, perhaps merely not negative, and often only an acceptable equilibrium, it was simply there or not, explicit as a chord. And you couldn't just evoke it. 'Or God knows, cheer it on.'

For even a cure could rampage, to a fine or classic result. On the day Heather (diagnosis, 'involutional despair') was leaving to resume touring with the company she had been invalided out of two years before, she reported to me: 'That art therapy aide I loathe, the one that's always encouraging but really believes we're all too eccentric to make real worthy use of our talents. . . . So when I came to say goodbye — for I'm really trying, y'know, she said: "Now Heather, smile. Like they say Leonardo even meditated with a smile." And I said: "And breathed from the diaphragm"— and barfed all over her smock.'

Then she hugged me, Heather did. We had never. 'Remember me, Carol. Memory is faith.' —

And now I have. With a smile.

When I let myself in, the Shelter-Pak left behind when I'd rushed out is sprawled just inside the door. Its sides are caved in, like a cat's after giving birth. Each day I have mined it more. On foot, one keeps a hard core of necessaries ever at reach. Now they have entrenched themselves in the places that habit appoints. Toothbrush in the bathroom glass, jacket on the hook. Towel and extra panties on the bathroom line. My wallet still lies within, along with a passport case big enough for all the archive of identity I must present to keep my allowance coming. I have no need here for alley comforts like the pewter flask for water, and the collapsible cup, so they too are in the pocket reserved. In the pocket next to those, the sanitaries, and a small pouch containing a nail scissors, file and tweezers in golden German brass, that I bought the minute I came out of jail. The hospital had confiscated them, then returned them when I left. They are more than implements. They are history. Like the one prescription, which is out of date.

The keys are still in my hand. I always pause over what to do with them. On the table they are too prominent. Up on a shelf is iffy; I might forget which, and once have. Finally, I pick a shelf and let one of the two keys hang over the edge. There is no key-pocket in the Shelter-Pak.

Hours later, I am still leaning over the checker board. Unfolded, in the clearer light here, its noble squares present themselves like a vale I can enter, a contested realm that those behind the bar of a single vision may view.

In Martyn's large dictionary, the definitions of the noun 'game' runs and romps through seven inches of the finest print. I like best the one that reads: 'A diversion of the nature of a contest, played according to the rules and decided by superior skill, strength, or good fortune.' I indeed have had my rules; the strength may well be in question. As to fortune, whose score is ever truly in? One synonym, 'an undertaking,' daunts me. And 'a person's policy' makes me rueful. I have nothing so organized.

Down that long column of print huntsmen sport and play; beneath it are batteries of quotes from the awesome personages a dictionary prefers: Wolsey. Byron. Buonaparte.

Outside the 'office' is that single line of drums. They know what they play for, or knew. But they are not me.

The nobility of the old games lies in the alternatives — never in the score. I touch my forehead to the checker board's mirror-glaze, the better to see my adversary. The counters can remain in their bag; they are not needed.

I am the red. I am the black.

The phone has rung twice during my occupancy. Once, a bond salesman: 'Is this the lady of the house? May I speak to your spouse?' — who hung up when I did not immediately reply, leaving me to fabricate rejoinders all afternoon. 'Waal, it's me who has the money.' . . . 'Sorry, she's not here.'

The second call, only last week, was from the woman who was once Martyn's wife. She had sounded warm, husky, irregular, indeed a person from a caravan, and hard-nosed on what she was after. She wanted to leave Martyn her annual address, 'But he'd have to write by return mail,' yet gave it to me. 'Thameside, can you spell it?' I said yes, I could spell Thames, and she softened. 'The children are mad for tennis. We're to settle in as near Wimbledon as we can manage.'

Finding that hilarious — will she haul them out of Squatterville to dress them in whites? — I kick my feet in the air. Are the caravans too being wooed away from their solemn abstentions? The feet, now that I notice them as more than vehicles, are still slim and arched; walking hasn't flattened them. But the Stabilizers are shabby. Almost tramp.

'So Martyn's in Africa. Once again. And you are —?'

Nervy of her. 'I work in the — use the office.'

'Um.' I hear her surmise.

'And use the tub.'

'Tub?' She tinkles it.

'Well, you know the New York climate.' I hear myself providing the sophisticated return her accent demands. In college we used to chat to each other in fake accents. Since then I haven't had much real access to a phone.

'Ah.' I hear her revising me. 'I don't, actually. Never been to New York. Of course the children are wild to go.'

I begin to hear how she underwrites her life. As Martyn hinted.

'Those must be your kids up on the bulletin board.'

'Bulletin board? . . .Ah yes. Always the impresario, isn't he? . . . So he's posted the pics I sent on, has he? I shall tell them. You can't do much of that in a caravan. . . . Or you don't. . . .Well . . . thanks very much, Miss —?'

'Smith. Carol Smith.'

'Miss Smith. Well, then —'

'Please. . . it's your call. . . but could we reverse charges? I want to ask you something.'

'About Martyn, eh? Never mind the charges. Fire away.'

'No, about caravans. Are they like our trailers? Or more like a bus?'

'They were gypsy vans. When my Rom great-grand-mother lived in one, they would have been carts. Now you wouldn't know them for that. Or only a few.' A long pause. 'Once you put the curtains up, it's a house on wheels, whatever else. And when the chi — the kids — kick up a rux, to go to school. Mad for it.'

I see the children circling the vans, slavering, to make them stop.

'A house that moves —' I say.

'Or gets pushed,' she says with a sigh. 'Why? You fancy one?'

'Oh no. No, I live out of my backpack.'

'Ah. Hostels.'

'No traveling, no. Except around the city. Outdoors.'

'Hul-lo. A slogger.' I hear her added whisper: *hence the tub*. . . . 'Beg pardon.'

I look at my shoe. 'That's okay. That's what we do. Oh, not Martyn. Persons like me.'

'Persons —' she tinkles. 'You Americans are so — formal. You are, aren't you? American?'

I know what she's asking. What color I am. I won't give her that satisfaction. Martyn knows why she left him, though he won't say. She wanted the children to be white.

'Oh, very —' I say. 'We all are.'

'Well, thanks —' I say, into the pause at the other end. 'You've been most kind.' I'd half like to admit to her how little I know Martyn, yet I'm not sure whether that's true. 'Why don't you send your picture along? He could hang it on the bulletin board.'

'Thank you, Miss Smith.' But she hasn't hung up yet. When it comes, it's not tinkle. 'I did.'

After, I think of how at the start of her call I wanted dearly to talk to another woman of maybe my age and middle education, it being so long since I had. But the feminine digs deep. So much still running in the dark sluice that willy-nilly is shared, that sorority denies. Yet could we have talked about houses?

Houses that stand still will have ever the same qualities. But a house that moves? Maybe even harder to rid yourself of than what I tote? With no kids to yell — *Stop!*

— On the ward there was a rich seventeen-year-old whose family had solved their status quo another way — they had five residences. They themselves were what moved. Which had put her where she was. When she called her parents she had to check the calendar. We often found her weeping. 'The liars. They should be at Shallygar. For the salmon fishing. They swore they would be. But I suspect they're holed up with that nasty German couple — at Bonn.' The truth is on both her face and ours. They don't want her call.—

This has been my first international call — to the real overseas. Bermuda was a mere tropic away, and only to an airline. Do the newspapers that shuttle the modern age along every morning forget or not admit how many like us lag? Or see only the smart haircut.

What this old-style phone system is said to lack is not always so, however. You can often see the person at the other end of the line.

One step though, I will go. Be brave, Carol. Buy that calendar.

At the stationer's, the line of lottery buyers is straggling out past me. I always wait until the last has gone. As they come in they are furtive, or even muttering some prayer. Once they've put down money they sweep a royal look around at the rest of us. Each of the men must have some secret place at the ready to store his ticket to the future; the hand is always quicker than the eye. Among them it is not proper to talk. The women may chat at the owner, particularly if they've had a previous near miss, but they push their luck into a corner of the purse, as if it must be ignored.

The owner remains impassive, his eyes on his small daughter. Small enough to be pre-teen, wise enough to be twenty, she has the curved nostrils and long eyes of a beauty-to-be, and perfect manners. On the afternoons when her mother works elsewhere she is the little mother of the store. Though now and then the father reins her in. No woman ever tends his counter. Darkish males, uncles or cousins in this Indian or Pakistani clan, do so, in substitution so steady that one cannot keep track. Toward evening, cookery smells waft from the rear, and sometimes a farther clatter; there may be a backyard. The clan may even have bought this rundown four-story on the district's fringe. Over west, on the avenue's corner, there is even a bar, from which the lottery customers may come. None are ever countrymen of the owner; these and he must know too well what he sells. And what they should buy.

I admire this establishment. Also the network it must belong to. They help keep the city a public place in a way that the plazas and the great buildings where all landlords are absentee can never mime. Privacies are in view here, even in control. My alleyways, that sell nothing, offer the same.

Meanwhile, I like coming in here, to be recognized. Is that weakness, in terms of the life I have opted for? A routine that will lead me back into the world of houses — and of family? — Are you afraid of family, Carol? Dr. Camacho never asked me this directly. It was assumed in our separate versions that all of us on the ward were. Or else had no family to be afraid of. — As in other respects, I am half and half.

Here at the stationer's there is surely a parable of the family. And lined up or not, in contrast, snapshots of the common luck. Each evening they and we are a kind of evidence. Our glances crisscross absently. But in the main they are not regarding me. People may never anywhere, much. I have to consider that it's I who am registering them. And have been, all along? . . . I know who would agree. This is what comes of registering him.

'Yes, Miss?' The owner is behind the counter. He knows me, if only as he knows us all. It's my turn.

He hands me the day's paper. And a letter. Addressed to me — me — in that large square hand, and with a foreign stamp. Taking it, a sensation quivers up my arm. All the notes and self-conscious epistles we four used to scatter when I was that college-girl. Since then a few bank notices,

on the trust, or public notices sent on by the welfare precinct. Never a letter addressed to me personally, at a known
address.

'Miss?' The owner is speaking to me. 'Today is the last
paper. The subscription is run out. But I can renew.'

I don't need to open the letter. My month is up. How
neatly Martyn has managed it. Of course I'll renew in his
name. Surely the owner can't care less what my status here
is, whether tenant or live-in, or however fly-by-night. Eyes
lowered, he is discreet with all who enter here.

'Yes, renew of course,' I say, plunging, but into what?
'Same name. But I haven't the money with me. I'll pay you
tomorrow.' I can use the 'green' still in the church salesman's
shopping bag.

He shakes his head. With reason? I have never spent a
dime in his store. 'Not necess-aree. We know the gentleman.' His forefinger doesn't quite touch the letter. He
knows that script better than me.

It's the little daughter who saves me, from what I can't
say. What would have been my question? About 'the gentleman?'

A delicate jangle at my elbow. She's tapping it. 'You live
in the place with the drums? He always promised I could
see them.'

A swift phrase from her father, not in English.

'Mother said yes, dear father.' Head bent over her joined
palms, bangles quiet. But she knows her power. 'Alas, he
was not free that day.' She nods up at me. 'He had to go to
re-hears-al.' The word stretches; she is proud of it. 'So for
twenty minutes, half an hour, may I?' Her wheedling shifts
between her father and me. 'I shall keep the time careful-

lee.' With a smart wriggle she lifts a wrist. I see — we all see — that she has a bright red wristwatch.

'It is for the Miss to say.' But he is proud too, that I see what a father is. When I signal yes he motions one of the younger men to accompany her. 'To escort back. But he is to wait outside your door.' There follows some jokery from her kinsmen, several of whom are always in the store. The young man detailed to go with us says, 'They tease that you don't play the drum, no woman does. So why? And that you are just showing off the watch.'

'I understand what they say per-fect-lee. I have not forgot.' She tosses her head at them.

As we head off, the father and I bow. He resembles any news vendor or stationer of his nationality, whichever that is, Paki or East Indian, whom you may see around the city. Study the man closer — the furrow of his brow, the curl of that lip, and he is perhaps a person. As with them all.

We are several doorways west of the corner bar. A half-block faces us, then the long avenue, down the middle of which is my door. She slips her right hand in mine — a shock. I am careful not to squeeze. Her steps are not mincing, but very short. I tailor my steps to her. Twice down the half-block, she glances at her left wrist. To enchant me a mere one of her tricks would do.

Sleepy-lidded, smoothing his polished black hair, the young man follows behind.

'He makes fun of my mother, she speaks no English; they none of them want her to learn,' she whispers. 'He there is my cousin. But I won't marry him.'

'Are you supposed to?'

She nods. 'The minute a girl gets the blood, they start on it. But my mother tells them. . . no.'

'But how old are you?'

'Old enough.'

'You speak fine English.'

'We all can, when we want to. We came first to Padding-ton.'

She sees I'm not sure where that is. 'London.'

'I have traveled. But not there.'

We are at the curb, waiting to cross the avenue. The traffic light is red.

'What's the farthest you have ever been?'

I consider. Church gardens, at night? The dayroom of a hospital? Prison corridors at dawn. Small towns, around Boston. A huge arena, not that far. Or the multiples of this city, from hock-shops to basement lairs, but always looking out to sea?

— Or the tidy island skies of Wedgwood blue, reflected poolside. Where the girl lying in the deckchair next to mine at siesta hears as I do the lazy voice floating down from the balcony: 'That bronze bikini suits Carey's friend's tan, doesn't it? Right down to the crotch.' For a sec my friend is silent, then: 'When Mum's drunk she always tries to excite Father. Probably has him by the coat-tail. In a sec we'll hear the door slam.' But we hear nothing. Carey's burnt-peach cheek blooms over me. The rest of her in her white suit is darker than me. 'Carol —' she breathes, 'we chums are going to make a bomb. Not to hurt anybody. Just to signify. Want to horn in?'—

The little fingers in mine are like twigs. I say: 'Bermuda. That's the farthest I've been.'

The trucks rumbling by prevent her from answering. On truck nights, opening my one free window, listening to them, heavy sounding or rattling light, I can about tell the hour it is between midnight and sunrise. And almost always, what day of the week it will be.

'That's only this hemisphere,' she says when she can.

We cross. She stops to sigh. 'But run by the British.' She glances at me sidelong. Most of her glances are. Her full face, if one can call such a small area that, is quite as handsome as the profile. But one feels that she's reserving it. 'Your gentleman, he tells my mother we were right to come here, even though at home my uncle, her brother, was a chemist. And my father a pharmacist. Uncle says the British let us rise. But somehow we are still in the same place.' She shrugs. 'But in London, the schools are not for babies. Like here.'

We are almost at Martyn's building.

'I thought your mother didn't speak English.'

The young man has stopped short behind us. So they all know where I live. It has a stoop. He leans there, a lanky young bird, with a beak too old for him.

'She doesn't.' She aims this at him. 'She was kept in the house because in London, our women, too many have jobs to sweep the airports. She wouldn't like to see. Or get respect on the street. But over here, since my aunt die, she takes care of uncle's kids. So she is still in the house.' She cocks her head up at me. 'She doesn't want to speak English; she is sad I speak it so much. But your gentleman, he can speak some of ours, eh? Through him my father goes to school. To get the account-ant's license, the CPA. This lazy one here, he thinks he'll just be my husband. And get the shop.'

The young man's face mottles, up to the slicked hair.

She wrinkles her little curved nose at him. 'I plan to be a gentleman's popsy, Cousin. Like the lady here.'

Her arm lifts just in time to shield her face from the slap. But not the watch.

It is one of those whose works are exposed; I can see those still jiggling. 'Only the crystal is smashed,' I say. But she mourns over it like for a pet. Then spins round and thrusts it at the cousin. 'Take it back to them. Show what you did.' And when he balks: 'Or I'll tell them you try to rape me. So you'll be sure of the shop.'

When he goes she calls after him: 'I shall come back on my own, tell them. In half an hour. I'll use this lady's clock.' She turns to me. 'He'll say I talk dirty because I go to the American school. Silly arse. Did they think I kept my ears glued, in Paddington?' She grins at me. 'Yes, they did.'

On the way upstairs I say: 'I'm not his popsy. Whatever that is. And not a lady, either.' When she doesn't reply I feel I am the child. 'But I know where to repair that watch. Over on Canal.'

'You think? They bought it at the free port, when we came here. But I am only given it now.'

Open the door of Martyn's place and you don't at once see the drums, in their line-up left of center of the glass wall. A couple are on stands, another pair hang on the wall; the two largest are poised on end, one in each corner of the nook. Some have designs painted or incised on the surface; some are amber-smooth, but fringed at the side with dangling tassels or braid. These are more instruments than would suffice for a troupe of six or eight; perhaps a performer played two, or kept a spare. A couple appear tawny new; most are darkened, no doubt by hand use. That there are no drumsticks is at once noticeable. And no players. These drums are meant to be heard; indeed, piled or up-ended or hung, they are like a stave from some song, written out in leather notes and still faintly sounding.

She paces down their line like good scholar. I see at once that they do not engage her. Finally she says: 'Not for rock-and-roll, eh?' and lets her eyes rove. 'What's that?'

'The office.'

She peers in. 'Ah, one of those com-puters. My father buys also. . . . Can I see the rest? Of the flat? . . . Okay!'

Passing the drums, she gives one a pat; it slightly re-sounds. 'Wo-oo. Veree na-tive. Like he said, when I ask. . . . We hear about those Africans from the estate manager here; my father too deals with him. . . .' When the earrings bounce the tiny bells reverberate like airs and graces from that other place, or time.

The bulletin board rivets her. She studies it for minutes. Is she really reading it? She devotes as much time to the postings far above her height as to the ones below. I am being given a lesson in the art of pretense, but what's she after? I pretend to read the paper, least I can do. While, like all in the shop, I bask in her charm — the profile, the bangles, the tinyness. The attention one must pay, wants to pay, like a fee.

When she whips around, the sandals clop. Always too big for her, the ones she wears, and too adult. 'Why don't you read your letter?'

Still in my hand, like a rent notice. 'Because I know what's in it.'

'He's not coming back!'

In the bald glare from the nearer bare window I see what I've never seen in the shop's murk. There's a graining of the skin, a curtaining of the eyes, a maturity of shoulder. She's not a dwarf; there's not that foreshortening of the limbs. But a — staginess? — that is not a child's. A miniature rather, for a family to cherish, even exhibit — and allow to pretend? That young cousin, is he being made to marry her?

'Why do you ask?' I say, but of course I know, and why she always carefully calls him 'the gentleman.' She has wanted to see his lair, his household, and any other trove she can spy. And why not? Maybe the child I have thought her to be is only in my own head — nobody else has ever said. I have not only lost years perhaps, but the very concept of what children are.

'Mind telling me what school you go to?'

'So you've caught on, have you.' She squints at me, as if glad I am smart. Sighs. 'I did go to that bloody baby-school, puh, high school, for a year. Which will not admit I am overqualified. So I quit. We are all angry. What if I sell my wedding jewelry my aunt left me, buy a motorbike, like my girlfriend in London, and go to be a messenger? I even find a place that will take me. If I will wear a sign and ride in the back. They keep me in then. So in the shop I play the tyke I was when we leave Paddington.' She has delivered all this with matching mime — clasped hands, upraised head. She spreads her hands, lifting them. 'But your gentleman — he caught on.' The voice lowers. 'He persuades the familee. My father re-a-lee. Because it is his grandmother who was so small, like me. They have plans for me to be a pharmacist — me? I will not spend my life in a shop. Not my American life.' She sits up, folds her arms. 'So he here, he tells them:

"In my shop," he says, "her size could be a plus." And a trouble too, but this he tells only me. He lets me decide.' She draws herself up, allowing me her true outline, a hint of breasts. The rich laugh that comes from her is full-size. 'I am senior student in theater, age eighteen — what if the birth certificate says less? — High School of Performing Arts. But that loafer, my cousin, he has to escort me and take me home.'

And out of wisdom on both sides, it would be decreed that she not come here. We are both one of Martyn's kind arrangements. And there on the table the letter lies.

She's eyeing it. 'And how old are you?' she asks, in the tit-for-tat kids use. There's more of the child in her than she admits. How do I answer her, I the pretender as well?

'Older than I look.'

'That's what they say in the shop. But younger than him. So very suitable, yet. For the child-bearing.'

'You're — out of your skull.'

'Barmy, that means? No, they are fond of him. They want to see him settled.'

And out of her reach.

What I resent is that she's making me see Martyn as I see too well he is. I could keep him in absentia until now. 'He's forty-six. His mother was almost that when she had him. She's British. He has a half-brother in the military, who's pro-apartheid to the gills, has pursued him all over the map, and once arrested him.' I wave toward the bulletin board. 'It's all there.'

'A — a Brit . . .Fancee.' She rallies. 'May I see the rest of the flat?'

'Go ahead.'

Once she's down the hall I open the letter.

Dear Carol:
My mother did not win her election. She thinks she did.
At ninety-two, perhaps she has the last word. My brother
and I are at her bedside.
Please keep my plant alive.

Martyn

From the bathroom there is a cry. What silly accident —?
She is that small. I rush there.

She's rapt, in front of the photograph. That array of
people, strung out by twos, threes, singles, along their —
stockade? In which the old browntone, printed on heavy
cardboard, melds all skin? 'I knew it. I knew it. They are
from South India, his people. Like us.' She stands on
tiptoe. 'Those there.'

I see now that there are two groups. The group she
points to? Like the others, their skin color has been assumpted
into the cardboard. If they are not all taller, or leaner, theirs
is another posture. Both groups are clad for hot weather,
and in white, but not alike. 'And those others?'

'Servants, perhaps.' Her bangles shake dismissively. 'Once
we left, we no longer had them.'

I know it's not Paddington she refers to.

Suddenly I want her out. It's not only Martyn she's made
me see — the helper, standing at his mother's bedside. She's
been giving me a character, making me more than I have set
myself to be. She has put her hand in mine.

'Why aren't you at school?'

Her brows go up. 'It's the holiday. We are in recess. . . .

Oh brother - er. I must help the mom . . . what time is it?'

'I don't keep a clock.'

She's not daunted. 'You are right. A clock keeps you.' She shrugs. 'Not to worry. Let them send for me. So . . . let's go.' She blows a kiss to the photograph.

'Back to the store?'

'No.' She leads me back down the hall, as if the place is hers. Of course it is not mine. I have to keep that in mind. Habit must be watched.

We are at the table where the letter is, like opposing communicants. For a minute we stand so, then I push the envelope to her. She examines the postmark greedily.

'Pretoria. Where is that?'

'South Africa. The capital.' I have long since looked it up. 'In the South African War, Churchill was imprisoned there.'

'Ah, him.'

'But in 1899 he escaped to Mozambique.' I hope she doesn't ask me where that is. 'Then in 1900 it was captured by the British.'

'Mozambique?'

'Pretoria.' I have got all that out of Martyn's desk encyclopedia, including a brief concluding statement, which she is welcome to. '"Half the population is of European descent."'

'But not Martyn!'

My turn to stare.

'I know what he is, people like them, from the newspapers,' she mumbles. 'I wouldn't say to his face. Nor in front of the others.'

So, continents apart, these passions grow. Hers for him.

His for me? I feel it in the letter vibrating on that meager, school-teachery table. All his dumb objects speaking for him. For the helper. Plus this girl he wouldn't have counted on. He doesn't count up.

Only I do, ungiving, unresonant. Sticking to my guns, that went off a long time ago.

I push the letter to her.

She reads it. 'But you don't have a plant.'

'My rent. To buy one. But I haven't paid up.'

'Ah, a joke.' But her head hangs; she's not stupid. She toys with the letter. 'But look — the postmark was a month ago.'

'The mail from there is slow, maybe.' I draw in my breath. 'Though the news from everywhere is so quick.'

My daily reading has brought me into the world I had forgot. One wider even than the outdoors, the outside. For days I have been wanting to tell someone, anybody, how when I walk down this street on a business day, listening to the lunch-hour crews exchanging telly-movie news-bytes, in the way street-talk does now, a world-news streams to me on the crowd's own wires, clogging my ears like a fur they sell.

But she does not hear it.

'So the old lady, his mother, is taking her time to die,' she says. 'We have one like that in the family. Nobody loves her, but we are very polite.' She has found the pile of papers I save and made a tuffet of them, sitting on it with her arms hunched around her knees. 'So he will stay on. And if I am not careful, I will marry my cousin. At school, they say I am not actress. I am too polite.'

Not too polite to cry. The tears roll down like beads. She

doesn't sob. To hold her is to console me as well. This warm creature, a woman, but fitting in my arms like a child. She has her own handkerchief.

'And you are so strong,' she says, jumping up. 'You talk to no one about yourself. You do not even need to know what holiday it is.'

I have never seen myself like that. And now, more than willing to talk, to people grazed on the street, or next to me in the night niches. 'Talk? Not locally maybe. That is true. Or not in your store. Because to me you all are like a — a tapestry, that I watch.'

Her chin goes up; she stamps her foot. 'Yes, that's what we Asians are to you, aren't we? Something to hang on a wall. But not to be.' Her shoe has come off. Like her wishes, it is maybe too big for her.

'Sorry. That's what comes of talking too much to a machine.'

'You talk to it?'

'I talk to it — yes. But not out loud.' A work period requires that I sit and think, always addressing that old-model confidante. But I do not always type. Would that be less odd to her, or more so? I am not sure I want to trust her. Not when normality is burgeoning round me like one of those pop-up books, where a page-turning child can slide a castle up from behind its moat, or see dolphins rise and fall in an unending ultramarine.

She has fallen into a reverie of her own. That quicksand of the intensely young. Her head lifts. 'I was wrong about the drums. They are for anybody. . .like this place. All the same no-color. And that little office, so empty — sweet. With nobody pushing. . . . A sleeping beauty place. You belong here. You should stay.' She looks up at me, then down, in mute sacrifice.

Nobody in my renewing life has yet spoken to me like that. With a child's kindness — like a freshet. A kindness in miniature, that you carry with you after, a cameo.

'I'm no beauty. But thanks.' I take a deep breath. 'I have been asleep.'

She is still cherishing the room, his room. 'But where do you sleep, really? There are no beds.'

'In my bag.' It has been pushed into its corner, where it lies ready. The corner nearest the door. 'Or sometimes —.' I point down the hall. 'Or — one of those.'

I can't tell what she thinks of that. In sudden reflex, she looks at her wrist. Then away.

'If we wait, a light comes on in the office. At six.'

'Too long. I better not.' She would like to.

But we don't have to decide. There's a knock on the door. She draws back.

'Your cousin? If it's him, I'll walk back with you.'

'If my mother would come — but they won't let her.'

'I could just not answer the door. But telephone to say you're safe. . . . And a — a free agent.' Why do I add that? I know you can't legislate for a person. Yet it was what they kept telling me.

'A what?' She laughs. For a wild moment I imagine that she had been the 'popsy' here before I came. A secret visitor. And has come to see the new occupant in their exchanged lair? . . . In the slammer, in a cell down the row from mine, a woman who was in for having pulled a knife on her rival had been a heroine to the whole facility.

Another knock.

What's making my heart so light, my walk so graceful? . . . The style you adopt when you already have a companion with you? Or you are a free agent? I open the door.

The stationer no longer has his eyes lowered to a counter. He is a father, nodding coolly to me, extending a firm arm to her. His glance ranges the room, under brows that meet like a visor. Later he'll be able to describe it. Maybe to the mother who would have wished to see it on her own.

There is a red welt on his cheek. He has been energized. What he says to her I will never know.

Arm in arm, they seem to be breathing in unison, viewing me from a world that is more than the weather-in-the-streets. A world where events make the seasons: a birth, a marriage, an emigration; death makes the inheritance, cousins are the ligaments. And the house is the core.

She is slipping off one of her glass bangles, a soft, ambery one, shifting it from her wrist to mine. Considering whether to add another. 'No —' she says. 'You would not wish to make a noise.'

In the glass office a time-switch turns on a lamp at six, morning and evenings. At first this had seemed like an intrusion. Causing me on my third day here to certify the time, by the phone. Now I welcome the lamp like a greeting, each time. In prison, as in hospital, the soul becomes a monologuist, no matter how surrounded. The physical speaks louder than any person; we are never deaf to that, even when asleep. At present, on daylight saving time, the outside is still bathed in saffron light. . . . *There.*

The light has gone on; it's six. The gentle glow from

without and within is seamless. An hour when walls melt. When having had company leaves a glow one wants to parlay. Into that haze of chatter and the presence of flesh.

All this is new to me. Or so long gone that memory is outstripped. If this is the norm, I am swimming nude in it. — Say 'bare-assed,' Carol. The way slouching the under-under has taught you. Forget your roots. That's a debt you once owed. You've paid up.—

Her last words ringing in my ears like my epitaph, I am digging in the abyss of my bag for the packet I have managed to keep always with me, ignored, yet semi-consciously counted in. Though forgotten, lately, under the slow crunch of the present, that has seduced me, that will do me in?

My fingers scrape bottom, scrounge only loss. . . . Repeat. . . . Dense and reliable as the fabric is, it has worn. Will it still save a life? Perhaps — if not as planned.

Here they are. Slipped down between torn lining and canvas — and waiting for judgment day? Dr. Camacho's postcards.

It's past six pm of the following day. The beacon light inside 'Africa' has flicked on-and-off for wake-up, though I never went to bed. Soon it will switch me to evening. All day long the windows have been sealed or closed against the street. The only sound here is the salesman's air-conditioner, now and then confirming the temperature and me, with its mm-hmmm. What I am about to do is to add my own noise. For postcards, you only need a pen.

I've never used the word processor full-scale. An old

model I know, it's friendly enough. But mind outstrips even those synapses. It's not a question of speed. Though at times my fingers fly over the keyboard scarcely touching. At times I cannot bear to look at the screen. I have at times recorded with my eyes closed. As for printing out, Martyn's equipment is on the blink, but I shall not call that repair service.

I prefer not knowing what is stored there, what is lost. Any residue is therefore a reasonable counterpart of what I am: in recovery — a mind.

It's possible I will leave a note for Martyn, giving him leave to print whatever survives. Because it is the history of my own survival, and I want somebody to know. And because the only way to thank the helper is to let the load be shared. As I have shared, if so weightlessly, the burden of his house.

All of that. And because I am saying goodbye.

So will end the case record? Except for the brief summary always demanded — *pro forma* is the phrase — of any 'Worker' going off case.

For that, Dr. Camacho's U.S. mail cards will be ideal. Some faithfully written upon over the years but never sent; some still blank. Long out-of-date as to postage, but an extra stamp will rectify. Perhaps the obvious interval between the old rate and the present one will give pause to some. Yet though the public reports on me have long been accessible, my guess is that any who might collate those with my private story are few.

Once I might have wished for that. But the daily round

no matter how minimal — does it shrink the 'manifesto impulse?' Or merely put it in scale?

Yet in the pile of newspaper, all in order by date, is one that came some days ago. When I leave will I set it on top? I don't always read the paper through, but this account was front page. . . .

I had cooked a meal for myself that night, excusing the formality, even laughing at myself, on the grounds that I would soon be back to scratch.

Once — there were tramps. They were considered part of the rolling stock of the nation. In those days they carried no ethical burden in their bundles-on-sticks. Riding the rails, they foraged and scavenged; in towns they were said to mark secretly certain backdoors as being easy handouts. Rollickers all, they were seen either as men who could not cope with the civil life, or chose not to. In turn, no one marked how it was with them when their time came to sicken and die. That was not in the legend.

My aunts' cookbook had a recipe for Hobo Stew, a simple one-pot mess sometimes resorted to. My stew, cooked in Martyn's one pot, was even simpler: canned beans, hotted up. But buying an onion to add is a domestic act. I had rarely cooked here, beyond coffee and tea. As in the pad, I have been reluctant to broach my usual outside diet — cold, raw, tinned, with take-outs in the dead of winter, and in summer a treat from a stall.

There's no course of hardening for streetlife. It's just that ease is too easy to get used to. If it's not meant to last. Yet should sticking to principle bar enjoyment? I found myself cautioning: Carol, cozy up. In a minute I'll reach for the folded paper brought in earlier that day, along with the tampons that are a luxury resumed. I enter drugstores easily now.

In the hospital they had issued us sanitary pads only, and afterwards I had continued to use those, out of the very habit of passive obedience the hospital both exploited and said they were trying to rid us of. In any event, under the pills, one's period can vanish, or be scant. But I have apparently normalized in this area as well. So, like the man I glimpse now and then on my nights in the park, who has a cellular phone he beds down with — I join with modern equipment as I can. 'Guy just handed me it,' he'd told me. 'Outside a Third Avenue bar I hang out near. Wanted it out of his sight; he can't pay the rent on it. Neither can I. Maybe it was on a drug-gang hotline? So far, nothing on it. But the cops see me talking on it, I don't get chased.'

Tonight I won't be chased. Soon, at month's end, I plan to be gone. Deserting those very seductions that have helped put me right. Back to those streets that most will see as what I can't be cured of. But tonight — I'm thinking — I am cozy. Not doll-cozy, like a child. Adult cozy, in the housed style of those who are in control. The meal, however modest, is achieved, and full in the belly. In the small of my back is the ache-y release that comes from the menstrual flow. When the body, without theory, once more relinquishes motherhood. Surely I'm not brooding on that. Merely savoring the feel of that pseudo-child's fingers in my own. Maybe no one has a true concept of what children are until you have one — and even then. What you need, Carol, is the larger view. So reach for it, your freebie newsheet. I do.

And there, on the front page, is our story. *Radical Fugitive Turns Herself In.*

Which one?

Minna, the labor unionist. Who has plea-bargained, turned state's evidence, or done whatever is professional.

A 'bulldog' detective is quoted. "'Never gave up on it. She was the mastermind. Others were just amateurs.'" There hadn't been much of a case to be pursued; why had he?

According to him, the owners of the damaged house — parents of Laura's boyfriend, had refused to pursue, and had since died. Nor would the son-and-heir to the building cooperate. He and Laura had obviously never needed to go underground, having married instead. Interviews refused.

Another named suspect, our Doris, mother of two, was now in treatment for breast cancer, diagnosis poor. But it was Minna's culpability that had kept him at it. "'Because of how she had snuck under, hey? Teaching our American children, pretty-please as all get out.'" In an L.A. high school. "'Advisor to the seniors. Chaperoned them at the prom, no less. Top salary with all benefits.'"

But Carey, where is she?

She is there. Second Section.

Minna, that gray space of a human, is not, maybe by photographer's choice. But Carey is. Full-length, in front of the hotel she was once hired to manage, and now owns. *Not In Bermuda* is the logo on the hotel's tee-shirt she wears. "'We do that so as not to embarrass them,'' Madame Fleurisse, as she prefers to be known, said mischievously. There have been rumors that she functions as a madam, but she denies the story as nonsense, alleging that for her customer-friends, some of them royal, there is no need. "They have each other." The island where the hotel is located is underdeveloped, "And will so remain."'

The language of her interview is as queenly as her foot-high up-do coif. "'If you're said to be in that trade, might at least follow suit.'"

But the legs in the white shorts look the same. The two darkish children lean against her whites. A boy and a girl. "'I had a third, but it died." Recently? "No — the first.'"

Their father? "'An American. From Boston, out of the Bahamas.'"

I see her sobbing on my shoulder. Did she follow him? Or he her?

For there is money; the island is a fief. "'My inheritance.'"

From her father, the well-known diplomat? "'Good Lord, no.'" From her mother, who has stood by her.

Dead?

"'Indeed not. The children call her Nanna Dowager. The whole island does. My mother has come into her own.'"

Madame's 'husband' — or the father of her children merely? — had pleaded with her to bear his son and daughter on American soil. "'But of course I could not.'" Or would not? Her reply: "'We are British subjects, all of us.'" The children bear her name. Her real one. But of course, if there should ever be a need for her to testify in behalf of a certain party, she would come.

For Minna?

"'You bats?" Madame replied.'

Then for whom?

According to the detective, there was a fifth young woman at first thought to be an accessory. 'Kind of an innocent hanger-on. When the house went, we found out later she wasn't even there. Did some months in jail though, had a breakdown later — we weren't proud of that.' Where was she now?

All parties had lost track of her. '"She traveled under several names later,"' the detective said. '"Like she wanted to hide. Until there was a case, no need to keep tabs. So we let ourselves lose track. Do it all the time."'

'"We five were all innocents," Madame Fleurisse said. "Minna wanted real targets. But we others just wanted to sign on. Maybe do a bit of damage. But not to hurt. And thanks to that accident — we didn't. Yes, it was indeed an accident," she said. "We barely got out of there. I'd been afraid that Minna and the others were centering more on target that day than we'd agreed. Central Park Fountain, actually. At midday. So I — well, in the scuffle it did go off. Lolly lost a finger, I understand — we fled our separate ways. But it must have been worth it to her. The parents wouldn't go back to the place. She and her boyfriend rebuilt."'

I can see them at it. The boy wanted us all out. We never even called him by name. He was just Laura's. She would rebuild him as well.

'"The one you call the hanger-on," Madame Fleurisse said. "We kind of did it for her, really. Even Laura, who is a bit of a louse. Even poor Dora who's not much of a — just a nice sweet love. And Emmy, when her mind was hers. Maybe even Minna, the party hack, though she meant to do it in that style she always socked us with — *Realpolitik*.

We were all using that girl, in our minds. She was the only real cause we'd ever come that close to. So we used her. And lost her. She was the real bomb."'

Had Madame Fleurisse any message for her co-conspirators?

'"That is the message," Madame Fleurisse said.'

But when asked the real name of the fifth woman, she would not reveal.

I am standing up. Reading that last, I stare into the photo's eyes as if I can force it to say. As if those cool eyes could hear me call: 'Okay, Carey, it's safe to. Or if you're just holding it in your heart to leave me be, wherever I am now. Don't. Go ahead.'

Or if she can't recall anything but the 'Smith'? Not that hard to believe. Brought up by a string of short-term nannies who departed before they even got a suntan, she had their loose habits of endearment, calling me 'Dickeybird', 'Hop-to-it,' 'Peachblossom,' 'Thomasina Thumb,' after all the books they must have read to her, hoping to stop her ears against the brute business in the room above.

'It's okay, if you don't remember it. I'm remembering for both of us.' But the photo does not reply.

I am still standing up. I don't cry. Blood is running down my leg. That seems as it should be. When a message pierces like the arrow always waited for.

I am the bomb.

'What is Lust?'

When the minister my aunts favored because he was

more than a preacher declared that text from the Sunday pulpit the congregation was not alarmed. Taking it for merely part of his What is the Way? sermons, that had included What is Church? Charity? Family? Episcopal? — the answer to each being Love. However, the aunts, whose donations at times could be only stuffs from our attic that the minister's wife did over for her blouses and his ties, had noticed at once that although he was wearing his robe, his tie was one of the loud ones from the local haberdashery. And in the vestry, in a meeting called for after the service, he did indeed reveal that he was leaving for a foreign mission, along with another woman, since his wife did not believe that either lust or Botswana was Love.

At the time, my eighteen-year-old body would have settled for any reasonable solution. I would discover, like many, that college was almost as good as a migration. There I learned that sex, even when restricted to two persons, could be engaged in almost as a communal activity. What else was group-biking to campsites just too far to return from that night, where after woodfire and song, boys and girls slipped away to become men and women. It was autumn, when at dusk the sun and the moon might both be in the sky, and for better or worse that would later be an image retained.

In prison, sex would come with a knife. In hospital, sex was forbidden, or frowned upon. In the halfway house, that boy and I had mostly swapped our woes. Later there would be a few dirty tricks in garages, with those who saw I was too beat to say no. In time, the medication, pushing me one stage past vulnerable, took care of me in its impersonal way. One is neutered. What is Lust, or indeed Love?

Whatever rages behind the tiny nipples of the queenly little creature who had been here — and who had given every hint that she expected to be full-size in the marriage bed and in child-bed also — has never happened to me. I have never been avid for one person. Yet I have hoped to hear from passion.

The virtue of the street is that you do not expect. I never looked that in the face before. And the political, even my young stance on it — can it so shrink the personal that you no longer dare?

Now another life is lapping at me, as if I loll in a nest of little animal tongues. And someone is avid for me.

Not strange that I believe this. Everything here is a bulletin board for him. His walls embrace me. The newspapers pile, like lazy or neglected conversation. Some talk we have already had, some we might. The paleface drums wait on call. While, in the bathroom, watched by those stiff half-ancestors of his, who whether they were the turbaned masters or their barelegged servants, were light-years apart from the mutton-chopped men and busked women who were half mine — I become the girl I might have been, wrapped lover-waiting, in her warm towel.

It's there that lust overtakes me, cupping my hand to breasts ripe and comely, spreading my legs to empty air. My fingernails, sharpened to ladylike ovals, scrape the tile. I filed the nails to go with the bangle on my wrist, recalling how the giver had saddened at the sight of their blunt squares. In my ears the blood thumps, ready. I suck water from the spigot, smooth my hot cheeks with his hands, stand up, beating my head with my fists, and run from Martyn and myself, out into the hall.

That same night I begin sleeping in the bags hung there, one to a night, and night after night. For this I must give up my divided routine. I don't find what I'm looking for. His smell.

When long after dark, some nights later, a letter is slipped into the commercial mail slot that all tenant doors here retain, I hoist myself up from the floor, where I have been lying face down, and walk on all fours monkey-style to pick it up; it seems to me that I am truly animal now. If one that yearns to speak. But I have not been idle here. Someone from the stationer's, noting that I haven't been by, will have brought the letter; I can guess who. When I complete the task that has kept me inside here, I'll read it, as a proper end to that labor. The earliest clippings and the dustiest are at the top, far above those I'd read. That must have been the reason for the ladder hung in the hall's dark corner, a homemade set of wooden rungs, but from its dust not since disturbed. I find these simple household actions touching; perhaps he would think the same of what is in my pack.

What I have been doing now is putting Martyn's history together. 'Collating' it, as my two Boston scholars would have said. So that I may ponder what has brought him to make the offer he has, to a woman with a history like mine. When I think of his hostility to the PAK, as to some pet I over-cherish, I have to smile — and he is at once in the room. My intent is not that. Perhaps I shouldn't open this second letter at all.

The postmark is not from Pretoria but from Durban. I had heard of that city and its industries, at that rally where Martyn had observed me. We had come in protest against

American companies who had investments in South Africa; in our ignorance we hadn't thought of the banks.

— For Laura, who had retroactively adopted the Holocaust though none of her family had been involved, *apartheid* had been merely 'one of those separations.' Her voice, so deaf to others, weathers the past well.

'I understand they plotz them into three colors,' she'd said, as we'd entered the arena. 'Whites, pure blacks — natives, y'know? — and coloreds. Mixed. Which includes Asians as well. And the tribals are in separate townships. My mother's been to Soweto, organizationally. She claims it was just *de facto* Mississippi. But she met some whites in South Africa who were benign, most of them Jews of course. Though not all.' She'd reached out to pat Carey. 'What's "de facto" mean?' Dora had asked. Carey said: 'And I suppose your mother picked up some art?' —

Forgive them. That is what memory can do. And sometimes, not too late.

I wonder now whether Laura's mother met any British. Below the clippings, whose slow descent to the eye-level present is a chronology, there is a small bookshelf, divided in three. In the first section are small mementos obviously British: a pipe rack with the seal of the Manchester maker; a small fake barometer from the Greenwich observatory, with the weather mark Always Fair; and an initialed silver traveling clock — are they the baggage a mother might impose? In the third section are her books. The space between is bare. I have put Martyn's first letter there. The second joins it. His past rises from this speaking wall, part of the smell I crave.

Martyn's mother writes nursery tales, in the language

she calls *Worldese*. She has revised Mother Goose in it, in terms culled from English, Dutch, Hindustani, Arabic, and French — 'all the basics one needs.' That's on an early book-jacket; on a later one she apologizes, regretting that she had not included Russian and Japanese. According to the book-jackets she has run for Parliament many times, but never made it. 'I run so that people may read.'

Martin must have spoken *Worldese* early. Educated in Capetown, which he bolted from, then Sydney, where an Australian uncle had property that for a time he helped manage, he first turns up in the news as an organizer of sports events for their native population, 'with international competition in mind.' Then it is Antwerp, where he does a movie short, using handsome drug addicts, all talking Afrikaans. 'Filmed in the gray mists of racial violence,' a foreign review says. I look closer at the photo. Not us. Not specifically. But I have learned from other clips what Afrikaans means.

Martyn's elder half-brother, full son of his landowner father, is a power in the national police. 'For certain the young hot-head deserves the sentence,' he was quoted at the time Martyn was jailed, and later hadn't denied his role in that. 'Safer there. And he wasn't in long. But he's clever, you know, like his doctor father. Coloreds make good scientists — look at India. But my kinsman — for this I don't deny — must now make his protests from abroad. Not from the Transvaal. Or any roads that lead to it.' And so Martyn had done, in any media that led to talk.

'I have one son who's been in pokey, one who houses and feeds me,' his mother reports. 'Is it any wonder I have to run for office?'

'The more recent her interviews, the more incendiary,' the Manchester Guardian reports: 'And the official photos larger. Is the lady making history or navigating it?' Scrawled in ink in the margin of that clipping, in flowing script that must be hers: 'Hah. Same as you, dear boy. Both.' In the photo in the last newsclip on her, she is seated, cane at side. 'Don't use it. Shows where I stand.' The cane has a pennant on it, the party's lettering on it not decipherable. She is wearing a lace head-dress. 'Dowagers have perks. And can you say for sure the Queen Mother didn't send me it?'

Few of the notices on Martyn himself are from his own country. Barring the jail ones, they tend to be in university-student rags, or broadsides with no source indicated. The singing troupe, opening in France and elsewhere, and a one-act play performed at a Rights conference in Bern, get what must be wide coverage.

I see how the Martyn I knew so briefly has himself learned to escape. Yet does what he must. In Bern, a young woman from a Human Rights magazine interviews him. 'Though known as a brilliant monologist in his stage, screen, and song documents, and as an appealing actor in works not his own, he has no public dialogue. Rumor has it that his mother, a long-term dissident, is hostage in some way to that silence, but this both he and she deny. An octogenarian, and a character admired if not beloved even by rightists, she campaigns from home, whether under house arrest is not known.'

On the small shelf of her publications all so cannily for children, there is a thin cookbook not hers: *750 Dishes From Overseas*, compiled in1945 by one Ivy Priestnall Holden of Cambridge, England, published 'for New York and British palates,' covering Europe but also 'novelties' from Canada and the British colonies. The compiler is deferent to the known cuisines but her heart is wide open to the colonials. All the recipes are by local women. Most are identified by province: 'A Canadian Woman.' 'A New Zealand House-wife.' They speak in one voice. As if over the shoulder, with timid authority, their hands meanwhile busy at a dozen other tasks.

While I eat deli- or take-out dinners I have to get from blocks away, these women are my company. I allot them their hairdo's, from spitcurls to high combs, their complexions, spotty to creamy, their weights. Some are massively breasted — best mother-style. Some are thin, with a colonial anxiety not always due to geography. A woman can be colonial in her own country. In her own house.

Yet when the newspapers get me down, or a bad outside night has, I huddle in their company. I return to them, as to one of the 'soap' operas not seen since the ward, when we were all too spaced out to change the program, many of us swaying from left to right. That sway, between whatever poles, may be in my consciousness, if not my body, to the end. I'll handle that. But are these women the 'serial,' not mine, that will travel forever at my side? Martyn's mother has made me their spy.

South Africa's recipes are the last in the book, which is inscribed by her to her daughter-in-law. 'Herein is the coffeebread that Martyn so much likes. You'll find that the servants make it better. We don't have the touch.'

Now the book has landed back here. No servants in a caravan? Or to be fair, had Martyn and his wife likely never had them? But studying this text, as I do, she would learn

Martyn's geography: Cherry fritters à la Natal . . . Zambesia Compote . . . Pretoria Pudding . . . ('always a delight with the children') . . . (Which one is certain to have?) . . . Veldt Date Porridge. . . Kenya Pineapple Gateau . . . Bloemfontein and Daloaga Bay Steak.

I riffle through for Durban. Ah, here:

TENNIS Sundaes From Africa: 'Out here in Africa, tennis and sundaes are synonymous. But our sundaes are such that any girl can make for herself, even if she be inexperienced.' The flavor for Durban is peach.

My heart opens and closes for these three people. For a man sweating out his sundaes. There is no tennis racquet here.

I fell asleep. Waking from those deeps at what must be long past midnight, I sense that velvet lack of movement into which even a city of clarions may fall. I am in an acute state of perception. The dream is just around the corner, the present sharp in the nostrils.

I see my legs stretched before me. That want to walk.

I smell the odor of being.

I taste the vim of the apple I ate before sleep, cracking the pips for their almond tang.

I hear — my heart.

I touch — hand to hand, clasping gratitude.

I breathe me in, slowly. I may not embrace the bizarre. But I know it exists. I plash in a modest backwater of well-being, knowing well that I am nude until I reach the clothes on the shore.

Don't boast, Carol. Keep a little caution-powder handy.

Just don't salt the coffee with it. Or tell too many people, maybe not anybody, what you now know is at last wrong-right with you.

Nothing much really. Only what smug millions expect of themselves daily. Or plod along sweetly unconscious that they are wearing its crown.

Oh, Carol honey. Honey honey honey. Love it or leave it, you know damn well what's the matter with you.

You're sane.

'Nothing's so pedestrian as sanity,' a patron who was giving the hospital some millions in return for his cure was reported as saying, over drinks with the gratefully assembled board of directors. 'But fellas, it leads to such . . .panoply.' The trusty who was serving the drinks as part of his own cure broke into hysterical laughter, afterwards informing the ward that the old boy had spittled his *p*'s. That night the trusty required sedation, being unable to get the phrase out of his head. The ward was restive too. We thought we knew what that word meant. And what sanity was. So did he.

My next session with Dr. Cee, I asked him: 'What's the word "panoply" mean?' He'd had to look it up. 'Let's see — ah. It means, "a complete set of armor."'

'I thought so —' I said.—

Martyn's letter, gummy with travel, is still up on that shelf. I know why I'm not opening it — or not yet. It may be offering me a job. Something more than this devotion to the manual of myself. Anyone may have such a manual, puzzled over, only to be tucked away, or now and then taken out for instruction, like the pamphlet that comes with the cordless iron, the VCR, the video screen that will turn the dining-room into a rainforest, the digital box that will answer all calls from outer life on the cheap. A real job comes from that outer life.

I have a choice. Maybe that's the job?

Memory is Faith, my actress friend assured me. And went out on the road again, with a second company.

I wish Heather were here. Not so we could celebrate.

So we could hug.

Bag is packed. Plumped again with all the personals that had seeped from it. In my weeks here have I acted like some sloppy mistress whose man is away with the tidy wife?

Once outside again, I know how it will be. Unable to scatter, I'll begin to cherish every neatness I can scrape up. The soft, glycerined air of restrooms one cannot even enter unless respectably pre-cleansed — and where one cannot rest. Or, dropping lower in the social scale, and if you have found a store that still stocks Sterno, the campsite fuel — the bunged pot on the improvised hob under some bridge. There's no glow, but the pot steams. . . . The bit of company — just enough, when a passing stumble-bum brays: 'I was a Boy Scout once.' And stumbles on past, almost politely, far enough on from me so he can pee. Then moves on. . . .

Where are they moving? Good question. Where did I, during those years when I deemed myself to be on the barricades — because I was nowhere else? Even so, in any planned life I adopt, will my bones ever forget that movement? Where the violences to be met were not legendary, as in a war, but pitiful. And the politenesses too. The street is a low-class war. But should anybody ask — a woman there has full privileges.

Nobody much does ask, or not much, about what goes on in the minds of the walking population. Or people do ask and then forget those who are not sufficiently in-a-slot. But now and then, in one of the scheduled parades that this city adores, a man will join it, dragging a banner without motto, of a meaning known only to him. But he marches; he too is on view.

I have packed the checker board. Red-and-black, black-and-red, will it remind me not only of the fates but of the possibilities? Or will it be just one of those games that help you turn your back on the newspapers? Or is it both?

There are games that tell you where to 'Go,' but merely on the game-board. There are battles to be fought on a screen, where one can murder, conquer and travel the universe; there's one at the stationer's, though I have never seen any of the luck-seekers stop to play. No matter how wide or thick or far its trick dimensions seem to be, it cannot empower them to win the lottery; you have to leave a video in order to live. No wonder, if at times you want to creep into it and stay.

Not far from the halfway house there was a hall offering those anodynes. It was after a sneaked visit there that the boy and I first crept into bed together. 'I could murder you for real,' he shuddered, which only made us creep the closer — until one night, he did half-try. I was the one to be banished, for safety's sake, they said.

Stop, memory. You too can be delay.

Outside, the weather is getting colder. The autumn sky is that icy blue which triumphs even over city dust. Downstairs, the street is empty. Commerce has gone for the night; cars are few. Today I walked along the Hudson, from the George Washington Bridge, to which I had subwayed, down to Seventy-Second Street, staying always as near the river as the city will let you go. A 'walk' is not the same as finding yourself where-ever and slogging on, but for keeping in training it will do.

When I came to the low stone barricade where Alphonse and I had met, I lingered, becalmed. It felt like an anniversary, at least for me. When that play was reviewed, with the cast list printed, I read that Alphonse had taken Martyn's place as Wall. He'll be a slender substitute, but as valiant as able. I'll be forever grateful to him. Though I've no plans to keep in touch. When it comes to people, there is a one-to-one continuity I must still lack. Though they may burn like candles in my mind.

As I left Riverside Drive, the west was banked with sunset clouds, those autumnal ones, so piled that one might walk on them, toward winter. At night now, Martyn's building is barely heated, but since it is classed as non-residential, those tenants who secretly household must not complain. I may have met one or two at dusk, nondescript except for their attaché cases; ostensibly they are merely working late. To them I'm perhaps a secretary doing the same. They are the moles of the city, not its rats. 'Quality rats prefer the waterfront. Even to the garbage. Best of all they want to be where children are.' That was Alphonse's lore. He treated the city as if he was courtier to a mad queen. When I get home, I thought, I'll send him a card.

Before I leave, I'll send them all cards, those persons who have their niches in my life. That way, I'll practice the continuity. Some would call it love.

Home?

Dangerous as any four-letter word in English.

In German, *Heimat*, said with a holy whine. The French are smarter; they cut it in two, and apportion a mite of its power to everybody: *chez moi, chez soi*. Meanwhile, keeping the 'house'— *à la maison* — an official pace away.

Inhabit home or leave it — I'm thinking as I came in here — it's whereby you have to explain your life.

When I came in from that walk, the cards on the table confronted me still, and the letter on its shelf. It's possible not to open a letter at all, or to stash it until one is safely away. But that wouldn't be fair, to a person so fair to me that I waver under the burden. No, I'll read the letter before I go. Surely it will contain love. That I'll carry with me. Also those cards, written while I too was traveling — in the byways of the mind.

But never sent. Some might be recent, others not; it was a dateless time. Some would be only a sentence or two, scatty and quick. Those were the hardest to write, and leave be. Some brood longer, on the life I was living. But not merely on the mode of the streets, which is public knowledge, whose warps any passerby can see. What if that same life is assumed as conscious experience? An indulgence, say, that no priest can give?

I set out the cards at random. A ghostly solitaire. Laid out by someone who doesn't quite know how to play.

To Carmen Rodriguez, that madonna of the inside, before whom even the roaches bow. Who seems to me in recall like a saint's picture in one of those nooks off a nave. But who hangs her headbands on a plaster Virgin rescued from an ashcan.

'—Remember me to the roaches. I drink tea from your cup.'

To Daisy Gold, whose carry-all held all the sorrows of Job, though more freely distributed.

'—A welfare worker is not supposed to "identify" with the client. You did. Thanks. —'

To Mungo, whose contradictions were like a sea with all its waves in reverse:

'—You helped me walk on glass. Thanks —'

To Angel, who was the first to offer me newspapers. Touched by God, that boy, in the best way: smarter than his parents, but still nice to them.

'—I'm reading the news now. Enjoy the bike. And don't ever change your name. Thanks —'

Tact — I think, reading those. I must be making the break to it. But for honesty's sake, I hope it doesn't go too far.

Turning up an angry card to Ms. Mickens, I can chuckle off that concern:

'—To Bryna Mickens, Substitute:

—Call me anytime. I'm in social work —'

When I open Martyn's letter I see it is postmarked eight days ago.

My mother has received her memorial. My elder brother,

the head-of-police, attended with men of his unit. Readers of my mother's books attended also, mostly Anglo couples with their children and children's children, for whom my mother's fierce blend of South African flora-fauna and Brit principle was thought to be ideal.

At the graveside my brother and I stood together. Sharpshooters managed to wing us both. The crowd stood fast. So did the unit. I was proud of both sides.

My brother is in hospital, but will survive, to live on my mother's land, which rightly goes to him; it was his father's. The monies from the books, which apparently lie unspent, and any future earnings therefrom, come to me. Some I will take out of the country if I can. Any theater I have in me I get from her, and she wouldn't care where it's used. The balance will go to the troupe.

My dear Carol: If you will live with me half the year, I will walk outside with you the other half — either six months to begin as you choose.

I should be able to return within the next week.

Love,
Martyn

The scene at the graveside is so vivid to me that what he proposes at first scarcely pushes in. The brother and his men are in uniform, a khaki the color of dark honey, that doesn't show sweat; their caps are absolutely level, their foreheads red with righteousness. The crowd, mostly women and children, pressed together thin as books read at bedtime, are on a shelf of tableland, to one side. Some who might be women from the cookbook are among them. The coffin, on a mechanized platform, sinks slowly out of sight. The corpse, who surely would have preferred to be lowered by human effort, does not protest. The sharpshooters, a duo at a distance only the dead can see without binoculars, make the sign of the cross before they fire. *Ping*. A sound like a witty remark. I cannot see what Martyn is wearing. But two men fall.

What's his wound? Wou-ound. The sound reverberates in those foothills I cannot see.

Not so serious that the hospital won't soon release him. And he can walk. I take heart at the word 'winged.'

I step out of the shell of myself. I take heart.

October 29th

The six o'clock light comes on. Two days have passed. My month is long since up, yet I am still here. No need to bring out the checkers to tell me why. I'm not foolish enough to think that one ever stops playing games with oneself. So I sit here, in wonder at how I have been weaned.

When I went to the stationer's again, resuming that routine, the daughter and her cousin were not there, but as I accepted the newspaper the father handed me, he unbent. 'She's at school,' he said. 'On her motorbike.' He would have said more, but just then the woman lurking in the rear stepped forward to reveal herself, the mother, all sinuous garment and coiled hair. 'Thank you,' I say to the father, and as I pass, the mother echoes it. She does not say for what. But she knows the English for it. It's well past dinner-time, the lottery customers are gone — but I'm in luck. I am now part of their story. The city has begun to let me in.

I am no longer angry at Martyn's offer. At first I thought he mocked the way I had lived, and assumably planned to go on living. The trouble is — I see how he might. What's a Jeanne d'Arc, if no one sees her burning?

My childhood did not allow anger. If there was reason for rage, whether on someone else's part or mine, I was programmed to remain oblivious. Of how our breasts swelled, the voice muttered, the fist sounded in the palm — a stand-in for the enemy we could not afford to have.

This time, I catch my own posture, swollen and inarticulate. The solitary glass bangle at my wrist, silent for want of a companion, reminds me. Anger without just cause is the psyche's noise. I think how Martyn would burst out laughing at the sight of me, and am ashamed.

I glance over at the line of drums. They and I have a small secret that I will not confide even to a machine.

October 31st

One recognition of a day's date even the confirmedly dateless are allowed. Maybe a street seller thrusts a flyer in your hand and you hold onto it, so as to keep track of when your next welfare check is due? Or the collector of aluminum cans for turn-in money, loading his barrow, turns up a half-empty, that if left unopened would have been good for two years yet — and shakes his head at that beery improvidence.

But date two entries, as I now have, and you join the calendared planet, all the way back to Copernicus. With maybe a clutch of Aztecs and Chaldeans at your elbow. To say nothing of Stonehenge.

Dusk comes earlier now. The year turns, and I don't need a weatherman to tell me so. Venture out, and I see all the astrology of the street. Jealousy nips me. Do I want to join the charts?

Saunter anywhere in a city's dust and you are forced to mark the two divided streams of the populace. First, always first, the mainstream of those who have appointments with tunnels, subways, buses or limos, no matter what their position is in society, and whether or not they are going home. Sooner or later they will — and home implies the calendared life. Everybody there takes for granted that days have labels. Life is conducted behind a curtain of numerals: bank statements, salaries, taxes, that sound their warning bells morning to evening, a background music that some repress, many enjoy.

Side by side with that flowing current, are those who live in the dateless country, their hobbled transportation likely to be themselves. In prison, the only date is your sentence, in hospital it's your feared or craved for 'release.' Once outside, we special ones meld with the commoners — those so low or dumb or hapless that they have been ousted even from the ranks of the resident poor.

But we are not that. We are the freed.

That's what the SW's don't understand.

Before Daisy Gold I had a man worker, given me by design. A cozy hipster with a ring in his ear and an extra in his nose for weekends; for our confabs he wore both. 'You can have a job, Carol, and still hang loose. Look at me. You don't have to be passive, dear, to be cool. And I myself spend the wee hours in a shelter, once a month.' All the lingo he had learned from his shrink he shook out on me.

'You're trying to rape me with theory, Manny,' I told him. 'I could complain.' But to be smart only spurs their interest.

He and a photographer friend wanted to do a documentary on me, for some nights following me on camera to wherever I crashed. Finally I say to them: 'If I had a pad, I'd call the cops on you. As it is, well — scram. I'm not a documentary. I'm a case record.' I see how he and the friend exchange glances. 'Carol —' Manny says. 'How'd you get so clean?'

They had found me in that spot near the George Washington Bridge, where I'd set up the Sterno. The night before, a girl sharing the archway with some of us, had had a miss and bled all over me before we got her into a cab and to Columbia Presbyterian, where she O.D.'d. 'The nurses let me wash up,' I tell him. The guy with the camera raises his flash but Manny stops him. 'Why —' he says to me, 'why do you so love the abyss?'

I remember how the hot came up in my cheeks, the way it does when you hear a piece of your story, from somebody else. And the truth drags out of you. 'I came from where the horrors are. I have to be where they still are. Or I don't feel — honorable.'

The six pm light comes on. Light is never humdrum, but the zigzag of pleasure at this near-ceremonial has lessened. I am too used to it.

When Manny was transferred to another precinct, he gave me a present. 'It's a vita. An employment history. Got it from that record of yours — hey? So what if they date, some? Lot of janes re-entering the work force. You could use this any time.'

On the ward you could talk about your 'life' until doomsday, all the while knowing you were on hold. A girl who later took pills said to Heather and me: 'When you commit suicide — do you "do yourself in?" Or out?' She always wore her dark glasses, even to the Thursday films. When they found her, months later, in an abandoned cemetery, the skeleton was still wearing its shades.

I never considered suicide. 'Ah Carol —' Dr. Cee said, in that probing which never touches you but whose fingers you can feel in your brain, 'you're pro-life.'

They had such an orderly facsimile charted for us: Mondays for single therapy, Wednesdays for group, Fridays, if on the mend, you went downtown unsupervised, but in twos — how could they counterpart the real pile of straws that faced each of us? That faces me, the fur district, and man-woman-and-chick — citywide?

The night the girl miscarried and then O.D.'d, when I got back from the Presbyterian I found my fire had been tended by the others under the archway. A wine and hash party was the idea, each addict to his own, with coffee for coming down. 'We could pool for eats,' I said, and they stared at this innocent, but tolerated. 'You see what she did —' one said, excusing me, 'it gives you an appetite.' So I could break out my wiener and soda picked up on the way back. No one else ate. But a campfire breeds talk.

Not all of the four had been inside. The two buddies I figured had been thieving soon skipped, once they were high, letting drop —'Lotta cars just asking for it, on the lower Drive.' The two who were left, a former 'tec who wore a thick toupee for warmth, and a black girl who wore a chainmail of beads, carried a suitcase, and could pass for being off to a weekend, were agreed. 'You lose your apartment, you can't hold onto your job. You lose your job, you can't keep up the apartment. I'm not a homeless,' she said. 'I'm a secretary, when I can get it. But you have to have a phone. Tonight — I just ran out of relatives.' The detective said, 'I have a habit, yes. But I don't steal for it. Do a little business for that, and you get by. But I can't save up, neither.'

I was new to it then. To how almost all of those you meet on the road are in the ward of themselves.

And walking, walking, on the proud stilts of a philosophy — wasn't I?

Down below, the street light goes on. The sky is a gasp of pink. Outside-versus-inside holds the moment in clarity. Like used to happen in that bay window, the last of daylight breathing over our game.

Your turn, Carol. Pull a straw.

I am going to pull one straw from the pile.

The flower market over east will still be open. I sometimes stroll past for the fresh ozone from trees and plants set out on the sidewalk, and in the rear of the store the bouquets waiting like movie stars for delivery to restaurants. Plus in the window a few corsages for the pre-theater trade.

I won't buy an orchid. But before I leave here, I'll pay my rent.

On the way, I'm thinking how the wait for Martyn has been like one long evening. None quite so calm as this one, the night when one decides — to decide.

At the market, only one stall is still open, the last of the Greek ones still catering to weddings, and to the belly-dancer cafés. No plants. But a trellis within is hung with frail bunches in the watercolor hues that dried flowers always are. I buy several bunches. They will rustle into winter on their own.

It's 9 pm Saturday, the Sunday papers will be out. I like knowing this fact of the city's household. Stopping at a vendor I pick up a Times, part of what my metropolitan holding brings in. But I can't carry it all, my arms are full.

'Just give me the Help Wanted,' I tell the vendor, an Afghani by the look of him. He is not surprised. So laden, blending with others passing on their late hunt for fruit and vegetables, one saunters or plods, destination pleasantly displayed. There's no adventure-to-come beyond the ampleness of food, and time. At the week's end, for those on the calendar. Will that now include me?

I take a crossblock, down which there is one of those dust-riddled parks the city has ordained for new high-risers, as vents meant to keep the buildings from pressing workers permanently in. There are no sleepers there yet. They'll be at the small carousings but will arrive later. When weather is clement the under-population rises to take possession.

I sit down. A bench is always halfway. When I press the stems of the flower bunches between its slats they look as if grown there — the kind of papery bloom a bench in a city would have. On which I myself might spend the night in my version of the 'public shelter' guaranteed me — but only if the authorities care to provide me with a phone on which I could call emergency 911.

The front page of the Help Wanted is all Temps, every agency ad yodeling like a band of alpinists. MANPOWER** Reap the Benefits, THE HOTTEST, 'Your Options Are Wide Open, TIGER**' is Excellence, STOP HOPING Dial A JOB. . . . If I can't handle Wordperfect or Windows systems they'll train me. To operate a Macintosh I see that 50 wpm is a must. Some promise medical and services, and paid vacations. None supply housing, but with a GLAM-OUR JOB in GLAMOUR CO's, or even HI FRIDAY PAY I could perhaps get in at the Y?

There's no place to pee near this park. The office patronage doesn't need one. Neither do I at the moment, but I am remembering how hard it is for women on the outside. To scrounge about, and find nothing, even the coffee-shop denying it has a 'facility,' because it's seen you before. To have a place of your own — is that copping out? Or the place where all the compromises begin? Let them. I un-hitch my flowerbed, and walk off.

The corner I'm nearing belongs to the anti-fur activist. She's still there. She knows me, but she has no nodding acquaintances. She can't change focus. Her anger has to stay pure.

'Excuse me —' I say. 'I pass you so often — I'm staying nearby. And you keep such long hours. Where do you relieve yourself?'

'Don't worry about me. Take this.' When I take the petition I'm to sign she says: 'The super in the building on the corner lets me, the basement toilet. He's a sympathizer. He loves dogs, cats, all animals. He says where he comes from they ate cat. And dog.' When she shudders her mass of frizzy hair ripples in the breeze.

'Why go just for anti-fur?' I say. I honestly wonder. 'Why not for people who live on the edge? Or babies with AIDS.'

'You're one of those, eh?' The voice is hoarse, the eyes narrow. 'Maybe when they skin people so they can wear the pelt in winter, I will. Or breed them, like for fox and mink.' She slaps at the petition. 'So will you take this home and sign it, or won't you?' Her bare arm is no hairier than mine, but her teeth are pointy — could argument have focused them also?

'Oh of course,' I say. 'I too am an animal.'

And pass on quickly, not knowing whether to laugh or cry. 'Whew, Martyn,' I would say if he were here, 'it's no slouch is it, being an activist?' And we would laugh together. We would certainly not cry.

I stop in my tracks. He is here. He has entered my monologue. Correction. He has been in it all this time — and all the while listening — as plainly as if actually perched on the edge of the desk in the glass office, casually swinging a leg in its paddle-shaped shoe. I can hear that voice, lazy in cadence, swift in reply, see that face by turns broad and hawk-thin, somber as a bust of Caesar speaking, or stretching to tell a joke — an actor's face, taking you into its mood, but never insincere. I can even reproduce, in fair facsimile, the gist of what he might say.

Whatever his counsel, will his presence haunt my meditation wherever I go? And even my acts?

'And where are you going, Carol?' the voice says, not so casual after all.

Halfway down the block, at Martyn's building, the lamp-post at the curb is lit, its pear-shaped iron finial veiled by smog. In this city-on-the-sea, which no longer smells of the sea, the empty avenues yawn like the jaws of barracudas swimming in the rubble left to them. Yet its street lamps glow with operetta romance. As if no masses for neglected souls are to be sung here, only the lacy choruses out of *La Bohème*. My musical aunt used to allow no one to touch that Red Seal record, murmuring as the faded scratching ended: 'Poignant, to a degree.'

At this hour, maybe past 10 pm, any loners walking would loom like Jonahs spat out of those shark-jaws, but tonight there's no one. At the top of Martyn's building my borrowed window is the sole one lit. Standing up there, one sees the solitary lamp below, its iron stanchion glistening. If there were someone leaning there — I say again to Martyn — it could be a painting.

As I near it, there is someone. A man loafs there, one palm and elbow against the post, head cocked toward it. But this is not a painting.

He doesn't yet see me. A vision would not.

I keep walking. He sees me.

Am I seeing double? An image in my head, and a man waiting?

'Carol. Carol.'

I have never had visions. Nor seen double.

This is sanity, a deep wave of it stretching me top to toe.

The flowers rustle, crushed against him. 'Wall.'

Blending, almost the same wood-mushroom color, except for the pink around the bandage on his shoulder, we have exchanged limbs, tongues. Our bodies fit. Nuzzling, we have mingled our animal scents. We are lying side-by-side now, but separate. It has amused him to take down the other Shelter-Pak from its hook in the hall.

'We had no room for beds here. Six men, sometimes eight. As well as me.'

And now — one woman. I have a sense of his usually crowded life. Of how he seemed when we met. Easy with friends. Ensconced in them. And then — to plump for a life with me? 'It's been a fine shakedown for me,' I say, choosing the word carefully.

Above us is that woman's snapshot of her offspring. All born since she left, but how long were she and Martyn together before? I feel again the intensity of her call.

'They won't be coming back,' he's saying. 'That troupe. Or any other. They adored the theater — it lifted them out of the ruck. But now, they want to be back in.'

And him?

We're pussyfooting, walking on eggs, and mutually aware of that. Still heavy with the physical, happy with it. But one emerges, if not sad, still oneself.

'I won't be going back there — not for a long time. If ever.' But the 'ever' sounds shaky. The only part of him that does.

'You're no expatriate. I can tell.'

He takes my hand across the spread-out packs we're lying on. 'That word, I can hear it preach from my own youth. . . . When now — we can step across countries like they're mudpuddles. Chat a man up from another continent like he's standing next to you at the urinal. . . . No one's going to be able to keep one nation stamped on the heart.'

I have my eyes closed. 'I love listening to you. You're so literate.'

Hearing him chuckle, I open my eyes. I see he knows when I tease. 'Pot calls kettle —' he says.

'Know what a "temp" is, Martyn? . . . Over there on your table. The Help Wanted columns.'

'My table again, is it? So quick?' He flicks the newspaper with a toe. 'Who wouldn't know what a "temp" is? Half my friends have worked that way, in their time. Some still are.'

'For me, it's a start. People like me — we are the expatriates.'

'Not to me.'

But I am staring at the floor. At the largest roach I ever saw, scuttling past. My hand has fogotten its reflex. Left it at the barrio. But the creature — inch-and-a-half surely — has stopped in its track.

'You're right —' I say again. . . . If I stay, will I be saying that constantly? 'Clean up your corner, and the roaches just go downstairs, or up. . . . But it's the first I've seen here.'

'Not a roach. A waterbug. Come through the pipes now and then. Ate the binding on one of my mother's books — they like paste and glue. What can it be after? . . . . Ah.'

The flowers, in a jar on the floor.

The bug is still immobile. 'They freeze when you notice them. But watch.' He bends toward it.

Gone. Over the door-sill and down the hall. Martyn laughs. 'Back to the bathroom pipes. Well, every creature deserves its lair.' He's not looking at me. We fall quiet, picking at the stuff of our Shelter-Paks. 'But fancy, poor thing. Not knowing your flowers were real.' His face is so droll I have to stroke it. Not a mythic face. You have to learn it each time. Yet steadfast. Like a lesson I should already know.

'That photo in the bathroom, Martyn. Who are they?'

'The household in which my real father grew up. His grandmother served there. The family she was in service to were jewelers, come to Africa from Bombay. Somebody snapped the whole lot, family and servants, at an outing. My great-grandmother is the tall girl at the left. Toting the basket. She died in that household. How she got the photo is anybody's guess. Maybe so that when her grandson, my father-to-be, went off to school she could give it to him. Her husband, my great-grandfather, was far away, in service as major-domo to a British family, the one into which my mother married — young, and what would later be called "socially intemperate" . . . .When his grandson — my father — was shot, that photo was found in his effects.'

He sounds brusque, with reason. 'Your family story, Martyn. More of a tangle even than mine.'

'You forget. I don't know beans about your beginnings.'

'Well — let's say we've both had a brush with the aristo-crats.'

And suddenly that seems hilarious. When we're done, he says: 'That we met at all. Oughtn't we send Alphonse a bouquet?'

Strange, to hold hands after sex, instead of before.

'Carol. You're not thinking of being — just temporary — here?'

The glass enclosure is all sunshine. If I were in there, at my volunteer work, it would be time for a noon break.

'I've been dreaming the past. And avoiding the future.'

'Time to reverse. My brother and I — at mother's death-bed we agreed to reconcile. Or to try.'

'She sounded — great. I've been reading her notices.'

'She had some of the qualities of greatness, yes. But all of its attitudes.'

'That dowager head-dress. La.'

'She had a foot in both camps. Calling me her white sheep, and my blondie sib her black one. Me her love-child, and him her misbegotten. And enjoying all of it.'

Lying back, we seek each other's warmth. But I am smelling him on me — and me on me. I jump up. 'Dibs on the shower.'

'All yours.' But as I linger, rueful, he can tell what I'm remembering. 'Mean of me. To decamp like that. But I had to catch a plane.' He jumps up. 'On second thought, that shower will do for the two of us.'

It does. Even though we must keep his bandaged shoulder well away.

Afterwards, enfolded as best we can in the one towel, he bows to the photograph. 'Hope you approved what you saw.'

Then we shout in one voice: 'I'm starving!'

For a minute he cradles me, murmuring happily, 'Going to have to learn how to talk separately. Lucky we're not in a play.'

And whoosh — stiffening in his arms, I am separate.

A second ago, I was as proudly naked as he. Now, am I wanting to huddle again into the worn, smeared shoes and bundled-up garb of — martyrdom? . . .Don't admit that word, Carol. . . . But my skin, clean as candlewax from the double shower, and heavy with stand-up sex — does it hunger sneakily for singleness? Scorning his hotplate, on which I've had a month's savory coffee and in-from-the-afternoon tea, do I yearn again for the breezy sleazy arcades where one can crouch into sleep — unscheduled, unordered? Except by the lock-step pace I called my own? Where I walk in allegiance with other untouchables. In mute sympathy with the smells that never signify. In the play that has no audience.

While Dr. Cee, a specialist in those, wrings his hands?

'There's only the one deli, Martyn, not too far from here. You've been hours en route — how many hours is it from South Africa? Put on some warm clothes. Then go snooze.' Shivering, in forethought I pull my crumpled ones from the bathroom hook that holds his pants and shirt, and mine. I close the bathroom door on him.

Sliding into my T-shirt, I target the backpacks lying in the bright sun-pocket at the room end of the hall. I must be careful to take the one packed. With all my unworldly goods.

'Just where do you think you're off to?'

It's no bright errand, I know that. 'Just going for sandwiches.'

Splayed against the open bathroom door, Martyn's whole body has turned as red as his face. That snarl — who would expect the hushed sweet burr issuing from it. 'No, Carol. Very neat. But not worthy of you. Not needed. Nobody's sending you out, love, ever again.'

The games fly up.

We are sitting at the table. In our snatched-up crew necks and tan pants we could be any couple sitting on a sand dune.

He had caught me just as I was bending to hoist my load.

It was easy; I too was in shock. He had jammed my two lives together. How he knew what I had been sent away for so long ago, I couldn't fathom. Martyn could play the part of spy with aplomb, I was sure, should he have wished to bother. Yet I trusted him. That was the trouble.

Forcing me back to the bathroom, making me dress, putting on his own clothes, he had growled at the backpack: 'If I could burn that piece of fancy double-think, I would.' But he knew he would be burning me.

I am facing the glass office. The line of drums is on my left. We are eating from the same box of crackers he fed me when I first came to tea. 'How did you know? About the sandwiches.'

He slouches in the straight chair.

'I grew up with politicals. There's always a buried something else. At the bottom of their best convictions. When we met at the play, you and I, I had half a mind to leave you be. But I couldn't. Nor when I left. Instead — I took the ticket, like those in Ahmed's shop do, and hoped for the best. Because I knew better than them, I had more than a tinker's chance. And more to gain.'

'So the stationer's name is Ahmed,' I say. And it's he who's surprised.

'I'm learning, that's all. I've been learning since you left. Go on.'

'All the time I was in Africa, in my head things went badly for you, Carol. It's called perspective. And as anybody who draws from the figure only will tell you, it's a trick. She's like a stunning *idée fixe*, I told myself. But with a flaw in it you can put your fist through.' He swings a leg. 'And so you can. And come through with a fistful.' He eats the cracker. Gets himself a glass of water. Sits up straight. 'The bullet in my arm put me right. If I'd died without seeing you again. So I hopped a plane. And on the plane, saw the London newspapers. With a recap of that story.'

And knew it for mine?

'You were the only clue. I knew it must be you.'

'You put two and two together.'

He is nodding, almost asleep. His head lifts. 'And two and two made five.'

And he sits up, crackling with the energy your own wit can lend you.

'I phoned her from the plane. "Madame had had dozens of calls since the interview," I was told, and would see no one. But I back-tracked, some hundreds of miles, and flew to the island anyway. Stormed the castle.' He smiles, not at me. The way all men did when they saw Carey. 'I'd a hunch — there are passports we carry. Like skin. Perhaps the clerk at the hotel described me. She sure reneged when she saw me. Did she recognize me, from the rally? Or merely the name of who I said had introduced us? She recognized him.'

He leans forward to grasp my hands. 'I didn't tell her anything, about the years between. That belongs to you. To her credit, she didn't ask. It looked to be a short take. I didn't see how to mention you. But she keeps those kids by her, like passports too. Or tokens. And just as I was about to make off, the boy says: "Are you a friend of my father's?" And I say: "Not that I know of. But of a long ago friend of your mother's. One of five."'

I see a pink stain on the sleeve of his shirt, but he fends me off. 'It's only serous fluid. They said the wound might seep.' He finishes the water. 'She's a cool one. "I live by living in the present," she says. "I'm not a loyal person." . . . And I believe her. With one exception. So I say, "But a message like yours deserves an answer. That fifth girl — the one you lost — whatever happened to her, she's made use of it. She has — found herself. . . . . Madame doesn't say anything. But the kid, he's about thirteen, he leans forward and says: "How?" — and I don't know how to answer him. But you have to answer a child. . . . So I say: "A kind of pilgrimage." And he says, "For what? Where?" And I say, "She herself would have to say. But even on this island there must be people she'd be doing it for."

'Madame doesn't say anything, only to the children — "Go and play." But when I leave, I find she's followed me out to the patio. "They're adopted," she says. "Nobody these days I'd want to be having children for. So, I invented myself, eh?" . . . Like a question. Like she's still doing that.'

The cracker-box is empty. He crushes it. 'She followed me to the cab. Tells the driver to wait. When she comes back she leans in on me. "So Carol found our target for us, did she?" she says, "When we'd only sent her out for sandwiches. And found you in the bargain. Lucky bomb." . . . And as the cab starts off, she shoves me this envelope.' The bandaged arm tosses me it.

She said 'Carol.' She did remember.

The creamy envelope, thick as bone, has landed near the cracker-box. Two unrelated shapes. No wires, no waddings. I see that other table again, in still life. The agent of destruction on it is as mum as any known, even a noose. I hear the girl carrier from Canada: *Here it is, the canister sinister.*

He's got up and is rooting in the fridge, his back to me. A big man, he needs his food. 'Wanted to open it. Didn't want you hurt. Then I remind myself — you've a nerve, Martyn. What Carol's survived, who's stronger than that?'

The envelope contains a note and a check. Written in the same big, loose sprawl in which she invited me to that other island, our senior year, the note says: 'Hang on for us. This is a bribe. — Carey.' The check, large or small according to one's lights, and for the exact amount, never concealed from my classmates, of my annual trust fund interest payment, is signed *Madame Fleurisse*.

I'm not hurt. The best one can ask for is to be remembered; even the street-souls I walk with don't require more. As for the check, will it be spent? Those used to playing only for chips are inclined to spend freely. 'Money must not become an emotion,' my practical day-aunt would say. 'Of course not,' the music-aunt would reply, giggling. 'It's simply more than we can afford.'

By then, with me home from school but out of the town's spectrum, they could reveal themselves — and I now assess them — as the cheerful, quirky, undowntrodden pair they were.

Yet in that household, with me as their charge, there would be no dreaming of men, of the sort that bubbles between even the stuffiest mothers, and their daughters: remembrances of courtship, coy allusions to after-prom kisses: 'And there he was at the football game, with that other girl. But he came back, baby. Else you wouldn't be here.' — Nor did I have father or brother to join in the badinage — 'Ah, they get us in the end, don't they, boys?'

I'd had no adolescent 'assist' — I was told — toward those reveries of the probable partner that could push many a girl toward the dullest substitute. What partner could those two dream up for me? Or my four friends?

I'd grown up thinking of males as 'the opposite.' But in me, what the college nurse in her sex survey termed 'full-blooded' would opt to have such sex as came my way. Moony and kicky in the backs of cars, or the bushes. With a crowd my day-time friends never knew about. On the stone floor with a prison guard, and retching afterward. Mute reachings in the hospital and the halfway house, little more than the foreplay of psyches trying to repair one another.

Then, nothing. In my walking I had been chaste. As in the Cat Club. As in the barrio. . . . Touched by God, I had never ogled a cafe lounger up the stairs. Fumbled after, I had never let a supper-sharing bum spread my legs.

Now Martyn has breached all that. Aided by my own warming, eager flesh. That sordid virgin is gone. But do I believe his epitaph to her history? Strong?

Martyn has dug out two apples. Pale-green orbs from Washington State, that I had planned to admire, then eat, one each day. We munch them like kids who have discovered Mom's hidden treat.

'Refrigerators are kind to me,' I say. 'They're always giving me surprises.' Like the old box that Daisy Gold praised. Inside, on shelves roomier than here, there had waited the squeaky-clean woman I am now.

'I'll be kinder,' Martyn says, getting up slowly. 'I'll bring us dinner. Jamaican place the troupe liked, over on Fourteenth. I'd planned to buy you lots of dinners. But this one — I'd like to bring home.'

His jacket is hung on the one hook near the door. Mine is beneath. It's worn, but still respectable. He smooths it. 'The slavey they were blowing up the world for. And they sent her out for sandwiches.'

The core of my humiliation. He's put his finger on it.

'Police caught me with the goods. I ate the evidence. Waiting in the station house.'

'T'll tell the restaurant they can be free with the spice.'

I watch as he pats his wallet, shifts it from jacket to slacks. Male gestures, built on pockets, have a sweet forthrightness ours don't have.

As he hoists his coat on, the postcard on the bulletin board catches his eye. He reads.

'The state of my world —' I falter. 'You're not obligated.'

Those sandy eyebrows that have scratched my belly, they shadow the eyes. 'A tea party. Against the state of mine. Or what should be mine.'

'So, I want to release you from your offer.'

'Granted,' he says with a rush. 'I thought about it all the way over. In the air. It was a false offer. It was for you. To get you. Not for —' He looks up at the bulletins, at that scrap of a card, white against the yellowed clips — 'your messages. You'll have yours. I'll have mine. Play-acting. Versus acts. Don't expect we'll ever resolve that rhythm. And why should we? Been around a long time, that rhythm. Our addition to the planet's. And we can only play it by ear. . . . And that's a long speech. Easier on a postcard. Maybe I'll post one. "To Carol. With love."'

He strides to the table, fiddling with the housekeys that

I'd put out to remind me to leave them for him at the stationers. 'But I'll do one thing for sure. Buy a bed.'

At the door he stops. Is he afraid to leave me? 'Damn. My sleeve's wet through.'

I help him peel the jacket off. His shirt-sleeve is sticky-wet. The dressing underneath soaked. 'They changed it for me in the plane. The altitude. You swell.'

'The hospital for you.'

'Right. In the morning. St. Vincent's. I know it well. We had bouts of pneumonia here. One pleurisy. They would strip to go barefoot.' He sighs. 'No, there's a spare dressing in my bag. Give it here.'

The wound is encrusted, not pretty, but neat.

'Not inflamed. They told me what to look for, if it seeped.' He opens the sealed dressing, but his one hand is clumsy.

'Here, let me.' I look for red streaks down the arm, but there are none. As I wrap the new dressing, I am careful not to have it adhere to the blond grizzle of hair, and insert one finger between dressing and underarm, so as not to bind.

'You do a neat job.'

'Saw it done. In the jug. Woman slashed another one. I was a trusty by then. Took her to the infirmary. This is serous fluid? That was blood. Lots.'

'You need to see blood? To show sympathy?'

'No.' My voice is shaky.

'But you thought you did.'

He's written 'Love' once. And just now said it. Can I?

'It's such a relief —' I burst out. 'Not to puzzle a person .'

He says, 'I hear what you say.'

At the door, jacket on again, he says: 'May take awhile.

Not a short-order joint. And they can do African. You dip the meat-sauce from a bowl, using the vegetables or leaves as scoops. There are no implements. Everybody at the one bowl. A ritual to make one cry. With a peculiar comfort. . . . I'll be back as soon as I can. I'll halloo from downstairs.' He sees my face. 'Trust me? To come back.'

I take breath. 'Trust me? To stay?'

When he's gone I do a number of things. I return the Shelter-Pak that belongs here to its hook in the hall. There's no hook for mine. Hung over the other it will bulk in the narrow aisle. In the cabinet under the bulletin board there's a hammer and nails. I drive in a long nail and hang my pack. Inside, there's a money pocket where I put the disability check when it first comes. Cashing it gives me a bad time. Soon that must stop. I stuff Carey's check in the pocket, well down. I doubt that I'll ever cash it, but I'll keep it. It's blood money. And that belongs in the record.

I am walking in a circle. Past the two letters from Martyn, on the bulletin board where I have posted them, near the snapshot of his wife's children. Past the office, on whose front panel the decal of a continent still clings. And finally, past the postcards on the table. Under the newly written ones is the promised one to Dr. Cee, written the winter I was released, but never sent. What I had wanted to say, what I said, had left no room for the address.

Left foot twitches, toward the door. Right arm, ramrod, stays. I have appointments. With a keyboard. With a line of drums. With a long list of persons whom I may not see again. With the dead, as well.

I stop at the window, exhausted. It is his turn to go for food, and I am grateful. We'll eat the food that requires a bowl but no implements. A country that still harbors such a custom must have its graces. As will a home. He'll buy a bed. I'll buy — another towel? I won't query whether the oldest child in that snapshot isn't more than a trifle darker than the two younger ones. That may be what only a mother, or a woman of color who will keep her mouth shut, is entitled to see. Though should we have none of our own, would it be time to tell?

When he comes back, and we've eaten, I'll show him how I have learned to play the drums: slap-and-smooth with the palm, smooth and slap-slap, pound-pound, and thrum thrrumm-m. I'm no drummer, but to each his song. The more I play, the more I'm sure of to whom I owe the irregular rhythms I was born with.

To that impractical person who giggled close to me but never came nearer. Who danced like a pigeon when she heard certain airs, but was distressed when I wanted a musical instrument. Who lent me to wear, the day I graduated, an enameled pin — 'from the attic,' though never before seen there and vanished again, the day after I wore it — made of an old Canadian coin. Who said once, not looking anywhere special: 'Poignant. To a degree.' The more I thrum, the clearer I see her. My amateur mother — the musical aunt.

Nothing that happens behind a window can't be solved — is the way I'm feeling. I'm not bandaged; nobody's shot me. But I've been winged.

I wish I had been at the window in time to watch Martyn walk away just now. A man's back, ignorant that it's being watched, tells you more about the man. You can better judge the weight of the load he carries, that he thinks hidden when you and he are face to face. You can't shoulder it, you have your own, and even when wounded he's the stronger. Can you slog alongside?

In from the cold, can I live as others do, yet keep in mind those who remain outside?

On Martyn's table, bottom of the pile of postcards are two others long-since inscribed. I extract the first one, written that same winter, also never sent. 'Write me how it is out there,' Dr. Cee had said, and I had, in a tiny orthography once taught us in art therapy.

In the naive ups and downs of our summer, fish might float through air that is like bright water behind the trees; even on a sandy street you might be walking on sky; this is how the world should be, was begun.

Winters, the sky fall-falls in bits that clog the ankles; fish scrounged from other climates lie behind the fishmonger's plate-glass, at nine bucks a throw. The only birds about are those who companion you in the gray stone niches, or in the pavement hot-spots where we can ruffle those feathers we still own. People who are still called people have vanished behind closed doors. Doors are sacred entrances, to churches where we don't belong.

I hadn't needed to mail it. His gift had achieved its purpose. A postcard is really for the sender. It tells you where you are. The orthography is excellent.

The second card, inscribed in a rougher hand, bears no

recipient. Yet it's clear whom I'm addressing. I see how that other self of myself saw its mission to be:

> The collective reality — what an ogre it can be. But outside it and underneath it are those who do not speak.
> Here I am. Here we are.
> The state of the world is also the state of us.
> We are the state within the state.
> We send you this card ———.

And I must now reply:

> You alleyways that harbored me, who can shoulder your load alone? Do so, and isn't it only a tramp's bundle-on-a-stick?
> Now I'm on the ward of the ordinary. Pray for me. That as I become workaday enough to buy a watch, which is not the worst of fates, I will do more by it than count my days. That I won't merely luxuriate in what I believe. That when I'm old I won't be frightened at what I've become.

Hell, it's time. Not for either the 6 am or the 6 pm light to flick on; I know that much. By the time-sense deeper in the bone, independent of light, he should be back by now — shouldn't he? This is the householder itch, the family unease that wants everybody safely in. Just so the day aunt used to stand in the candle-lit bay, waiting for the night aunt to return, a worm of worry extending from her bent form, but not affecting me. I knew my place. Yet one night I burst out jealously: 'Why do you worry so about her?' And the answer came from behind that crouched shape: 'Because she has no fear.' And like a bitter-lemon keynote I only now hear, 'Nor do you.'

Will Martyn fear for me? Will I fear for him, the domestic drip-dripping on us like the spots of candle wax not found on the window-seat until the next day. 'Candles are for company, but you don't have company, why are you always burning them?' a schoolmate said to me. 'We have to get rid of them,' I'd answered. 'They're from the blackout during a war.'

Repetition will woo Martyn and me, as it's weaned me here. But I can imagine there'll be enough of the bare. We'll see to it. Unless the world gets there first. Which in one way or other it will. What do I know about the state of the world, except that it is us? In every house as in every alley — and at every grave. The sharpshooters are always anonymous.

While the keys held in common hang on the hook where one person left them — I see them up there, and the other leaves them behind. In trust. But why had he bothered to say he would halloo? A halloo is from afar. Has he too felt the doubleness already stealing like a sweet fog around us? Perhaps he'll phone his doubts from the restaurant. Or, never having got to it, from the street. 'Afar' wouldn't have to be Africa. Or not yet.

I drop to my knees, near the phone. Willing it to ring. Willing it not to, if the message is bad. There is a need, I'm sure, for — could one call it 'singletude,' as apart from living single? One would slip away now and then from the doubleness. Even in stealth, maybe. To walk, waist untwined, swinging in the alpine air of the lone meditation, ears stoppled against all communication from another skull. Only to come back sated, shivering with eagerness for the dual, as if reeled in on a tape. But one can't urge that vision over a phone.

Then I hear it. A halloo, not far. As near as the window I rush to is to a lamppost four storys below. He and it are not a painting; there's too much of him. He holds a wide, shallow bowl, covered in foil. Vinyl and string grocery bags depend from his one arm, and from around his neck; the wounded arm has none. He is a one-armed wall, offering a banquet. And he has company.

The Indian girl, in shiny black helmet, jumpsuit and boots, leans on the motorbike like an aviatrix. The bike has the cousin in tow. They are both looking up, but with the eyes only. Her helmet is too big for her, his too small for him.

Martyn manages a one-hand, three-fold motion. Signalling: these two — may I bring them up? For what's in the bowl?

I spread my arms wide, wide.

Girl, bike, cousin spring to action. As she directs him to park the bike inside our door, I see they've swapped manners. She's no longer polite. He is. As he up-ends the bike she blows me a kiss through the handlebars.

Martyn has already disappeared. Four stories, and that load. And the bike will have to be pulled up on the landing. Just enough time. I open the housedoor a crack.

There's no straightening up to be done. Except for the empty crackerbox on the table. And the two cards lying there.

I'll tuck them in the backpack pocket, where I put Carey's

check. Nuzzle the money as they will, they can't sweeten it. But as papers of record they belong with it.

Not that I need to keep these soul-bytes in sight, like the calendar put on a shelf to remind you that the convenience store around the corner — the one that gives you credit, is trying to hang on. I always know who I am, and where; that's been the trouble. I'm one of those. Sink to the depths and it's because you know what you are. Or when you rise toward those heights you are almost capable of. I snap the pocket closed over the jumble that can't be thrown away.

I hear the three coming nearer. Heavy steps. One burdened man, and one in tow, packages thumping against the rail. They sound like the movie music that signals Fate is creeping toward somebody's come-uppance. The audience hopes to get its money's worth.

The girl makes no noise. But I suspect her destiny, and the cousin's as well. The clan will close over them, but not quite. There is after all the bike.

The door is flung wide. Martyn stands there, laden like the god of gifts, carrying the bowl that will make us cry. Been a long walk from Fourteenth Street, but he won't let us see that. Does he know his destiny, this slightly wounded man? Does he know ours?

I am the record. That's a destiny, as far as it goes. But something has been added. I have company.

Martyn's face does not change at the sight of me. Warmed maybe, by what we've been through. But not astounded. The two faces flanking his are, the tiny one screwed in delight, the cousin's still led by its nose.

Is that sheen on Martyn's face sweat? Or pride?

I have remembered the bit of glory he held out to me. As

I'll remember the two cards, shining now in their dark pocket, with an incandescence once mine.

I am the bomb. I could run for parliament. From an inherited seat. Slap-slap and a smooth thrru-um, I am playing the drums.

For all of us.

So ends the record.

Now — the required statement:

Open the door, Carol, to Carol Smith.

Case closed.

Hortense Calisher

AGE
A Love Story

'a luminous, accessible, well crafted,
lovely book' — *Chicago Tribune*

Rupert is an honored American poet; Gemma a retired
architect. They live happily and comfortably in a Greenwich
Village apartment; the setting, for over thirty years, of their
married life. Each with a previous marriage behind them —
which left her with two daughters and him with the promise
of greatness — they are now facing the challenge of old age
together. Both, in their own way, defy the inevitability of
death, and yet both are busy preparing for it. The alternating
entries of their private journals, which make up the body of
Calisher's text, tell a story of familiarity and the fear of loss,
love and uncertainty of the future, meanings and habits.
With rare verve and panache, Hortense Calisher has
confronted a difficult and often neglected subject —
and has triumphed magnificently.